D0469068

Great Horse Stories

Compiled by
James Daley

DOVER PUBLICATIONS, INC.
Mineola, New York

Bibliographical Note

This Dover edition, first published in 2010, is a new selection of fifteen short stories reprinted from standard texts. Please see the acknowledgments for additional bibliographical information. This new anthology includes an introductory Note.

International Standard Book Number

ISBN–13: 978-0-486-47669-8
ISBN–10: 0-486-47669-3

Manufactured in the United States by LSC Communications
47669308   2019
www.doverpublications.com

Acknowledgments

"Carved in Sand" by Erle Stanley Gardner. Reprinted by permission of the Queen Literary Agency.

"Shadow Quest" by William F. Nolan. Reprinted by permission of William F. Nolan.

"The Summer of the Beautiful White Horse" from *My Name is Aram* by William Saroyan, copyright © 1939 and renewed 1966 by William Saroyan. Reprinted by permission of the Trustees of Leland Stanford Junior University.

Note

HELEN Thomson once said that, "In riding a horse, we borrow freedom." This statement, as simple as it is poetic, seems to sum up the joy of horses as well as a sentiment ever could. As any equestrian will tell you, riding a horse is at the same time a sport, a relationship, a thrill-ride, and a deep encounter with nature—that's what makes it so meaningful to so many.

Hopefully, the stories in this anthology will be able to capture at least a little bit of this vast and varied experience. From the pride and trials of Anna Sewell's "Black Beauty" to the childhood longing of William Saroyan's "The Summer of the Beautiful White Horse," *Great Horse Stories* contains tales that aim to touch on the incredibly wide array of experience and emotion felt by horse lovers everywhere. Not limiting itself only to traditional horse stories, however, this anthology also includes great mysteries like Doyle's famous "Silver Blaze," science fiction such as William F. Nolan's classic "Shadow Quest," and suspense stories like the great "Carved in Sand" by Erle Stanley Gardner.

Whatever your tastes may be, if you love horses, you'll love these great horse stories.

Enjoy!

JAMES DALEY

Contents

Black Beauty: Young Folks' Edition

Anna Sewell

I. My Early Home

THE first place that I can well remember was a pleasant meadow with a pond of clear water in it. Over the hedge on one side we looked into a plowed field, and on the other we looked over a gate at our master's house, which stood by the roadside. While I was young I lived upon my mother's milk, as I could not eat grass. In the daytime I ran by her side, and at night I lay down close by her. When it was hot we used to stand by the pond in the shade of the trees, and when it was cold we had a warm shed near the grove.

There were six young colts in the meadow beside me; they were older than I was. I used to run with them, and had great fun; we used to gallop all together round the field, as hard as we could go. Sometimes we had rather rough play, for they would bite and kick, as well as gallop.

One day, when there was a good deal of kicking, my mother whinnied to me to come to her, and then she said: "I wish you to pay attention to what I am going to say. The colts who live here are very good colts, but they are cart-horse colts, and they have not learned manners. You have been well-bred and well-born; your father has a great name in these parts, and your grandfather won the cup at the races; your grandmother had the sweetest temper of any horse I ever knew, and I think you have never seen me kick or bite. I hope you will grow up gentle and good, and never learn bad ways; do your work with a good will, lift your feet up well when you trot, and never bite or kick even in play."

1

I have never forgotten my mother's advice. I knew she was a wise old horse, and our master thought a great deal of her. Her name was Duchess, but he called her Pet.

Our master was a good, kind man. He gave us good food, good lodging and kind words; he spoke as kindly to us as he did to his little children. We were all fond of him, and my mother loved him very much. When she saw him at the gate she would neigh with joy, and trot up to him. He would pat and stroke her and say, "Well, old Pet, and how is your little Darkie?" I was a dull black, so he called me Darkie; then he would give me a piece of bread, which was very good, and sometimes he brought a carrot for my mother. All the horses would come to him, but I think we were his favorites. My mother always took him to town on a market-day in a light gig.

We had a ploughboy, Dick, who sometimes came into our field to pluck blackberries from the hedge. When he had eaten all he wanted he would have what he called fun with the colts, throwing stones and sticks at them to make them gallop. We did not much mind him, for we could gallop off; but sometimes a stone would hit and hurt us.

One day he was at this game, and did not know that the master was in the next field, watching what was going on; over the hedge he jumped in a snap, and catching Dick by the arm, he gave him such a box on the ear as made him roar with the pain and surprise. As soon as we saw the master we trotted up nearer to see what went on.

"Bad boy!" he said, "bad boy! to chase the colts. This is not the first time, but it shall be the last. There—take your money and go home; I shall not want you on my farm again." So we never saw Dick any more. Old Daniel, the man who looked after the horses, was just as gentle as our master; so we were well off.

II. The Hunt

BEFORE I was two years old a circumstance happened which I have never forgotten. It was early in the spring; there had been a little frost in the night, and a light mist still hung over the woods and meadows. I and the other colts were feeding at the lower part of the field when we heard what sounded like the cry of dogs. The oldest of the colts raised his head, pricked his ears, and said, "There are the hounds!" and cantered off, followed by the rest of us, to the upper part of the field, where we could look over the hedge and see several fields beyond. My mother and an old riding horse of our master's were also standing near, and seemed to know all about it. "They have found a hare," said my mother, "and if they come this way we shall see the hunt."

And soon the dogs were all tearing down the field of young wheat next to ours. I never heard such a noise as they made. They did not bark, nor howl, nor whine, but kept on a "yo! yo, o, o! yo, o, o!" at the top of their voices. After them came a number of men on horseback, all galloping as fast as they could. The old horses snorted and looked eagerly after them, and we young colts wanted to be galloping with them, but they were soon away into the fields lower down; here it seemed as if they had come to a stand; the dogs left off barking and ran about every way with their noses to the ground.

"They have lost the scent," said the old horse; "perhaps the hare will get off."

"What hare?" I said.

"Oh, I don't know what hare; likely enough it may be one of our own hares out of the woods; any hare they can find will do for the dogs and men to run after"; and before long the dogs began their "yo; yo, o, o!" again, and back they came all together at full speed, making straight for our meadow at the part where the high bank and hedge overhang the brook.

"Now we shall see the hare," said my mother; and just then a hare, wild with fright, rushed by and made for the woods. On came the dogs; they burst over the bank, leaped the stream and came dashing across the field, followed by the huntsmen. Several men leaped their horses clean over, close upon the dogs. The hare tried to get through the fence; it was too thick, and she turned sharp around to make for the road, but it was too late; the dogs were upon her with their wild cries; we heard one shriek, and that was the end of her. One of the huntsmen rode up and whipped off the dogs, who would soon have torn her to pieces. He held her up by the leg, torn and bleeding, and all the gentlemen seemed well pleased.

As for me, I was so astonished that I did not at first see what was going on by the brook; but when I did look, there was a sad sight; two fine horses were down; one was struggling in the stream, and the other was groaning on the grass. One of the riders was getting out of the water covered with mud, the other lay quite still.

"His neck is broken," said my mother.

"And serves him right, too," said one of the colts.

I thought the same, but my mother did not join with us.

"Well, no," she said, "you must not say that; but though I am an old horse, and have seen and heard a great deal, I never yet could make out why men are so fond of this sport; they often hurt themselves, often spoil good horses, and tear up the fields, and all for a hare, or a fox, or a stag, that they could get more easily some other way; but we are only horses, and don't know."

While my mother was saying this, we stood and looked on. Many of the riders had gone to the young man; but my master was the first to raise him. His head fell back and his arms hung down, and every one looked very serious. There was no noise now; even the dogs were quiet, and seemed to know that something was wrong. They carried him to our master's house. I heard afterwards that it was the squire's only son, a fine, tall young man, and the pride of his family.

They were now riding in all directions—to the doctor's, and to Squire Gordon's, to let him know about his son. When Bond, the farrier, came to look at the black horse that lay groaning on the grass, he felt him all over, and shook his head; one of his legs was broken. Then some one ran to our master's house and came back with a gun; presently there was a loud bang and a dreadful shriek, and then all was still; the black horse moved no more.

My mother seemed much troubled; she said she had known that horse for years, and that his name was Rob Roy; he was a good horse, and there was no vice in him. She never would go to that part of the field afterwards.

Not many days after, we heard the church-bell tolling for a long time, and looking over the gate, we saw a long strange black coach that was covered with black cloth and was drawn by black horses; after that came another and another and another, and all were black, while the bell kept tolling, tolling. They were carrying young Gordon to the churchyard to bury him. He would never ride again. What they did with Rob Roy I never knew; but 'twas all for one little hare.

III. My Breaking In

I was now beginning to grow handsome, my coat had grown fine and soft, and was bright black. I had one white foot and a pretty white star on my forehead. I was thought very handsome; my master would not sell me till I was four years old; he said lads ought not to work like men, and colts ought not to work like horses till they were quite grown up.

When I was four years old, Squire Gordon came to look at me. He examined my eyes, my mouth, and my legs; he felt them all down, and then I had to walk and trot and gallop before him; he seemed to like me, and said, "When he has been well broken in he will do very well." My master said he would break me in himself, and he lost no time about it, for the next day he began.

Every one may not know what breaking in is, therefore I will describe it. It means to teach a horse to wear a saddle and bridle, and to carry on his back a man, woman, or child; to go just the way they wish, and to go quietly. Besides this, he has to learn to wear a collar, and a breeching, and to stand still while they are put on; then to have a cart or a buggy fixed behind, so that he cannot walk or trot without dragging it after him; and he must go fast or slow, just as his driver wishes. He must never start at what he sees, nor speak to other horses, nor bite, nor kick, nor have any will of his own, but always do his master's will, even though he may be very tired or hungry; but the worst of all is, when his harness is once on, he may neither jump for joy nor lie down for weariness. So you see this breaking in is a great thing.

I had, of course, long been used to a halter and a head-stall, and to be led about in the fields and lanes quietly, but now I was to have a bit and bridle; my master gave me some oats as usual, and after a good deal of coaxing he got the bit into my mouth and the bridle fixed, but it was a nasty thing! Those who have never had a bit in their mouths cannot think how bad it feels; a great piece of cold hard steel as thick as a man's finger to be pushed into one's mouth, between one's teeth, and over one's tongue, with the ends coming out at the corner of your mouth, and held fast there by straps over your head, under your throat, round your nose, and under your chin; so that no way in the world can you get rid of the nasty hard thing; it is very bad! at least I thought so; but I knew my mother always wore one when she went out, and all horses did when they were grown up; and so, what with the nice oats, and what with my master's pats, kind words, and gentle ways, I got to wear my bit and bridle.

Next came the saddle, but that was not half so bad; my master put it on my back very gently, while Old Daniel held my head; he then made the girths fast under my body, patting and talking to me all the time; then I had a few oats, then a little leading about; and this he did every day till I began to look for the oats and the saddle. At length, one morning, my master got on my back and rode me around the meadow on the soft grass. It certainly did feel queer; but I must say I felt rather proud to carry my master, and as he continued to ride me a little every day, I soon became accustomed to it.

The next unpleasant business was putting on the iron shoes; that too was very hard at first. My master went with me to the smith's forge, to see that I was not hurt or got any fright. The blacksmith took my feet in his hand, one after the other, and cut away some of the hoof. It did not pain me, so I stood still on three legs till he had done them all. Then he took a piece of iron the shape of my foot, and clapped it on, and drove some nails through the shoe quite into my hoof, so that the shoe was firmly on. My feet felt very stiff and heavy, but in time I got used to it.

And now having got so far, my master went on to break me to harness; there were more new things to wear. First, a stiff heavy collar just on my neck, and a bridle with great side-pieces against my eyes, called blinkers, and blinkers indeed they were, for I could not see on either side, but only straight in front of me; next there was a small saddle with a nasty stiff strap that went right under my tail; that was the crupper. I hated the crupper—to have my long tail doubled up and poked through that strap was almost as bad as the bit. I never felt more like kicking, but of course I could not kick such a good master, and so in time I got used to everything, and could do my work as well as my mother.

I must not forget to mention one part of my training, which I have always considered a very great advantage. My master sent me for a fortnight to a neighboring farmer's, who had a meadow which was skirted on one side by the railway. Here were some sheep and cows, and I was turned in among them.

I shall never forget the first train that ran by. I was feeding quietly near the pales which separated the meadow from the railway, when I heard a strange sound at a distance, and before I knew whence it came—with a rush and a clatter, and a puffing out of smoke—a long black train of something flew by, and was gone almost before I could draw my breath. I galloped to the further side of the meadow, and there I stood snorting with astonishment and fear. In the course of the day many other trains went by, some more slowly; these drew up at the station close by, and sometimes made an awful shriek and groan before they stopped. I thought it very dreadful, but the cows went on eating very quietly, and hardly raised their heads as the black, frightful thing came puffing and grinding past. For the first few days I could not feed in peace; but as I found that this terrible creature never came into the field, or did me any harm, I began to disregard it, and very soon I cared as little about the passing of a train as the cows and sheep did.

Since then I have seen many horses much alarmed and res-tive at the sight or sound of a steam engine; but, thanks to my good master's care, I am as fearless at railway stations as in my own stable. Now if any one wants to break in a young horse well, that is the way.

My master often drove me in double harness, with my mother, because she was steady and could teach me how to go better than a strange horse. She told me the better I behaved the better I should be treated, and that it was wisest always to do my best to please my master. "I hope you will fall into good hands, but a horse never knows who may buy him, or who may drive him; it is all a chance for us; but still I say, do your best wherever it is, and keep up your good name."

IV.　Birtwick Park

I T was early in May, when there came a man from Gordon's, who took me away to the Hall. My master said, "Good-bye, Darkie; be a good horse and always do your best." I could not say "good-bye," so I put my nose in his hand; he patted me kindly, and I left my first home. I will describe the stable into which I was taken; this was very roomy, with four good stalls; a large swinging window opened into the yard, making it pleasant and airy.

The first stall was a large square one, shut in behind with a wooden gate; the others were common stalls, good stalls, but not nearly so large. It had a low rack for hay and a low manger for corn; it was called a box stall, because the horse that was put into it was not tied up, but left loose, to do as he liked. It is a great thing to have a box stall.

Into this fine box the groom put me; it was clean, sweet, and airy. I never was in a better box than that, and the sides were not so high but that I could see all that went on through the iron rails that were at the top.

He gave me some very nice oats, patted me, spoke kindly, and then went away.

When I had eaten my oats, I looked round. In the stall next to mine stood a little fat gray pony, with a thick mane and tail, a very pretty head, and a pert little nose. I put my head up to the iron rails at the top of my box, and said, "How do you do? What is your name?"

He turned round as far as his halter would allow, held up his head, and said, "My name is Merrylegs. I am very handsome. I carry the young ladies on my back, and sometimes I take our mistress out in the low cart. They think a great deal of me, and so does James. Are you going to live next door to me in the box?"

I said, "Yes."

"Well, then," he said, "I hope you are good-tempered; I do not like any one next door who bites." Just then a horse's head looked over from the stall beyond; the ears were laid back, and the eye looked rather ill-tempered. This was a tall chestnut mare, with a long handsome neck; she looked across to me and said, "So it is you have turned me out of my box; it is a very strange thing for a colt like you to come and turn a lady out of her own home."

"I beg your pardon," I said, "I have turned no one out; the man who brought me put me here, and I had nothing to do with it. I never had words yet with horse or mare, and it is my wish to live at peace."

"Well," she said, "we shall see; of course, I do not want to have words with a young thing like you." I said no more. In the afternoon, when she went out, Merrylegs told me all about it.

"The thing is this," said Merrylegs, "Ginger has a habit of biting and snapping; that is why they call her Ginger, and when she was in the box-stall, she used to snap very much. One day she bit James in the arm and made it bleed, and so Miss Flora and Miss Jessie, who are very fond of me, were afraid to come into the stable. They used to bring me nice things to eat, an apple, or a carrot, or a piece of bread, but after Ginger stood in that box, they dared not come, and I missed them very much. I hope they will now come again, if you do not bite or snap." I told him I never bit anything but grass, hay, and corn, and could not think what pleasure Ginger found it.

"Well, I don't think she does find pleasure," says Merrylegs; "it is just a bad habit; she says no one was ever kind to her, and why should she not bite? Of course, it is a very bad habit; but I am sure, if all she says be true, she must have been very ill-used before she came here. John does all he can to please her; so I think she might be good-tempered here. You see," he said, with a wise look, "I am twelve years old; I know a great deal, and I can tell you there is not a better place for a horse all round the country than this. John is the best groom that ever was; he has been here fourteen years; and you never saw such a kind boy as James is, so that it is all Ginger's own fault that she did not stay in that box."

V. A Fair Start

THE name of the coachman was John Manly; he had a wife and one child, and lived in the coachman's cottage, near the stables.

The next morning he took me into the yard and gave me a good grooming, and just as I was going into my box, with my coat soft and bright, the squire came in to look at me, and seemed pleased. "John," he said, "I meant to have tried the new horse this morning, but I have other business. You may as well take him around after breakfast; go by the common and the Highwood, and back by the water-mill and the river; that will show his paces."

"I will, sir," said John. After breakfast he came and fitted me with a bridle. He was very particular in letting out and taking in the straps, to fit my head comfortably; then he brought a saddle, but it was not broad enough for my back; he saw it in a minute, and went for another, which fitted nicely. He rode me first slowly, then a trot, then a canter, and when we were on the common, he gave me a light touch with his whip, and we had a splendid gallop.

"Ho, ho! my boy," he said, as he pulled me up, "you would like to follow the hounds, I think."

As we came back through the park we met the squire and Mrs. Gordon walking; they stopped, and John jumped off. "Well, John, how does he go?"

"First rate, sir," answered John; "he is as fleet as a deer, and has a fine spirit, too; but the lightest touch of the rein will guide him. Down at the end of the common we met one of those traveling carts hung all over with baskets, rugs, and such like; you know, sir, many horses will not pass those carts quietly; he just took a good look at it, and then went on as quiet and pleasant as could be. They were shooting rabbits near the Highwood, and a gun went off close by; he pulled up a little and looked, but he did not stir a step to right or left. I just held the rein steady and did not hurry him, and it's my opinion he has not been frightened or ill-used while he was young."

"That's well," said the squire, "I will try him myself tomorrow."

The next day I was brought up for my master. I remembered my mother's counsel and my good old master's, and I tried to do exactly what he wanted me to do. I found he was a very good rider, and thoughtful for his horse, too. When he came home, the lady was at the hall door as he rode up. "Well, my dear," she said, "how do you like him?"

"He is exactly what John said," he replied; "a pleasanter creature I never wish to mount. What shall we call him?"

She said: "He is really quite a beauty, and he has such a sweet, good-tempered face and such a fine, intelligent eye—what do you say to calling him 'Black Beauty'?"

"Black Beauty—why, yes, I think that is a very good name. If you like, it shall be his name"; and so it was.

When John went into the stable, he told James that the master and mistress had chosen a good sensible name for me, that meant something. They both laughed, and James said, "If it was not for bringing back the past, I should have named him Rob Roy, for I never saw two horses more alike." "That's no wonder," said John; "didn't you know that Farmer Grey's old Duchess was the mother of them both?"

I had never heard that before; and so poor Rob Roy who was killed at that hunt was my brother! I did not wonder that my mother was so troubled. It seems that horses have no relations; at least they never know each other after they are sold.

John seemed very proud of me; he used to make my mane and tail almost as smooth as a lady's hair, and he would talk to me a great deal; of course, I did not understand all he said, but I learned more and more to know what he meant, and what he wanted me to do. I grew very fond of him, he was so gentle and kind; he seemed to know just how a horse feels, and when he cleaned me he knew the tender places and the ticklish places; when he brushed my head, he went as carefully over my eyes as if they were his own, and never stirred up any ill-temper.

James Howard, the stable boy, was just as gentle and pleasant in his way, so I thought myself well off. There was another man who helped in the yard, but he had very little to do with Ginger and me.

A few days after this I had to go out with Ginger in the carriage. I wondered how we should get on together; but except laying her ears back when I was led up to her, she behaved very well. She did her work honestly, and did her full share, and I never wish to have a better partner in double harness. When we came to a hill, instead of slackening her pace, she would throw her weight right into the collar, and pull away straight up. We had both the same sort of courage at our work, and John had oftener to hold us in than to urge us forward; he never had to use the whip with either of us; then our paces were much the same, and I found it very easy to keep step with her when trotting, which made it pleasant, and master always liked it when we kept step well, and so did John. After we had been out two or three times together we grew quite friendly and sociable, which made me feel very much at home.

As for Merrylegs, he and I soon became great friends; he was such a cheerful, plucky, good-tempered little fellow, that he was a favorite with every one, and especially with Miss Jessie and Flora, who used to ride him about in the orchard, and have fine games with him and their little dog Frisky.

VI. Merrylegs

MR. Blomefield, the vicar, had a large family of boys and girls; sometimes they used to come and play with Miss Jessie and Flora. One of the girls was as old as Miss Jessie; two of the boys were older, and there were several little ones. When they came, there was plenty of work for Merrylegs, for nothing pleased them so much as getting on him by turns and riding him all about the orchard and the home paddock, and this they would do by the hour together.

One afternoon he had been sent out with them a long time, and when James brought him in and put on his halter, he said: "There, you rogue, mind how you behave yourself, or we shall get into trouble."

"What have you been doing, Merrylegs?" I asked.

"Oh!" said he, tossing his little head, "I have only been giving those young people a lesson; they did not know when they had enough, so I just pitched them off backwards; that was the only thing they could understand."

"What?" said I, "you threw the children off? I thought you did know better than that! Did you throw Miss Jessie or Miss Flora?"

He looked very much offended, and said: "Of course not; I would not do such a thing for the best oats that ever came into the stable; why, I am as careful of our young ladies as the master could be, and as for the little ones, it is I who teach them to ride. When they seem frightened or a little unsteady on my back, I go as smooth and as quiet as old pussy when she is after a bird; and when they are all right I go on again faster, you see, just to use them to it; so don't you trouble yourself preaching to me; I am the best friend and the best riding-master those children have. It is not them, it is the boys; boys," said he, shaking his mane, "are quite different, they must be broken in, as we were broken in when we were colts, and just be taught what's what. The other children had ridden me about for nearly two hours, and then the boys thought it was their turn, and so it was, and I was quite agreeable. They rode me by turns, and I galloped them about, up and down the fields and all about the orchard, for a good hour. They had each cut a great hazel stick for a riding whip, and laid it on a little too hard; but I took it in good part, till at last I thought we had had enough, so I stopped two or three times by way of a hint. Boys think a horse or pony is like a steam engine, and can go as long and as fast as they please; they never think that a pony can get tired, or have any feelings; so as the one who was whipping me could not understand, I just rose up on my hind legs and let him slip off behind—that was all; he mounted me again, and I did the same. Then the other boy got up, and as soon as he began to use his stick, I laid him on the grass, and so on, till they were able to understand, that was all. They were not bad boys; they don't wish to be cruel. I like them very well; but you see I had to give them a lesson. When they brought me to James and told him, I think he was very angry to see such big sticks. He said they were not for young gentlemen."

"If I had been you," said Ginger, "I would have given those boys a good kick, and that would have given them a lesson."

"No doubt you would," said Merrylegs; "but then I am not quite such a fool as to anger our master or make James ashamed of me; besides, those children are under my charge when they are riding; I tell you they are entrusted to me. Why, only the other day I heard our master say to Mrs. Blomefield, 'My dear madam, you need not be anxious about the children; my old Merrylegs will take as much care of them as you or I could; I assure you I would not sell that pony for any money, he is so perfectly good-tempered and trustworthy'; and do you think I am such an ungrateful brute as to forget all the kind treatment I have had here for five years, and all the trust they place in me, and turn vicious, because a couple of ignorant boys used me badly? No, no! you never had a good place where they were kind to you, and so you don't know, and I am sorry for you; but I can tell you good places make good horses. I wouldn't vex our people for anything; I love them, I do," said Merrylegs, and he gave a low "ho, ho, ho," through his nose, as he used to do in the morning when he heard James' footstep at the door.

VII. Going for the Doctor

O NE night I was lying down in my straw fast asleep, when I was suddenly roused by the stable bell ringing very loud. I heard the door of John's house open, and his feet running up to the Hall. He was back again in no time; he unlocked the stable door, and came in, calling out, "Wake up, Beauty! you must go well now, if ever you did"; and almost before I could think, he had got the saddle on my back and the bridle on my head. He just ran around for his coat, and then took me at a quick trot up to the Hall door. The Squire stood there, with a lamp in his hand. "Now, John," he said, "ride for your life—that is, for your mistress' life; there is not a moment to lose. Give this note to Dr. White; give your horse a rest at the inn, and be back as soon as you can."

John said, "Yes, sir," and was on my back in a minute. The gardener who lived at the lodge had heard the bell ring, and was ready with the gate open, and away we went through the park, and through the village, and down the hill till we came to the toll-gate. John called very loud and thumped upon the door; the man was soon out and flung open the gate.

"Now," said John, "do you keep the gate open for the doctor; here's the money," and off we went again.

There was before us a long piece of level road by the riverside; John said to me, "Now, Beauty, do your best," and so I did; I wanted no whip nor spur, and for two miles I galloped as fast I could lay my feet to the ground; I don't believe that my old grandfather, who won the race at Newmarket, could have gone faster. When we came to the bridge, John pulled me up a little and patted my neck. "Well done, Beauty! good old fellow," he said. He would have let me go slower, but my spirit was up, and I was off again as fast as before. The air was frosty, the moon was bright; it was very pleasant. We came through a village, then through a dark wood, then uphill, then downhill, till after an eight miles' run, we came to the town, through the streets and into the market-place. It was all quite still except the clatter of my feet on the stones—everybody was asleep. The church clock struck three as we drew up at Dr. White's door. John rang the bell twice, and then knocked at the door like thunder. A window was thrown up, and the doctor, in his night-cap, put his head out and said, "What do you want?"

"Mrs. Gordon is very ill, sir; master wants you to go at once; he thinks she will die if you cannot get there. Here is a note."

"Wait," he said, "I will come."

He shut the window and was soon at the door. "The worst of it is," he said, "that my horse has been out all day, and is quite done up; my son has just been sent for, and he has taken the other. What is to be done? Can I have your horse?"

"He has come at a gallop nearly all the way, sir, and I was to give him a rest here; but I think my master would not be against it, if you think fit, sir."

"All right," he said; "I will soon be ready."

John stood by me and stroked my neck. I was very hot. The doctor came out with his riding-whip. "You need not take that, sir," said John; "Black Beauty will go till he drops. Take care of him, sir, if you can; I should not like any harm to come to him."

"No, no, John," said the doctor, "I hope not," and in a minute we had left John far behind.

I will not tell about our way back. The doctor was a heavier man than John, and not so good a rider; however, I did my very best. The man at the toll-gate had it open. When we came to the hill, the doctor drew me up. "Now, my good fellow," he said, "take some breath." I was glad he did, for I was nearly spent, but that breathing helped me on, and soon we were in the park. Joe was at the lodge gate; my master was at the Hall door, for he had heard us coming. He spoke not a word; the doctor went into the house with him, and Joe led me to the stable. I was glad to get home; my legs shook under me, and I could only stand and pant. I had not a dry hair on my body, the water ran down my legs, and I steamed all over—Joe used to say, like a pot on the fire. Poor Joe! he was young and small, and as yet he knew very little, and his father, who would have helped him, had been sent to the next village; but I am sure he did the very best he knew. He rubbed my legs and my chest, but he did not put my warm cloth on me; he thought I was so hot I should not like it. Then he gave me a pail full of water to drink; it was cold and very good, and I drank it all; then he gave me some hay and some corn, and, thinking he had done right, he went away. Soon I began to shake and tremble, and turned deadly cold; my legs ached, my loins ached, and my chest ached, and I felt sore all over. This developed into a strong inflammation, and I could not draw my breath without pain. John nursed me night and day. My master, too, often came to see me. "My poor Beauty," he said one day, "my good horse, you saved your mistress' life, Beauty; yes, you saved her life." I was very glad to hear that, for it seems the doctor had said if we had been a little longer it would have been too late. John told my master he never saw a horse go so fast in his life. It seems as if the horse knew what was the matter. Of course I did, though John thought not; at least I knew as much as this—that John and I must go at the top of our speed, and that it was for the sake of the mistress.

VIII. The Parting

I had lived in this happy place three years, but sad changes were about to come over us. We heard that our mistress was ill. The doctor was often at the house, and the master looked grave and anxious. Then we heard that she must go to a warm country for two or three years. The news fell upon the household like the tolling of a death-bell. Everybody was sorry. The master arranged for breaking up his establishment and leaving England. We used to hear it talked about in our stable; indeed, nothing else was talked about. John went about his work silent and sad, and Joe scarcely whistled. There was a great deal of coming and going; Ginger and I had full work.

The first of the party who went were Miss Jessie and Flora with their governess. They came to bid us good-bye. They hugged poor Merrylegs like an old friend, and so indeed he was. Then we heard what had been arranged for us. Master had sold Ginger and me to an old friend. Merrylegs he had given to the vicar, who was wanting a pony for Mrs. Blomefield, but it was on the condition that he should never be sold, and that when he was past work he should be shot and buried. Joe was engaged to take care of him and to help in the house, so I thought that Merrylegs was well off.

"Have you decided what to do, John?" he said.

"No, sir; I have made up my mind that if I could get a situation with some first-rate colt-breaker and horse-trainer, it would be the right thing for me. Many young animals are frightened and spoiled by wrong treatment, which need not be if the right man took them in hand. I always get on well with horses, and if I could help some of them to a fair start I should feel as if I was doing some good. What do you think of it, sir?"

"I don't know a man anywhere," said master, "that I should think so suitable for it as yourself. You understand horses, and somehow they understand you, and I think you could not do better."

The last sad day had come; the footman and the heavy luggage had gone off the day before, and there were only master and mistress, and her maid. Ginger and I brought the carriage up to the Hall door, for the last time. The servants brought out cushions and rugs, and when all were arranged, master came down the steps carrying the mistress in his arms (I was on the side next the house, and could see all that went on); he placed her carefully in the carriage, while the house servants stood round crying.

"Good-bye, again," he said; "we shall not forget any of you," and he got in. "Drive on, John." Joe jumped up and we trotted slowly through the park and through the village, where the people were standing at their doors to have a last look and to say, "God bless them."

When we reached the railway station, I think mistress walked from the carriage to the waiting-room. I heard her say in her own sweet voice, "Good-bye, John; God bless you." I felt the rein twitch, but John made no answer; perhaps he could not speak. As soon as Joe had taken the things out of the carriage, John called him to stand by the horses, while he went on the platform. Poor Joe! He stood close up to our heads to hide his tears. Very soon the train came puffing into the station; then two or three minutes, and the doors were slammed to; the guard whistled and the train glided away, leaving behind it only clouds of white smoke and some very heavy hearts.

When it was quite out of sight, John came back. "We shall never see her again," he said—"never." He took the reins, mounted the box, and with Joe drove slowly home; but it was not our home now.

IX. Earlshall

THE next morning after breakfast, Joe put Merrylegs into the mistress' low chaise to take him to the vicarage; he came first and said good-bye to us, and Merrylegs neighed to us from the yard. Then John put the saddle on Ginger and the leading rein on me, and rode us across the country to Earlshall Park, where the Earl of W—— lived. There was a very fine house and a great deal of stabling. We went into the yard through a stone gateway, and John asked for Mr. York. It was some time before he came. He was a fine-looking, middle-aged man, and his voice said at once that he expected to be obeyed. He was very friendly and polite to John, and after giving us a slight look, he called a groom to take us to our boxes, and invited John to take some refreshment.

We were taken to a light, airy stable, and placed in boxes adjoining each other, where we were rubbed down and fed. In about half an hour John and York, who was to be our new coachman, came in to see us.

"Now, Manly," he said, after carefully looking at us both, "I can see no fault in these horses; but we all know that horses have their peculiarities as well as men, and that sometimes they need different treatment. I should like to know if there is anything particular in either of these that you would like to mention."

"Well," said John, "I don't believe there is a better pair of horses in the country, and right grieved I am to part with them, but they are not alike. The black one is the most perfect temper I ever knew; I suppose he has never known a hard word or blow since he was foaled, and all his pleasure seems to be to do what you wish; but the chestnut, I fancy, must have had bad treatment; we heard as much from the dealer. She came to us snappish and suspicious, but when she found what sort of place ours was, it all went off by degrees; for three years I have never seen the smallest sign of temper, and if she is well treated there is not a better, more willing animal than she is. But she has naturally a more irritable constitution than the black horse; flies tease her more; anything wrong in her harness frets her more; and if she were ill-used or unfairly treated she would not be unlikely to give tit for tat. You know that many high-mettled horses will do so."

"Of course," said York, "I quite understand; but you know it is not easy in stables like these to have all the grooms just what they should be. I do my best, and there I must leave it. I'll remember what you have said about the mare." They were going out of the stable, when John stopped, and said, "I had better mention that we have never used the check-rein with either of them; the black horse never had one on, and the dealer said it was the gag-bit that spoiled the other's temper."

"Well," said York, "if they come here, they must wear the check-rein. I prefer a loose rein myself, and his lordship is always very reasonable about horses; but my lady—that's another thing; she will have style, and if her carriage horses are not reined up tight she wouldn't look at them. I always stand out against the gag-bit, and shall do so, but it must be tight up when my lady rides!"

"I am sorry for it," said John; "but I must go now, or I shall lose the train."

He came round to each of us to pat and speak to us for the last time; his voice sounded very sad. I held my face close to him; that was all I could do to say good-bye; and then he was gone, and I have never seen him since.

The next day Lord W—— came to look at us; he seemed pleased with our appearance. "I have great confidence in these horses," he said, "from the character my friend Gordon has given me of them. Of course they are not a match in color, but my idea is that they will do very well for the carriage while we are in the country. Before we go to London I must try to match Baron; the black horse, I believe, is perfect for riding."

York then told him what John had said about us.

"Well," said he, "you must keep an eye to the mare, and put the check-rein easy; I dare say they will do very well with a little humoring at first. I'll mention it to your lady."

In the afternoon we were harnessed and put in the carriage and led round to the front of the house. It was all very grand, and three times as large as the old house at Birtwick, but not half so pleasant, if a horse may have an opinion. Two footmen were standing ready, dressed in drab livery, with scarlet breeches and white stockings. Presently we heard the rustling sound of silk as my lady came down the flight of stone steps. She stepped round to look at us; she was a tall, proud-looking woman, and did not seem pleased about something, but she said nothing, and got into the carriage. This was the first time of wearing a check-rein, and I must say, though it certainly was a nuisance not to be able to get my head down now and then, it did not pull my head higher than I was accustomed to carry it. I felt anxious about Ginger, but she seemed to be quiet and content.

The next day we were again at the door, and the footmen as before; we heard the silk dress rustle, and the lady came down the steps, and in an imperious voice, she said, "York, you must put those horses' heads higher, they are not fit to be seen."

York got down, and said very respectfully, "I beg your pardon, my lady, but these horses have not been reined up for three years, and my lord said it would be safer to bring them to it by degrees; but, if your ladyship pleases, I can take them up a little more." "Do so," she said.

York came round to our heads and shortened the rein himself, one hole, I think. Every little bit makes a difference, be it for better or worse, and that day we had a steep hill to go up. Then I began to understand what I had heard of. Of course, I wanted to put my head forward and take the carriage up with a will as we had been used to do; but no, I had to pull with my head up now, and that took all the spirit out of me, and the strain came on my back and legs. When we came in, Ginger said, "Now you see what it is like; but this is not bad, and if it does not get much worse than this I shall say nothing about it, for we are very well treated here; but if they strain me up tight, why, let 'em look out! I can't bear it, and I won't."

Day by day, hole by hole, our bearing-reins were shortened, and instead of looking forward with pleasure to having my harness put on, as I used to do, I began to dread it. Ginger too seemed restless, thought she said very little. The worst was yet to come.

X. A Strike For Liberty

ONE day my lady came down later than usual, and the silk rustled more than ever. "Drive to the Duchess of B——'s," she said, and then after a pause, "Are you never going to get those horses' heads up, York? Raise them at once, and let us have no more of this humoring nonsense."

York came to me first, while the groom stood at Ginger's head. He drew my head back and fixed the rein so tight that it was almost intolerable; then he went to Ginger, who was impatiently jerking her head up and down against the bit, as was her way now. She had a good idea of what was coming, and the moment York took the rein off the turret in order to shorten it, she took her opportunity, and reared up so suddenly that York had his nose roughly hit and his hat knocked off; the groom was nearly thrown off his legs. At once they both flew to her head, but she was a match for them, and went on plunging, rearing, and kicking in a most desperate manner; at last she kicked right over the carriage pole and fell down, after giving me a severe blow on my near quarter. There is no knowing what further mischief she might have done, had not York sat himself down flat on her head to prevent her struggling, at the same time calling out, "Unbuckle the black horse! Run for the winch and unscrew the carriage pole! Cut the trace here, somebody, if you can't unhitch it!" The groom soon set me free from Ginger and the carriage, and led me to my box. He just turned me in as I was, and ran back to York. I was much excited by what had happened, and if I had ever been used to kick or rear I am sure I should have done it then; but I never had, and there I stood, angry, sore in my leg, my head still strained up to the terret on the saddle, and no power to get it down. I was very miserable, and felt much inclined to kick the first person who came near me.

Before long, however, Ginger was led in by two grooms, a good deal knocked about and bruised. York came with her and gave us orders, and then came to look at me. In a moment he let down my head.

"Confound these check-reins!" he said to himself; "I thought we should have some mischief soon. Master will be sorely vexed. But here, if a woman's husband can't rule her, of course a servant can't; so I wash my hands of it, and if she can't get to the Duchess' garden party I can't help it."

York did not say this before the men; he always spoke respectfully when they were by. Now he felt me all over, and soon found the place above my hock where I had been kicked. It was swelled and painful; he ordered it to be sponged with hot water, and then some lotion was put on.

Lord W—— was much put out when he learned what had happened; he blamed York for giving way to his mistress, to which he replied that in future he would much prefer to receive his orders only from his lordship. I thought York might have stood up better for his horses, but perhaps I am no judge.

Ginger was never put into the carriage again, but when she was well of her bruises one of Lord W——'s younger sons said he should like to have her; he was sure she would make a good hunter. As for me, I was obliged still to go in the carriage, and had a fresh partner called Max; he had always been used to the tight rein. I asked him how it was he bore it.

"Well," he said, "I bear it because I must; but it is shortening my life, and it will shorten yours too, if you have to stick to it."

"Do you think," I said, "that our masters know how bad it is for us?"

"I can't say," he replied, "but the dealers and the horse-doctors know it very well. I was at a dealer's once, who was training me and another horse to go as a pair; he was getting our heads up, and he said, a little higher and a little higher every day. A gentleman who was there asked him why he did so. 'Because,' said he, 'people won't buy them unless we do. The fashionable people want their horses to carry their heads high and to step high. Of course, it is very bad for the horses, but then it is good for trade. The horses soon wear up, and they come for another pair.' That," said Max, "is what he said in my hearing, and you can judge for yourself."

What I suffered with that rein for four months in my lady's carriage would be hard to describe; but I am quite sure that, had it lasted much longer, either my health or my temper would have given way. Before that, I never knew what it was to foam at the mouth, but now the action of the sharp bit on my tongue and jaw, and the constrained position of my head and throat, always caused me to froth at the mouth more or less. Some people think it very fine to see this, and say, "What fine, spirited creatures!" But it is just as unnatural for horses as for men to foam at the mouth; it is a sure sign of some discomfort, and should be attended to. Besides this, there was a pressure on my windpipe, which often made my breathing very uncomfortable; when I returned from my work, my neck and chest were strained and painful, my mouth and tongue tender, and I felt worn and depressed.

In my old home I always knew that John and my master were my friends; but here, although in many ways I was well treated, I had no friend. York might have known, and very likely did know, how that rein harassed me; but I suppose he took it as a matter of course that could not be helped; at any rate, nothing was done to relieve me.

XI. A Horse Fair

No doubt a horse fair is a very amusing place to those who have nothing to lose; at any rate, there is plenty to see.

Long strings of young horses out of the country, fresh from the marshes, and droves of shaggy little Welsh ponies, no higher than Merrylegs; and hundreds of cart horses of all sorts, some of them with their long tails braided up and tied with scarlet cord; and a good many like myself, handsome and high-bred, but fallen into the middle class, through some accident or blemish, unsoundness of wind, or some other complaint. There were some splendid animals quite in their prime, and fit for anything, they were throwing out their legs and showing off their paces in high style, as they were trotted out with a leading rein, the groom running by the side. But round in the background there were a number of poor things, sadly broken down with hard work, with their knees knuckling over and their hind legs swinging out at every step; and there were some very dejected-looking old horses, with the under-lip hanging down and the ears lying back heavily, as if there was no more pleasure in life, and no more hope; there were some so thin you might see all their ribs, and some with old sores on their backs and hips. These were sad sights for a horse to look upon, who knows not but he may come to the same state. I was put with some useful-looking horses, and a good many people came to look at us. The gentlemen always turned from me when they saw my broken knees; though the man who had me swore it was only a slip in the stall.

The first thing was to pull my mouth open, then to look at my eyes, then feel all the way down my legs and give me a hard feel of the skin and flesh, and then try my paces. It was wonderful what a difference there was in the way these things were done. Some did it in a rough, off-hand way, as if one was only a piece of wood; while others would take their hands gently over one's body, with a pat now and then, as much as to say, "By your leave." Of course, I judged a good deal of the buyers by their manners to myself.

There was one man, I thought, if he would buy me, I should be happy. He was not a gentleman. He was rather a small man, but well made, and quick in all his motions. I knew in a moment, by the way he handled me, that he was used to horses; he spoke gently, and his gray eye had a kindly, cheery look in it. It may seem strange to say—but it is true all the same—that the clean, fresh smell there was about him made me take to him; no smell of old beer and tobacco, which I hated, but a fresh smell as if he had come out of a hayloft. He offered twenty-three pounds for me; but that was refused, and he walked away. I looked after him, but he was gone, and a very hard-looking, loud-voiced man came. I was dreadfully afraid he would have me; but he walked off. One or two more came who did not mean business. Then the hard-faced man came back again and offered twenty-three pounds. A very close bargain was being driven, for my salesman began to think he should not get all he asked, and must come down; but just then the gray-eyed man came back again. I could not help reaching out my head toward him. He stroked my face kindly. "Well, old chap," he said, "I think we should suit each other. I'll give twenty-four for him."

"Say twenty-five, and you shall have him." "Twenty-four then," said my friend, in a very decided tone, "and not another sixpence—yes, or no?"

"Done," said the salesman; "and you may depend upon it there's a monstrous deal of quality in that horse, and if you want him for cab work he's a bargain."

The money was paid on the spot, and my new master took my halter, and led me out of the fair to an inn, where he had a saddle and bridle ready. He gave me a good feed of oats, and stood by while I ate it, talking to himself and talking to me. Half an hour after, we were on our way to London, through pleasant lanes and country roads, until we came into the great thoroughfare, on which we traveled steadily, till in the twilight we reached the great city. The gas lamps were already lighted; there were streets and streets crossing each other, for mile upon mile. I thought we should never come to the end of them. At last, in passing through one, we came to a long cab stand, when my rider called out in a cheery voice, "Good-night, Governor!"

"Hallo!" cried a voice. "Have you got a good one?"

"I think so," replied my owner.

"I wish you luck with him."

"Thank ye, Governor," and he rode on. We soon turned up one of the side-streets, and about half-way up that we turned into a very narrow street, with rather poor-looking houses on one side, and what seemed to be coach-houses and stables on the other.

My owner pulled up at one of the houses and whistled. The door flew open, and a young woman, followed by a little girl and boy, ran out. There was a very lively greeting as my rider dismounted. "Now, then, Harry, my boy, open the gates, and mother will bring us the lantern."

The next minute they were all round me in the stable yard. "Is he gentle, father?" "Yes, Dolly, as gentle as your own kitten; come and pat him." At once the little hand was patting about all over my shoulder without fear. How good it felt!

"Let me get him a bran mash while you rub him down," said the mother. "Do, Polly, it's just what he wants; and I know you've got a beautiful mash ready for me."

I was led into a comfortable, clean-smelling stall with plenty of dry straw, and after a capital supper, I lay down, thinking I was going to be happy.

XII. A London Cab Horse

My new master's name was Jeremiah Barker, but as every one called him Jerry, I shall do the same. Polly, his wife, was just as good a match as a man could have. She was a plump, trim, tidy little woman, with smooth, dark hair, dark eyes, and a merry little mouth. The boy was nearly twelve years old, a tall, frank, good-tempered lad; and little Dorothy (Dolly they called her) was her mother over again, at eight years old. They were all wonderfully fond of each other; I never knew such a happy, merry family before or since. Jerry had a cab of his own, and two horses, which he drove and attended to himself. His other horse was a tall, white, rather large-boned animal, called Captain. He was old now, but when he was young he must have been splendid; he had still a proud way of holding his head and arching his neck; in fact, he was a high-bred, fine-mannered, noble old horse, every inch of him. He told me that in his early youth he went to the Crimean War; he belonged to an officer in the cavalry, and used to lead the regiment.

The next morning, when I was well-groomed, Polly and Dolly came into the yard to see me and make friends. Harry had been helping his father since the early morning, and had stated his opinion that I should turn out "a regular brick." Polly brought me a slice of apple, and Dolly a piece of bread, and made as much of me as if I had been the Black Beauty of olden time. It was a great treat to be petted again and talked to in a gentle voice, and I let them see as well as I could that I wished to be friendly. Polly thought I was very handsome, and a great deal too good for a cab, if it was not for the broken knees.

"Of course there's no one to tell us whose fault that was," said Jerry, "and as long as I don't know I shall give him the benefit of the doubt; for a firmer, neater stepper I never rode. We'll call him Jack, after the old one—shall we, Polly?"

"Do," she said, "for I like to keep a good name going."

Captain went out in the cab all the morning. Harry came in after school to feed me and give me water. In the afternoon I was put into the cab. Jerry took as much pains to see if the collar and bridle fitted comfortably as if he had been John Manly over again. There was no check-rein, no curb, nothing but a plain ring snaffle. What a blessing that was!

After driving through the side-street we came to the large cabstand where Jerry had said "Good-night." On one side of this wide street were high houses with wonderful shop fronts, and on the other was an old church and churchyard, surrounded by iron palisades. Alongside these iron rails a number of cabs were drawn up, waiting for passengers; bits of hay were lying about on the ground; some of the men were standing together talking; some were sitting on their boxes reading the newspaper; and one or two were feeding their horses with bits of hay, and giving them a drink of water. We pulled up in the rank at the back of the last cab. Two or three men came round and began to look at me and pass their remarks.

"Very good for a funeral," said one.

"Too smart-looking," said another, shaking his head in a very wise way; "you'll find out something wrong one of these fine mornings, or my name isn't Jones."

"Well," said Jerry pleasantly, "I suppose I need not find it out till it find me out, eh? And if so, I'll keep up my spirits a little longer."

Then there came up a broad-faced man, dressed in a great gray coat with great gray capes and great white buttons, a gray hat, and a blue comforter loosely tied around his neck; his hair was gray, too; but he was a jolly-looking fellow, and the other men made way for him. He looked me all over, as if he had been going to buy me; and then straightening himself up with a grunt, he said, "He's the right sort for you, Jerry; I don't care what you gave for him, he'll be worth it." Thus my character was established on the stand. This man's name was Grant, but he was called "Gray Grant," or "Governor Grant." He had been the longest on that stand of any of the men, and he took it upon himself to settle matters and stop disputes.

The first week of my life as a cab horse was very trying. I had never been used to London, and the noise, the hurry, the crowds of horses, carts, and carriages, that I had to make my way through, made me feel anxious and harassed; but I soon found that I could perfectly trust my driver, and then I made myself easy, and got used to it.

Jerry was as good a driver as I had ever known; and what was better, he took as much thought for his horses as he did for himself. He soon found out that I was willing to work and do my best; and he never laid the whip on me, unless it was gently drawing the end of it over my back, when I was to go on; but generally I knew this quite well by the way in which he took up the reins; and I believe his whip was more frequently stuck up by his side than in his hand.

In a short time I and my master understood each other, as well as horse and man can do. In the stable, too, he did all that he could for our comfort. The stalls were the old-fashioned style, too much on the slope; but he had two movable bars fixed across the back of our stalls, so that at night, when we were resting, he just took off our halters and put up the bars, and thus we could turn about and stand whichever way we pleased, which is a great comfort.

Jerry kept us very clean, and gave us as much change of food as he could, and always plenty of it; and not only that, but he always gave us plenty of clean fresh water, which he allowed to stand by us both night and day, except of course when we came in warm. Some people say that a horse ought not to drink all he likes; but I know if we are allowed to drink when we want it we drink only a little at a time, and it does us a great deal more good than swallowing down half a bucketful at a time because we have been left without till we are thirsty and miserable. Some grooms will go home to their beer and leave us for hours with our dry hay and oats and nothing to moisten them; then of course we gulp down too much at once, which helps to spoil our breathing and sometimes chills our stomachs. But the best thing that we had here was our Sundays for rest! we worked so hard in the week, that I do not think we could have kept up to it, but for that day; besides, we had then time to enjoy each other's company.

XIII. Dolly and A Real Gentleman

THE winter came in early, with a great deal of cold and wet. There was snow, or sleet, or rain, almost every day for weeks, changing only for keen driving winds or sharp frosts. The horses all felt it very much. When it is a dry cold, a couple of good thick rugs will keep the warmth in us; but when it is soaking rain, they soon get wet through and are no good. Some of the drivers had a waterproof cover to throw over, which was a fine thing; but some of the men were so poor that they could not protect either themselves or their horses, and many of them suffered very much that winter. When we horses had worked half the day we went to our dry stables, and could rest; while they had to sit on their boxes, sometimes staying out as late as one or two o'clock in the morning, if they had a party to wait for.

When the streets were slippery with frost or snow, that was the worst of all for us horses; one mile of such traveling with a weight to draw, and no firm footing, would take more out of us than four on a good road; every nerve and muscle of our bodies is on the strain to keep our balance; and, added to this, the fear of falling is more exhausting than anything else. If the roads are very bad, indeed, our shoes are roughed, but that makes us feel nervous at first.

One cold windy day, Dolly brought Jerry a basin of something hot, and was standing by him while he ate it. He had scarcely begun, when a gentleman, walking toward us very fast, held up his umbrella. Jerry touched his hat in return, gave the basin to Dolly, and was taking off my cloth, when the gentleman, hastening up, cried out, "No, no, finish your soup, my friend; I have not much time to spare, but I can wait till you have done, and set your little girl safe on the pavement."

So saying, he seated himself in the cab. Jerry thanked him kindly, and came back to Dolly. "There, Dolly, that's a gentleman; that's a real gentleman, Dolly; he has got time and thought for the comfort of a poor cabman and a little girl."

Jerry finished his soup, set the child across, and then took his orders to drive to Clapham Rise. Several times after that, the same gentleman took our cab. I think he was very fond of dogs and horses, for whenever we took him to his own door, two or three dogs would come bounding out to meet him. Sometimes he came round and patted me saying in his quiet, pleasant way: "This horse has got a good master, and he deserves it." It was a very rare thing for any one to notice the horse that had been working for him. I have known ladies to do it now and then, and this gentleman, and one or two others have given me a pat and a kind word; but ninety-nine out of a hundred would as soon think of patting the steam engine that drew the train.

One day, he and another gentleman took our cab; they stopped at a shop in R—— Street, and while his friend went in, he stood at the door. A little ahead of us on the other side of the street, a cart with two very fine horses was standing before some wine vaults; the carter was not with them, and I cannot tell how long they had been standing, but they seemed to think they had waited long enough, and began to move off. Before they had gone, many paces, the carter came running out and caught them. He seemed furious at their having moved, and with whip and rein punished them brutally, even beating them about the head. Our gentleman saw it all, and stepping quickly across the street, said in a decided voice: "If you don't stop that directly, I'll have you arrested for leaving your horses, and for brutal conduct."

The man, who had clearly been drinking, poured forth some abusive language, but he left off knocking the horses about, and taking the reins, got into his cart; meantime our friend had quietly taken a notebook from his pocket, and looking at the name and address painted on the cart, he wrote something down.

"What do you want with that?" growled the carter, as he cracked his whip and was moving on. A nod and a grim smile was the only answer he got.

On returning to the cab, our friend was joined by his companion, who said laughing, "I should have thought, Wright, you had enough business of your own to look after, without troubling yourself about other people's horses and servants."

Our friend stood still for a moment, and throwing his head a little back, "Do you know why this world is as bad as it is?"

"No," said the other.

"Then I'll tell you. It is because people think only about their own business, and won't trouble themselves to stand up for the oppressed, nor bring the wrong-doer to light. I never see a wicked thing like this without doing what I can, and many a master has thanked me for letting him know how his horses have been used."

"I wish there were more gentlemen like you, sir," said Jerry, "for they are wanted badly enough in this city."

XIV. Poor Ginger

ONE day, while our cab and many others were waiting outside one of the parks where music was playing, a shabby old cab drove up beside ours. The horse was an old worn-out chestnut, with an ill-kept coat, and bones that showed plainly through it, the knees knuckled over, and the fore-legs were very unsteady. I had been eating some hay, and the wind rolled a little lock of it that way, and the poor creature put out her long thin neck and picked it up, and then turned round and looked about for more. There was a hopeless look in the dull eye that I could not help noticing, and then, as I was thinking where I had seen that horse before, she looked full at me and said, "Black Beauty, is that you?"

It was Ginger! but how changed! The beautifully arched and glossy neck was now straight, and lank, and fallen in; the clean, straight legs and delicate fetlocks were swelled; the joints were grown out of shape with hard work; the face, that was once so full of spirit and life, was now full of suffering, and I could tell by the heaving of her sides, and her frequent cough, how bad her breath was. Our drivers were standing together a little way off, so I sidled up to her a step or two, that we might have a little quiet talk. It was a sad tale that she had to tell.

After a twelvemonth's run off at Earlshall, she was considered to be fit for work again, and was sold to a gentleman. For a little while she got on very well, but after a longer gallop than usual, the old strain returned, and after being rested and doctored she was again sold. In this way she changed hands several times, but always getting lower down.

"And so at last," said she, "I was bought by a man who keeps a number of cabs and horses, and lets them out. You look well off, and I am glad of it, but I could not tell you what my life has been. When they found out my weakness, they said I was not worth what they gave for me, and that I must go into one of the low cabs, and just be used up; that is what they are doing, whipping and working with never one thought of what I suffer—they paid for me, and must get it out of me, they say. The man who hires me now pays a deal of money to the owner every day, and so he has to get it out of me, too; and so it's all the week round and round, with never a Sunday rest."

I said, "You used to stand up for yourself if you were ill-used."

"Ah!" she said, "I did once, but it's no use; men are strongest, and if they are cruel and have no feeling, there is nothing that we can do but just bear it—bear it on and on to the end. I wish the end was come, I wish I was dead. I have seen dead horses, and I am sure they do not suffer pain."

I was very much troubled, and I put my nose up to hers, but I could say nothing to comfort her. I think she was pleased to see me, for she said, "You are the only friend I ever had."

Just then her driver came up, and with a tug at her mouth, backed her out of the line and drove off, leaving me very sad, indeed.

A short time after this, a cart with a dead horse in it passed our cab stand. The head hung out of the cart tail, the lifeless tongue was slowly dropping with blood; and the sunken eyes! but I can't speak of them, the sight was too dreadful! It was a chestnut horse with a long, thin neck. I saw a white streak down the forehead. I believe it was Ginger; I hoped it was, for then her troubles would be over. Oh! if men were more merciful, they would shoot us before we came to such misery.

XV.

AT a sale I found myself in company with a lot of horses— some lame, some broken-winded, some old, and some that I am sure it would have been merciful to shoot.

The buyers and sellers, too, many of them, looked not much better off than the poor beasts they were bargaining about. There were poor old men, trying to get a horse or pony for a few pounds, that might drag about some little wood or coal cart. There were poor men trying to sell a worn-out beast for two or three pounds, rather than have the greater loss of killing him. Some of them looked as if poverty and hard times had hardened them all over; but there were others that I would have willingly used the last of my strength in serving; poor and shabby, but kind and humane, with voices that I could trust. There was one tottering old man that took a great fancy to me, and I to him, but I was not strong enough—it was an anxious time! Coming from the better part of the fair, I noticed a man who looked like a gentleman farmer, with a young boy by his side; he had a broad back and round shoulders, a kind, ruddy face, and he wore a broad-brimmed hat. When he came up to me and my companions, he stood still, and gave a pitiful look round upon us. I saw his eye rest on me; I had still a good mane and tail, which did something for my appearance. I pricked my ears and looked at him.

"There's a horse, Willie, that has known better days."

"Poor old fellow!" said the boy; "do you think, grandpapa, he was ever a carriage horse?"

"Oh, yes! my boy," said the farmer, coming closer, "he might have been anything when he was young; look at his nostrils and his ears, the shape of his neck and shoulder; there's a deal of breeding about that horse." He put out his hand and gave me a kind pat on the neck. I put out my nose in answer to his kindness; the boy stroked my face.

"Poor old fellow! see, grandpapa, how well he understands kindness. Could not you buy him and make him young again as you did with Ladybird?"

"My dear boy, I can't make all old horses young; besides, Ladybird was not so very old, as she was run down and badly used."

"Well, grandpapa, I don't believe that this one is old; look at his mane and tail. I wish you would look into his mouth, and then you could tell; though he is so very thin, his eyes are not sunk like some old horses." The old gentleman laughed. "Bless the boy! he is as horsey as his old grandfather."

"But do look at his mouth, grandpapa, and ask the price; I am sure he would grow young in our meadows."

The man who had brought me for sale now put in his word. "The young gentleman's a real knowing one, sir. Now, the fact is, this 'ere hoss is just pulled down with over-work in the cabs; he's not an old one, and I heard as how the vetenary said that a six-months' run off would set him right up, being as how his wind was not broken. I've had the tending of him these ten days past, and a gratefuller, pleasanter animal I never met with, and 'twould be worth a gentleman's while to give a five-pound note for him, and let him have a chance. I'll be bound he'd be worth twenty pounds next spring."

The old gentleman laughed, and the little boy looked up eagerly. "O, grandpapa, did you not say the colt sold for five pounds more than you expected? You would not be poorer if you did buy this one."

The farmer slowly felt my legs, which were much swelled and strained; then he looked at my mouth. "Thirteen or fourteen, I should say; just trot him out, will you?"

I arched my poor thin neck, raised my tail a little and threw out my legs as well as I could, for they were very stiff.

"What is the lowest you will take for him?" said the farmer as I came back. "Five pounds, sir; that was the lowest price my master set."

"'Tis a speculation," said the old gentleman, shaking his head, but at the same time slowly drawing out his purse, "quite a speculation! Have you any more business here?" he said, counting the sovereigns into his hand. "No, sir, I can take him for you to the inn, if you please."

"Do so, I am now going there."

XVI. My Last Home

ONE day, during this summer, the groom cleaned and dressed me with such extraordinary care that I thought some new change must be at hand; he trimmed my fetlocks and legs, passed the tar-brush over my hoofs, and even parted my forelock. I think the harness had an extra polish. Willie seemed half-anxious, half-merry, as he got into the chaise with his grandfather. "If the ladies take to him," said the old gentleman, "they'll be suited and he'll be suited; we can but try."

At the distance of a mile or two from the village, we came to a pretty, low house, with a lawn and shrubbery at the front, and a drive up to the door. Willie rang the bell, and asked if Miss Blomefield or Miss Ellen was at home. Yes, they were. So, while Willie stayed with me, Mr. Thoroughgood went into the house. In about ten minutes he returned, followed by three ladies; one tall, pale lady, wrapped in a white shawl, leaned on a younger lady, with dark eyes and a merry face; the other, a very stately-looking person, was Miss Blomefield. They all came and looked at me and asked questions. The younger lady—that was Miss Ellen—took to me very much; she said she was sure she should like me, I had such a good face. The tall, pale lady said she should always be nervous in riding behind a horse that had once been down, as I might come down again, and if I did she should never get over the fright."

"You see, ladies," said Mr. Thoroughgood, "many first-rate horses have had their knees broken through the carelessness of their drivers, without any fault of their own, and from what I see of this horse, I should say that is his case; but, of course, I do not wish to influence you. If you incline, you can have him on trial, and then your coachman will see what he thinks of him."

"You have always been such a good adviser to us about our horses," said the stately lady, "that your recommendation would go a long way with me, and if my sister Lavinia sees no objection, we will accept your offer of a trial, with thanks."

It was then arranged that I should be sent for the next day. In the morning a smart-looking young man came for me; at first, he looked pleased; but when he saw my knees, he said in a disappointed voice: "I didn't think, sir, you would have recommended a blemished horse like that."

"'Handsome is that handsome does,'" said my master; "you are only taking him on trial, and I am sure you will do fairly by him, young man; if he is not safe as any horse you ever drove, send him back."

I was led to my new home, placed in a comfortable stable, fed, and left to myself. The next day, when my groom was cleaning my face, he said: "That is just like the star that Black Beauty had, he is much the same height, too; I wonder where he is now."

A little further on, he came to the place in my neck where I was bled, and where a little knot was left in the skin. He almost started, and begun to look me over carefully, talking to himself. "White star in the forehead, one white foot on the off side, this little knot just in that place"; then, looking at the middle of my back—"and as I am alive, there is that little patch of white hair that John used to call 'Beauty's threepenny bit.' It must be Black Beauty! Why, Beauty! Beauty! do you know me? little Joe Green, that almost killed you?" And he began patting and patting me as if he was quite overjoyed.

I could not say that I remembered him, for now he was a fine grown young fellow, with black whiskers, and a man's voice, but I was sure he knew me, and that he was Joe Green, and I was very glad. I put my nose up to him, and tried to say that we were friends. I never saw a man so pleased.

"Give you a fair trial! I should think so, indeed! I wonder who the rascal was that broke your knees, my old Beauty! you must have been badly served out somewhere; well, well, it won't be my fault if you haven't good times of it now. I wish John Manly was here to see you."

In the afternoon I was put into a low Park chair and brought to the door. Miss Ellen was going to try me, and Green went with her. I soon found that she was a good driver, and she seemed pleased with my paces. I heard Joe telling her about me, and that he was sure I was Squire Gordon's old "Black Beauty."

When we returned, the other sisters came out to hear how I had behaved myself. She told them what she had just heard, and said: "I shall certainly write to Mrs. Gordon, and tell her that her favorite horse has come to us. How pleased she will be!"

After this I was driven every day for a week or so, and as I appeared to be quite safe, Miss Lavinia at last ventured out in the small close carriage. After this it was quite decided to keep me and call me by my old name of Black Beauty.

I have now lived in this happy place a whole year.

Her First Horse Show

David Gray

SHE folded the program carefully for preservation in her memory-book, and devoured the scene with her eyes. It was hard to believe, but unquestionably Angelica Stanton, in the flesh, was in Madison Square Garden at the horse show. The great arena was crowded; the band was playing, and a four-in-hand was swinging around the tan-bark ring.

What had been her dream since she put away her dolls and the flea-bitten pony was realized. The pony had been succeeded by Lady Washington, and with Lady Washington opened the epoch when she began to hunt with the grown-up people and to reflect upon the outside world. From what she had gathered from the men in the hunting-field, the outside world seemed to center in the great horse show, and most of what was interesting and delightful in life took place there.

Besides the obvious profit of witnessing this institution, there had arisen, later on, more serious considerations which led Angelica to take an interest in it. Since the disappearance of Lady Washington and the failure to trace her, Angelica's hope was in the show.

One of the judges who had visited Jim had unwittingly laid the bases of this hope. "All the best performers in America are exhibited there," he had said in the course of an interminable discussion upon the great subject. And was not Lady Washington probably the best? Clearly, therefore, soon or late Lady Washington would be found winning blue ribbons at Madison Square Garden.

41

To this cheering conclusion the doubting Thomas within her replied that so desirable a miracle could never be; and she cherished the doubt, though rather to provoke contrary fate into refuting it than because it embodied her convictions. She knew that some day Lady Washington must come back.

After Jim had sold Lady Washington, he had been informed by Chloe, the parlor-maid, how Angelica felt, and he repented his act. He had tried to buy the mare back, but the man to whom he had sold her had sold her to a dealer, and he had sold her to somebody who had gone abroad, and no one knew what this person had done with her. So Lady Washington had disappeared, and Angelica mourned for her. Two years passed, two years that were filled with doubt and disappointment. Each autumn Jim went North with his horses, but never suggested taking Angelica. As for Angelica, the subject was too near her heart for her to broach it. Thus it seemed that life was slipping away, harshly withholding opportunity.

That November, for reasons of his own, Jim decided to take Angelica along with him. When he told her of his intention, she gasped, but made no demonstration. On the threshold of fulfilling her hope she was afraid to exult: she knew how things are snatched away the moment one begins to count upon them; but inwardly she was happy to the point of apprehension. On the trip North she "knocked wood" scrupulously every time she was lured into a day-dream which pictured the finding of Lady Washington, and thus she gave the evil forces of destiny no opening.

The first hour of the show overwhelmed her. It was too splendid and mystifying to be comprehended immediately, or to permit a divided attention. Even Lady Washington dropped out of her thoughts, but only until the jumping classes began. The first hunter that trotted across the tanbark brought her back to her quest.

But after two days the mystery was no more a mystery, and the splendor had faded out. The joy of it had faded out, too. For two days she had pored over the entry-lists and had studied every horse that entered the ring; but the search for Lady

Washington had been a vain one. Furthermore, all the best horses by this time had appeared in some class, and the chances of Lady Washington's turning up seemed infinitesimal. Reluctantly she gave up hope. She explained it to herself that probably there had been a moment of vainglorious pride when she had neglected to "knock wood." She would have liked to discuss it with somebody; but Chloe and her colored mammy, who understood such matters, were at the "Pines" in Virginia, and Jim would probably laugh at her; so she maintained silence and kept her despair to herself.

It was the evening of the third day, and she was at the show again, dressed in her habit, because she was going to ride. Her brother was at the other end of the Garden, hidden by a row of horses. He was waiting to show in a class of park hacks. There was nothing in it that looked like Lady Washington, and she turned her eyes away from the ring with a heavy heart. The band had stopped playing, and there was no one to talk to but her aunt's maid, and this maid was not companionable. She fell to watching the people in the boxes; she wished that she knew some of them. There was a box just below her which looked attractive. There were two pretty women in it, and some men who looked as if they were nice; they were laughing and seemed to be having a good time. She wished she was with them, or home, or anywhere else than where she was.

Presently the music struck up again; the hum of the innumerable voices took a higher pitch. The ceaseless current of promenaders staring and bowing at the boxes went slowly around and around. Nobody paid any attention to the horses, but all jostled and chattered and craned their necks to see the people. When her brother's Redgauntlet took the blue ribbon in the heavyweight green-hunter class, not a person in the whole Garden applauded except herself. She heard a man ask, "What took the blue?" And she heard his friend answer, "Southern horse, I believe; don't know the owner." They didn't even know Jim! She would have left the place and gone back to her aunt's for a comfortable cry, but she was going to ride Hilda in the ladies' saddle class, which came toward the end of the evening.

The next thing on the program were some qualified hunters which might be expected to show some good jumping. This was something to be thankful for, and she turned her attention to the ring.

"I think I'll go down on the floor," she said to the maid. "I'm tired of sitting still."

In theory Miss Angelica Stanton was at the horse show escorted by her brother; but in fact she was in the custody of Caroline, the maid of her aunt Henrietta Cushing, who lived in Washington Square. Miss Cushing was elderly, and she disapproved of the horse show because her father had been a charter member of the Society for the Prevention of Cruelty to Animals, and because to go to it in the afternoon interfered with her drive and with her tea, while to go to it in the evening interfered with her whist, and that was not to be thought of. Consequently, when Angelica arrived, the horse show devolved upon Caroline, who accepted the situation not altogether with resignation. She had done Miss Cushing's curls for twenty years, and had absorbed her views.

Angelica would have preferred stopping at the hotel with Jim; but that, he said, was out of the question. Jim admitted that Aunt Henrietta was never intentionally entertaining, but he said that Angelica needed her womanly influence. Jim had brought up Angelica, and the problem sometimes seemed a serious one. She was now sixteen, and he was satisfied that she was going to be a horsewoman, but at times he doubted whether his training was adequate in other respects, and that was why he had brought her to the horse show and had incarcerated her at Aunt Henrietta's.

The girl led Caroline through the crowd, and took a position at the end, between the first and last jumps. As the horses were shown, they went round the ring, came back, and finished in front of them. It was the best place from which to watch, if one wished to see the jumping.

Angelica admitted to herself that some of the men rode pretty well, but not as well as some of the men rode at their out-of-door shows at home; and the tan-bark was not as good as turf. It was a large class, and after eight or ten had been shown, a striking-looking black mare came out of the line and started plunging and rearing toward the first jump. Her rider faced her at the bars, and she minced reluctantly forward. Just before they reached the wings the man struck her. She stopped short and whirled back into the ring.

From the time the black mare appeared Angelica's heart almost stopped beating. "I'm sure of it, I'm sure of it!" she gasped. "Three white feet and the star. Caroline," she said, "that's Lady Washington. He oughtn't to strike her. He mustn't!"

"Hush, miss," said Caroline. "We'll be conspicuous."

The man was bringing the mare back toward the jump. As before, he used his whip, intending to drive her into the wings, and, as before, she stopped, reared angrily, wheeled about, and came back plunging. The man quieted her after a little, and turned her again toward the hurdle. It was his last chance. She came up sulkily, tossing her head and edging away from the bars. As he got near the wings he raised his whip again. Then the people in that part of the Garden heard a girl's shrill excited voice cry out: "You mustn't hit her! Steady, Lady Washington! Drop your curb!"

The black mare's ears went forward at the sound of the voice. The young man on her back put down his uplifted whip and loosened the rein on the bit. He glanced around with an embarrassed smile, and the next instant he was over the jump, and the mare was galloping for the hurdle beyond.

Suddenly Angelica became conscious that several thousand people were staring at her with looks of wonder and amusement. Caroline clutched her arm and dragged her away from the rail. The girl colored, and shook herself free.

"I don't care," she said. "He shouldn't have hit her. She can jump anything if she's ridden right. I knew we'd find her," she muttered excitedly. "I knew it!"

Caroline struggled desperately through the crowd with her charge.

"Whatever will Miss Cushing say!" she gasped.

Angelica forgot the crowd. "I don't care," she said. "If Aunt Henrietta had ever owned Lady Washington she'd have done the same thing. And if you tell her I'll pay you back. She'll know that you let me leave my seat, and she told you not to." This silenced Caroline.

"There! He's fussed her mouth again," she went on. The black mare had refused, and was rearing at the jump next the last. The girl stood on tiptoe and watched impatiently for a moment.

"There she goes," she murmured, with a sigh. The judges had ordered the horse out.

Angelica tagged along disconsolately through the crowd till a conversation between two men who were leaning against the rail caught her ear.

"I wonder who that little girl was," said one. "The mare seemed to know her voice, but Reggie doesn't call her Lady Washington."

"No—Hermione," said the other. "He may have changed it, though," he added. "He gives them all names beginning with H."

"You'll have an easy time beating him in the five-foot-six jumps," said the first man. "It's a good mare, but he can't ride her."

Angelica wondered who they were, but they turned around just then, and she dropped her eyes and hurried after Caroline.

As they made their way through the crowd, a nudge from the maid took her thoughts from Lady Washington. She had been wondering how she would find the young man who had ridden her. She looked up and saw that a man was bowing to her. It was Mr. "Billy" Livingstone. Mr. Livingstone was nearly sixty, but he had certain qualities of permanent youth which made him "Billy" to three generations.

"Hello, Angelica!" he exclaimed. "When did you turn up! How you've grown!"

"I came up North with Jim," she replied.

"You should have let me know," he said. "You know Jim never writes any one. This is the first time I've been here. I'm just back from the country. Where's your box—that is, who are you with!"

"I'm here with my maid," said Angelica, with a somewhat conscious dignity. "Jim is with the horses."

Livingstone looked from the slender girl to the substantial Caroline, and the corners of his mouth twitched.

"I prefer to be alone this way," she explained. "It's more independent."

Mr. Livingstone thought a moment. "Of course that's so," he said. "But I think I've got a better plan; let's hunt up Mrs. Dicky Everett."

"Is she an old woman?" asked Angelica.

"Not so terribly old," said Mr. Livingstone. "I suppose you'd call her middle-aged."

"Thirty?" asked Angelica.

"Near it, I'm afraid," he answered.

"Well, I don't know," said Angelica. "That's pretty old. She won't have anything to say to me."

"She knows something about a horse," said Livingstone, "though, of course, she can't ride the way you do. If you find her stupid, I'll take you away; but I want you to come because she will be very nice to me for bringing you."

He turned to Caroline. "I'm a friend of Miss Stanton's brother. Go to your seat, and I'll bring Miss Stanton back to you."

Then he led the way up the stairs, and Angelica followed, wondering what sort of person Mrs. "Dicky" Everett might be.

She cheered herself with the thought that she could not be any older or more depressing than Aunt Henrietta, and if she was fond of horses she might know who owned Lady Washington.

Livingstone consulted his program. "It's down on this side," he said. She followed him mechanically, with her eyes wandering toward the ring, till presently they stopped.

"Hello!" she heard them call to Livingstone, as he stepped in ahead of her, and the next moment she realized that she was in the very box which she had watched from her seat among the chairs.

"I want to present you to my friend Miss Stanton," Livingstone said. He repeated the names, but they made no impression upon her, because there, standing in front of her, was the young man who had ridden Lady Washington.

"You seem to know each other," said Livingstone "Am I wasting my breath? Is this a joke?"

He looked at Angelica. She was speechless with mixed joy and embarrassment.

"Come here, my dear," said one of the two pretty women, "and sit down beside me. Miss Stanton," she went on to Livingstone, "very kindly tried to teach Reggie how to ride Hermione, and we are glad to have the chance to thank her."

"I don't understand at all," said Livingstone. "But there are so many things that I shall never understand that one more makes no difference."

Angelica's self-confidence began to come back.

"Why, he was riding Lady Washington with a whip," she explained. "And I just called out to him not to. You remember Lady Washington,—she was a four-year-old when you were at the Pines,—and you know you never could touch her with a whip."

"I remember very well," said Livingstone. "You flattered me by offering to let me ride her, an offer which, I think, I declined. When did you sell her?"

"Two years ago," said Angelica.

Then the other young woman spoke. "But how did you recognize the horse?" she asked. "You haven't seen it for two years."

"Recognize her!" exclaimed Angelica. "I guess if you had ever owned Lady Washington you would have recognized her. I broke her as a two-year-old, and schooled her myself. Jim says she's the best mare we ever had." Angelica looked at the woman pityingly. She was sweet-looking and had beautiful clothes, but she was evidently a goose.

"Miss Stanton won the high jump with the mare," Livingstone remarked, "at their hunt show down in Virginia."

"It was only six feet," said the girl, "but she can do better than that. Jim wouldn't let me ride her at anything bigger."

"I should hope not," said the lady by whose side she was sitting. Then she asked suddenly, "You are not Jimmie Stanton's sister?"

"Yes," said Angelica.

"I'd like to know why he hasn't brought you to see me!"

"He's awfully busy with the horses," the girl replied.

"He has to stop at the Waldorf and see about the show with the men, and he makes me stay with Aunt Henrietta Cushing." She stopped abruptly. She was afraid that what she had said might sound disloyal. "I like to stop with Aunt Henrietta," she added solemnly. "Besides, I've been busy looking for Lady Washington."

The young man whom they called Reggie, together with Mr. Livingstone and the lady beside Angelica, laughed openly at this allusion to Miss Cushing.

"Do you know her?" asked Angelica.

"Oh, everybody knows your Aunt Henrietta," said the lady.

"And loves her," added Livingstone, solemnly.

The lady laughed a little. "You see, she's connected with nearly everybody. She's a sort of connection of Reggie's and mine, so I suppose we're sort of cousins of yours. I hope you will like us."

"I don't know much about my relations on my mother's side," Angelica observed. The distinction between connections and relatives had never been impressed upon her. She was about to add that Jim said that his New York relatives tired him, but caught herself. She paused uneasily.

"Please excuse me," she said, "but I didn't hear Mr. Livingstone introduce me to you."

"Why," said Livingstone, who overheard, "this is Mrs. Everett. I told you we were coming into her box."

"I thought she must have stepped out," said Angelica.

"You told me she was middle-aged."

A peal of laughter followed.

"Angelica! Angelica!" Mr. Livingstone exclaimed.

"But you did," said Angelica. "I asked you if she was an old lady, and you said, 'Not so terribly old—middle aged.' And she's not; she's young."

"Things can never be as they were before," said Livingstone, mournfully, as the laughter died away.

"No," said Mrs. Everett.

There was a pause, and one of the men turned to Reggie. "What are you going to do about the five-foot-six jumps?"

"Let it go," said Reggie.

"It's a pity," said the other. "If you had met Miss Stanton earlier in the evening, I think she could have taught you to ride that mare. I wanted to see you win your bet."

"Bet?" said Livingstone.

"Reggie's such an idiot," said Mrs. Everett. "He bet Tommy Post that Hermione would beat his chestnut in the five-foot-six jumps, and Reggie can't make Hermione jump at all, so he's lost."

"Not yet; I've got a chance," said Reggie, good-naturedly. "Perhaps I'll go in, after all." The other men laughed.

"I should think you had made monkey enough of yourself for one evening," observed Palfrey, who was his best friend and could say such things.

"Five feet six would be easy for Lady Washington," said Angelica. "I can't get used to calling her by that new name." She hesitated a moment with embarrassment, and then she stammered: "Why don't you let *me* ride her?"

The people in the box looked aghast.

"I'm afraid it wouldn't do," said Reggie, seriously. "It's awfully good of you, but, you see, it wouldn't look well to put a lady on that horse. Suppose something should happen?"

"Good of me!" the girl exclaimed. "I'd love it! I want to ride her again so much!"

"Well," said Reggie, "I'll have her at the park for you tomorrow morning. You can ride her whenever you like."

A low cry of alarm ran through the Garden, and the conversation in the box hushed. A tandem cart had tipped over, and the wheeler was kicking it to pieces.

"I don't like that sort of thing," said Mrs. Everett, with a shudder.

They finally righted the trap, and the driver limped off to show that he was not hurt. The great crowd seemed to draw a long breath of relief, and the even hum of voices went on again. The judges began to award the ribbons, and Angelica looked down at her program.

"Dear me!" she exclaimed. "The saddle class I'm going to ride in is next. I'm afraid I'll be late. Good-by."

"Good-by," they all replied.

"Don't you come," she said to Livingstone. "It's just a step."

"I must keep my word with Caroline," he answered, and he took her to hear seat.

"She's immense, isn't she?" he said, as he came back. "I'm glad Reggie didn't let her ride that brute. She will be killed one of these days."

"She's going to be a great beauty," said Mrs. Everett.

"She looks like her blessed mother," said Livingstone. "I was very fond of her mother. I think that if it hadn't been for Stanton—"

"Stop!" interrupted Mrs. Everett. "Your heart-tragedies are too numerous. Besides, if you *had* married her you wouldn't be here trying to tell us why you didn't." And they all laughed, and cheerfully condemned the judging of the tandem class.

The negro groom who had come up with the Stanton horses met Angelica as she was going down-stairs into the basement where the stalls were. Jim had not appeared, so Angelica and Caroline had started off alone.

"Hilda's went lame behind, Miss Angie," the man said. "She must have cast huhself. They ain't no use to show huh."

Ordinarily this calamity would have disturbed Angelica, but the discovery of Lady Washington was a joy which could not be dimmed.

"Have you told my brother?" she asked.

"Yes, Miss Angie," said the man. "He was gwine to tell you."

"I want to see her," said Angelica, and they went on toward the stall. But what Angelica most wanted was to get among the horses and look for a certain black mare.

Hilda was very lame, and there was fever in the hock. Angelica patted her neck, and turned away with a side glance at Caroline, who, she feared, would rebel at being led through the horses' quarters. She walked down the row of stalls till she came to the corner, then up through another passage till she stopped at a big box-stall over the side of which stretched a black head set on a long, thoroughbred-looking neck.

The small, fine ears, the width between the eyes, the square little muzzle, were familiar; and there was a white star on the forehead. But Angelica did not enumerate these things. Horses to her had personalities and faces, just as people had them. She recognized Lady Washington as she had recognized Mr. Livingstone. She made a little exclamation, and, standing on tiptoe, put her arms about the mare's neck, and kissed it again and again.

"The dear! She remembers me!" the girl said, wiping her eyes. "It's Lady Washington," she explained to Caroline. She reached up to fondle the little muzzle, and the mare nipped playfully.

"Look out, miss," called the stable-boy, who was sitting on a soap-box; "she's mean."

"She's no such thing," said the girl.

"Oh, ain't she?" said the boy.

"Well, if she is, you made her so," retorted Angelica.

The boy grinned. "I ain't only been in the stable two weeks," he said. "She caught me on the second day and nigh broke me leg. You see her act in the ring? Mr. Haughton says he won't ride her no more, and she's entered in the five-foot-six jumps."

The girl looked thoughtfully at the boy and then at the horse. An idea had come to her. She was reflecting upon the last words Mr. Haughton had spoken before she left the box: *"You can ride her whenever you like."*

"I know," she said aloud. "I'm going to ride her in that class. I'm Miss Stanton. I used to own her, you know. My saddle is down there with Mr. Stanton's horses, and I want you to go and get it."

"Oh, never, Miss Angelica!" exclaimed Caroline. "Dear me, not that!"

"You hush," said Angelica.

The stable-boy looked at her incredulously. "I ain't had no orders, miss," he said. "I'll have to see William. Did Mr. Haughton say you might?"

"Of course he said I might," she replied.

The boy said no more and went off after William.

"Of course he said I might," she repeated half aloud. "Didn't he say I might ride her 'whenever I wanted to'? 'Whenever' is any time, and I want to now." She fortified herself behind this sophistry, but she was all in a flutter lest Jim or Mr. Haughton should appear. The thought, however, of being on Lady Washington's back, and showing people that she wasn't sulky and bad-tempered, was a temptation too strong to be resisted.

The boy came back with the head groom, to whom he had explained the matter.

"Why miss," said William, "she'd kill you. I wouldn't want to show her myself. Mr. Haughton, miss, must have been joking. Honest, miss, you couldn't ride Hermione." The man was respectful but firm.

"Think what Miss Cushing would say," said Caroline.

"But I tell you I can," retorted Angelica. She paid no attention to Caroline; her temper flashed up. "You don't seem to understand. I owned that mare when she was Lady Washington, and broke her all myself, and schooled her, too. Mr. Haughton hasn't any 'hands,' and he ought to know better than to raise a whip on her."

William grinned at the unvarnished statement about his master's "hands."

"Are you the young lady what called out to him in the ring?" he asked.

"Yes, I am," said Angelica. "And if he'd done what I told him to she would have won. Here's our Emanuel," she went on. "He'll tell you I can ride her. Emanuel," she demanded, as the negro approached, "haven't I ridden Lady Washington?"

"You jest have, Miss Angie," said Emanuel. "Why," said he, turning to William, "this heah young lady have rode that maah ovah six feet. She done won the high jump at ouah hunt show. That's Lady Washington all right," he went on, looking at the head poked out over the stall. "I got huh maahk on mah ahm foh to remembah huh."

The stable-boy grinned.

"Well, she never bit me," said Angelica.

"The young lady," said Willliam, doubtfully, "wants to ride her in the five-foot-six class. She says Mr. Haughton said she might."

"Oh, Miss Angelica," interposed Caroline, "you'll be kilt!"

"You're a goose," said Angelica. "I've ridden her hundreds of times."

"I don't know how Mistah Jim would like it," said Emanuel; "but she could ride that maah all right, you jest bet."

William was getting interested. He was not so concerned about Mr. Stanton's likes as he was that his stable should take some ribbons.

"Mr. Haughton said you might ride her?" he repeated.

"Of course he did," said Angelica; "I just left him in Mrs. Everett's box, and I've got my own saddle and everything."

"All right, miss," said William. "Get the saddle, Tim."

William did not believe that Mr. Haughton had given any such orders, but he had gotten into trouble not long before by refusing to give a mount to a friend of Haughton's whom he did not know and who came armed only with verbal authority. He knew that if any harm was done he could hide behind that occurrence.

"I want a double-reined snaffle," said Angelica. "Emanuel," she added, "you have the bit I used to ride her with. Bring my own bridle."

"I'm afraid you won't be able to hold her, miss," muttered William; "but it's as you say. Hurry up with that saddle," he called to the stable-boy. "We ain't got no time to lose. They're callin' the class now. You're number two, miss; I'll get your number for you."

"You'll be kilt! You'll be kilt!" said Caroline, dolefully. "Think what Miss Cushing will say!"

"Caroline," said Angelica, "you don't know anything about horses, so you hush." And then she added under her breath, "If I can only get started before Jim sees me!"

In the Everett box they were waiting for the five-foot-six class to begin. They called it the five-foot-six class because there were four jumps that were five feet six inches high; the others were an even five feet. It was the "sensational event" of the evening. Thus far the show had been dull.

"Those saddle-horses were an ordinary lot," observed Reggie.

"This isn't opening very well, either," said Palfrey. The first horse had started out by refusing. Then he floundered into the jump and fell.

"Let's not wait," said Mrs. Everett. But the words were hardly spoken when, with a quick movement, she turned her glasses on the ring. Something unusual was going on at the farther end. A ripple of applause cam down the sides of the Garden, and then she saw a black horse, ridden by a girl, come cantering toward the starting-place.

"It's that child on Hermione! You must stop it, Reggie!" she exclaimed excitedly.

Before any one could move, Angelica had turned the horse toward the first jump. It looked terribly high to Mrs. Everett. It was almost even with the head of the man who was standing on the farther side ready to replace the bars if they should be knocked down.

Tossing her head playfully, the black mare galloped steadily for the wings, took off in her stride, and swept over the jump in a long curve. She landed noiselessly on the tan-bark, and was on again. Around the great ring went the horse and the girl, steadily, not too fast, and taking each jump without a mistake. The great crowd remained breathless and expectant. Horse and rider finished in front of the Everett box, and pulled up to a trot, the mare breathing hard with excitement, but well-mannered.

Then a storm of cheers and hand-clapping burst, the like of which was never heard at a New York horse show before.

As the applause died away, Reggie rose and hurried out. "Let's all go," said Mrs. Everett.

Before they got through the crowd the judges had awarded the ribbons. There was only three other horses that went over all the jumps, and none of them made a clean score. There was no question about which was first. The judges ran their hands down the mare's legs in a vain search for lumps. She was short-coupled, with a beautiful shoulder and powerful quarters. She had four crosses of thoroughbred, and showed it.

"She's a picture mare," said one of the judges, and he tied the blue rosette to her bridle himself. Then the great crowd cheered and clapped again, and Angelica rode down to the entrance as calmly as if she were in the habit of taking blue ribbons daily. But inside she was not calm.

"I've got to cry or something," she thought.

At the gate some one came out of the crowd and took the mare by the head. Angelica looked down, and there were her brother and Reggie and Mrs. Everett's party. The Garden began to swim.

"Oh, Jim!" she murmured, "help me down. It's Lady Washington." Then she threw her arms around his neck and wept.

They were at supper in the old Waldorf Palm Room before Angelica was quite certain whether actual facts had been taking place or whether she had been dreaming. It seemed rather too extraordinary and too pleasant to be true. Still, she was sure that she was there, because the people stared at her when she came in dressed in her habit, and whispered to each other about her. Furthermore, a party of judges came over and asked Mrs. Everett to present them.

There never before was quite such an evening. It was after twelve, at least, and nobody had suggested that she ought to be in bed. One pleasant thing followed another in quick succession, and there seemed no end to them. She was absorbed in an edible rapture which Mrs. Everett called a "café parfait" when she became aware that Reggie's friend, Mr. Palfrey, had started to address the party. She only half listened, because she was wondering why every one except Mrs. Everett and herself had denied himself this delightful sweet. Grown-up people had strange tastes.

Mr. Palfrey began by saying that he thought it was time to propose a toast in honor of Miss Stanton, which might also rechristen Reggie's mare by her first and true name, "Lady Washington." He said that it was plain to him that the mare had resented a strange name out of Greek mythology, and in future would go kindly, particularly if Reggie never tried to ride her again.

He went on with his remarks, and from time to time the people interrupted with laughter; but it was only a meaningless sound in Angelica's ears. The words "Reggie's mare" had come like a blow in the face. She had forgotten about that. Her knees grew weak and a lump swelled in her throat. It was true, of course, but for the time being it had passed out of her mind. And now that Lady Washington had won the five-foot-six class and was so much admired, probably Jim could not afford to buy her back. It was doubtful if Mr. Haughton would sell her at any price.

Presently she was aroused by a remark addressed directly to her.

"I think that's a good idea," said Reggie. "Don't you?"

She nodded; but she did not know what the idea was, and she did not trust her voice to ask.

"Only," he continued turning to Palfrey, "it isn't my mare any more; it's Miss Stanton's. Put that in, Palfrey."

Angelica's mouth opened in wonderment and her heart stood still. She looked about the table blankly.

"It's so," said Reggie; "she's yours."

"But I can't take her," she said falteringly. "She's too valuable. Can I, Jim?"

"But Jim's bought her," said Reggie, hurriedly.

Angelica's eyes settled on her brother's face; he said nothing, but began to smile; Reggie was kicking him under the table.

"Yes," said Reggie; "when I saw you ride Lady Washington, that settled it with me. I'm too proud to stand being beaten by a girl; so I made Jim buy her back and promise to give her to you."

"Do you mean it?" said Angelica. "Is Lady Washington really mine?"

"Yes," he said.

She dropped her hands in her lap and sighed wearily. "It doesn't seem possible," she murmured. She paused and seemed to be running over the situation in her mind. Presently she spoke as if unaware that the others were listening. "I knew it would happen, though," she said. "I knew it. I reckon I prayed enough." She smiled as a great thrill of happiness ran through her, and glancing up, saw that all the rest were smiling, too.

"I'm so happy," she said apologetically. Then she bethought herself, and furtively reached down and tapped the frame of her chair with her knuckles.

"Well, here's the toast," said Mr. Palfrey, rising. "To the lady and Lady Washington." And they all rose and drank it standing.

The Adventure of Silver Blaze

Sir Arthur Conan Doyle

"I am afraid, Watson, that I shall have to go," said Holmes, as we sat down together to our breakfast one morning.

"Go ! Where to?"

"To Dartmoor—to King's Pyland."

I was not surprised. Indeed, my only wonder was that he had not already been mixed up in this extraordinary case, which was the one topic of conversation through the length and breadth of England. For a whole day my companion had rambled about the room with his chin upon his chest and his brows knitted, charging and re-charging his pipe with the strongest black tobacco, and absolutely deaf to any of my questions or remarks. Fresh editions of every paper had been sent up by our news-agent only to be glanced over and tossed down into a corner. Yet, silent as he was, I knew perfectly well what it was, over which he was brooding. There was but one problem before the public which could challenge his powers of analysis, and that was the singular disappearance of the favourite for the Wessex Cup and the tragic murder of its trainer. When, therefore, he suddenly announced his intention of setting out for the scene of the drama, it was only what I had both expected and hoped for.

"I should be most happy to go down with you if I should not be in the way," said I.

"My dear Watson, you would confer a great favour upon me by coming. And I think that your time will not be mis-spent, for there are points about this case which promise to make it an absolutely unique one. We have, I think, just time to catch our train at Paddington, and I will go further into the matter upon our journey. You would oblige me by bringing with you your very excellent field-glass."

And so it happened that an hour or so later I found myself in the corner of a first-class carriage, flying along, en route for Exeter, while Sherlock Holmes, with his sharp, eager face framed in his earflapped travelling cap, dipped rapidly into the bundle of fresh papers which he had procured at Paddington. We had left Reading far behind us before he thrust the last of them under the seat, and offered me his cigar case.

"We are going well," said he, looking out of the window, and glancing at his watch. "Our rate at present is fifty-three and a half miles an hour."

"I have not observed the quarter-mile posts," said I.

"Nor have I. But the telegraph posts upon this line are sixty yards apart, and the calculation is a simple one. I presume that you have already looked into this matter of the murder of John Straker and the disappearance of Silver Blaze?"

"I have seen what the *Telegraph* and the *Chronicle* have to say."

"It is one of those cases where the art of the reasoner should be used rather for the sifting of details than for the acquiring of fresh evidence. The tragedy has been so uncommon, so complete, and of such personal importance to so many people that we are suffering from a plethora of surmise, conjecture, and hypothesis. The difficulty is to detach the framework of fact— of absolute, undeniable fact—from the embellishments of theorists and reporters. Then, having established ourselves upon this sound basis, it is our duty to see what inferences may be drawn, and which are the special points upon which the whole mystery turns. On Tuesday evening I received telegrams, both from Colonel Ross, the owner of the horse, and from Inspector Gregory, who is looking after the case, inviting my co-operation."

"Tuesday evening !" I exclaimed. "And this is Thursday morning. Why did you not go down yesterday?"

"Because I made a blunder, my dear Watson—which is, I am afraid, a more common occurrence than anyone would think who only knew me through your memoirs.

The fact is that I could not believe it possible that the most remarkable horse in England could long remain concealed, especially in so sparsely inhabited a place as the north of Dartmoor. From hour to hour yesterday I expected to hear that he had been found, and that his abductor was the murderer of John Straker. When, however, another morning had come and I found that, beyond the arrest of young Fitzroy Simpson, nothing had been done, I felt that it was time for me to take action. Yet in some ways I feel that yesterday has not been wasted."

"You have formed a theory then?"

"At least I have got a grip of the essential facts of the case. I shall enumerate them to you, for nothing clears up a case so much as stating it to another person, and I can hardly expect your co-operation if I do not show you the position from which we start."

I lay back against the cushions, puffing at my cigar, while Holmes, leaning forward, with his long thin forefinger checking off the points upon the palm of his left hand, gave me a sketch of the events which had led to our journey.

"Silver Blaze," said he, "is from the Isonomy stock, and holds as brilliant a record as his famous ancestor. He is now in his fifth year, and has brought in turn each of the prizes of the turf to Colonel Ross, his fortunate owner. Up to the time of the catastrophe he was first favourite for the Wessex Cup, the betting being three to one on. He has always, however, been a prime favourite with the racing public, and has never yet disappointed them, so that even at those odds enormous sums of money have been laid upon him. It is obvious, therefore, that there were many people who had the strongest interest in preventing Silver Blaze from being there at the fall of the flag, next Tuesday.

"This fact was, of course, appreciated at King's Pyland, where the Colonel's training stable is situated. Every precaution was taken to guard the favourite. The trainer, John Straker, is a retired jockey, who rode in Colonel Ross's colours before he became too heavy for the weighing chair. He has served the Colonel for five years as jockey, and for seven as trainer, and has always shown himself to be a zealous and honest servant. Under him were three lads, for the establishment was a small one, containing only four horses in all. One of these lads sat up each night in the stable, while the others slept in the loft. All three bore excellent characters. John Straker, who is a married man, lived in a small villa about two hundred yards from the stables. He has no children, keeps one maid-servant, and is comfortably off. The country round is very lonely, but about half a mile to the north there is a small cluster of villas which have been built by a Tavistock contractor for the use of invalids and others who may wish to enjoy the pure Dartmoor air. Tavistock itself lies two miles to the west, while across the moor, also about two miles distant, is the larger training establishment of Mapleton, which belongs to Lord Backwater, and is managed by Silas Brown. In every other direction the moor is a complete wilderness, inhabited only by a few roaming gipsies. Such was the general situation last Monday night when the catastrophe occurred.

On that evening the horses had been exercised and watered as usual, and the stables were locked up at nine o'clock. Two of the lads walked up to the trainer's house, where they had supper in the kitchen, while the third, Ned Hunter, remained on guard. At a few minutes after nine the maid, Edith Baxter, carried down to the stables his supper, which consisted of a dish of curried mutton. She took no liquid, as there was a water-tap in the stables, and it was the rule that the lad on duty should drink nothing else. The maid carried a lantern with her, as it was very dark, and the path ran across the open moor.

"Edith Baxter was within thirty yards of the stables when a man appeared out of the darkness and called to her to stop. As he stepped into the circle of yellow light thrown by the lantern she saw that he was a person of gentlemanly bearing, dressed in a grey suit of tweed with a cloth cap. He wore gaiters, and carried a heavy stick with a knob to it. She was most impressed, however, by the extreme pallor of his face and by the nervousness of his manner. His age, she thought, would be rather over thirty than under it.

"'Can you tell me where I am?' he asked. 'I had almost made up my mind to sleep on the moor when I saw the light of your lantern.'

"'You are close to the King's Pyland training stables,' she said.

"'Oh, indeed! What a stroke of luck!' he cried. 'I understand that a stable boy sleeps there alone every night. Perhaps that is his supper which you are carrying to him. Now I am sure that you would not be too proud to earn the price of a new dress, would you?' He took a piece of white paper folded up out of his waistcoat pocket. 'See that the boy has this to-night, and you shall have the prettiest frock that money can buy.'

"She was frightened by the earnestness of his manner, and ran past him to the window through which she was accustomed to hand the meals. It was already open, and Hunter was seated at the small table inside. She had begun to tell him of what had happened, when the stranger came up again.

"'Good evening,' said he, looking through the window, 'I wanted to have a word with you.' The girl has sworn that as he spoke she noticed the corner of the little paper packet protruding from his closed hand.

"'What business have you here?' asked the lad.

"'It's business that may put something into your pocket,' said the other. 'You've two horses in for the Wessex Cup—Silver Blaze and Bayard. Let me have the straight tip, and you won't be a loser. Is it a fact that at the weights Bayard could give the other a hundred yards in five furlongs, and that the stable have put their money on him?'

"'So you're one of those damned touts,' cried the lad. 'I'll show you how we serve them in King's Pyland.' He sprang up and rushed across the stable to unloose the dog. The girl fled away to the house, but as she ran she looked back, and saw that the stranger was leaning through the window. A minute later, however, when Hunter rushed out with the hound he was gone, and though the lad ran all round the buildings he failed to find any trace of him."

"One moment!" I asked. "Did the stable-boy, when he ran out with the dog, leave the door unlocked behind him?"

"Excellent, Watson; excellent!" murmured my companion. "The importance of the point struck me so forcibly, that I sent a special wire to Dartmoor yesterday to clear the matter up. The boy locked the door before he left it. The window, I may add, was not large enough for a man to get through.

"Hunter waited until his fellow grooms had returned, when he sent a message up to the trainer and told him what had occurred. Straker was excited at hearing the account, although he does not seem to have quite realized its true significance. It left him, however, vaguely uneasy, and Mrs. Straker, waking at one in the morning, found that he was dressing. In reply to her inquiries, he said that he could not sleep on account of his anxiety about the horses, and that he intended to walk down to the stables to see that all was well. She begged him to remain at home, as she could hear the rain pattering against the windows, but in spite of her entreaties he pulled on his large mackintosh and left the house.

"Mrs. Straker awoke at seven in the morning, to find that her husband had not yet returned. She dressed herself hastily, called the maid, and set off for the stables. The door was open; inside huddled together upon a chair, Hunter was sunk in a state of absolute stupor, the favourite's stall was empty, and there were no signs of his trainer.

"The two lads who slept in the chaff-cutting loft above the harness-room were quickly aroused. They had heard nothing during the night, for they are both sound sleepers. Hunter was obviously under the influence of some powerful drug; and, as no sense could be got out of him, he was left to sleep it off while the two lads and the two women ran out in search of the absentees. They still had hopes that the trainer had for some reason taken out the horse for early exercise, but on ascending the knoll near the house, from which all the neighbouring moors were visible, they not only could see no signs of the favourite, but they perceived something which warned them that they were in the presence of a tragedy.

"About a quarter of a mile from the stables, John Straker's overcoat was flapping from a furze bush. Immediately beyond there was a bowl-shaped depression in the moor, and at the bottom of this was found the dead body of the unfortunate trainer. His head had been shattered by a savage blow from some heavy weapon, and he was wounded in the thigh, where there was a long, clean cut, inflicted evidently by some very sharp instrument. It was clear, however, that Straker had defended himself vigorously against his assailants, for in his right hand he held a small knife, which was clotted with blood up to the handle, while in his left he grasped a red and black silk cravat, which was recognised by the maid as having been worn on the preceding evening by the stranger who had visited the stables.

"Hunter, on recovering from his stupor, was also quite positive as to the ownership of the cravat. He was equally certain that the same stranger had, while standing at the window, drugged his curried mutton, and so deprived the stables of their watchman.

"As to the missing horse, there were abundant proofs in the mud which lay at the bottom of the fatal hollow, that he had been there at the time of the struggle. But from that morning he has disappeared; and although a large reward has been offered, and all the gipsies of Dartmoor are on the alert, no news has come of him. Finally an analysis has shown that the remains of his supper, left by the stable lad, contain an appreciable quantity of powdered opium, while the people at the house partook of the same dish on the same night without any ill effect.

"Those are the main facts of the case, stripped of all surmise and stated as baldly as possible. I shall now recapitulate what the police have done in the matter.

"Inspector Gregory, to whom the case has been committed, is an extremely competent officer. Were he but gifted with imagination he might rise to great heights in his profession. On his arrival he promptly found and arrested the man upon whom suspicion naturally rested. There was little difficulty in finding him, for he inhabited one of those villas which I have mentioned. His name, it appears, was Fitzroy Simpson. He was a man of excellent birth and education, who had squandered a fortune upon the turf, and who lived now by doing a little quiet and genteel bookmaking in the sporting clubs of London. An examination of his betting-book shows that bets to the amount of five thousand pounds had been registered by him against the favourite.

"On being arrested he volunteered the statement that he had come down to Dartmoor in the hope of getting some information about the King's Pyland horses, and also about Desborough, the second favourite, which was in charge of Silas Brown, at the Mapleton stables. He did not attempt to deny that he had acted as described upon the evening before, but declared that he had no sinister designs, and had simply wished to obtain first-hand information. When confronted with his cravat he turned very pale, and was utterly unable to account for its presence in the hand of the murdered man. His wet clothing showed that he had been out in the storm of the night before, and his stick, which was a Penang lawyer, weighted with lead, was just such a weapon as might, by repeated blows, have inflicted the terrible injuries to which the trainer had succumbed.

"On the other hand, there was no wound upon his person, while the state of Straker's knife would show that one, at least, of his assailants must bear his mark upon him. There you have it all in a nutshell, Watson, and if you can give me any light I shall be infinitely obliged to you."

I had listened with the greatest interest to the statement which Holmes, with characteristic clearness, had laid before me. Though most of the facts were familiar to me, I had not sufficiently appreciated their relative importance, nor their connection to each other.

"Is it not possible," I suggested, "that the incised wound upon Straker may have been caused by his own knife in the convulsive struggles which follow any brain injury?"

"It is more than possible; it is probable," said Holmes. "In that case, one of the main points in favour of the accused disappears."

"And yet," said I, "even now I fail to understand what the theory of the police can be."

"I am afraid that whatever theory we state has very grave objections to it," returned my companion. "The police imagine, I take it, that this Fitzroy Simpson, having drugged the lad, and having in some way obtained a duplicate key, opened the stable door, and took out the horse, with the intention, apparently, of kidnapping him altogether. His bridle is missing, so that Simpson must have put this on. Then, having left the door open behind him, he was leading the horse away over the moor, when he was either met or overtaken by the trainer. A row naturally ensued, Simpson beat out the trainer's brains with his heavy stick without receiving any injury from the small knife which Straker used in self-defence, and then the thief either led the horse on to some secret hiding-place, or else it may have bolted during the struggle, and be now wandering out on the moors. That is the case as it appears to the police, and improbable as it is, all other explanations are more improbable still. However, I shall very quickly test the matter when I am once upon the spot, and until then I really cannot see how we can get much further than our present position."

It was evening before we reached the little town of Tavistock, which lies, like the boss of a shield, in the middle of the huge circle of Dartmoor. Two gentlemen were awaiting us at the station; the one a tall fair man with lion-like hair and beard, and curiously penetrating light blue eyes, the other a small alert person, very neat and dapper, in a frock-coat and gaiters, with trim little side-whiskers and an eye-glass. The latter was Colonel Ross, the well-known sportsman, the other Inspector Gregory, a man who was rapidly making his name in the English detective service.

"I am delighted that you have come down, Mr. Holmes," said the Colonel. "The Inspector here has done all that could possibly be suggested; but I wish to leave no stone unturned in trying to avenge poor Straker, and in recovering my horse."

"Have there been any fresh developments?" asked Holmes.

"I am sorry to say that we have made very little progress," said the Inspector. "We have an open carriage outside, and as you would no doubt like to see the place before the light fails, we might talk it over as we drive."

A minute later we were all seated in a comfortable landau and were rattling through the quaint old Devonshire town. Inspector Gregory was full of his case, and poured out a stream of remarks, while Holmes threw in an occasional question or interjection. Colonel Ross leaned back with his arms folded and his hat tilted over his eyes, while I listened with interest to the dialogue of the two detectives. Gregory was formulating his theory, which was almost exactly what Holmes had foretold in the train.

"The net is drawn pretty close round Fitzroy Simpson," he remarked, "and I believe myself that he is our man. At the same time, I recognise that the evidence is purely circumstantial, and that some new development may upset it."

"How about Straker's knife?"

"We have quite come to the conclusion that he wounded himself in his fall."

"My friend Dr. Watson made that suggestion to me as we came down. If so, it would tell against this man Simpson."

"Undoubtedly. He has neither a knife nor any sign of a wound. The evidence against him is certainly very strong. He had a great interest in the disappearance of the favourite, he lies under the suspicion of having poisoned the stable boy, he was undoubtedly out in the storm, he was armed with a heavy stick, and his cravat was found in the dead man's hand. I really think we have enough to go before a jury."

Holmes shook his head. "A clever counsel would tear it all to rags," said he. "Why should he take the horse out of the stable? If he wished to injure it, why could he not do it there? Has a duplicate key been found in his possession? What chemist sold him the powdered opium? Above all, where could he, a stranger to the district, hide a horse, and such a horse as this? What is his own explanation as to the paper which he wished the maid to give to the stable-boy?"

"He says that it was a ten-pound note. One was found in his purse. But your other difficulties are not so formidable as they seem. He is not a stranger to the district. He has twice lodged at Tavistock in the summer. The opium was probably brought from London. The key, having served its purpose, would be hurled away. The horse may lie at the bottom of one of the pits or old mines upon the moor."

"What does he say about the cravat?"

"He acknowledges that it is his, and declares that he had lost it. But a new element has been introduced into the case which may account for his leading the horse from the stable."

Holmes pricked up his ears.

"We have found traces which show that a party of gipsies encamped on Monday night within a mile of the spot where the murder took place. On Tuesday they were gone. Now, presuming that there was some understanding between Simpson and these gipsies, might he not have been leading the horse to them when he was overtaken, and may they not have him now?"

"It is certainly possible."

"The moor is being scoured for these gipsies. I have also examined every stable and outhouse in Tavistock, and for a radius of ten miles."

"There is another training stable quite close, I understand?"

"Yes, and that is a factor which we must certainly not neglect. As Desborough, their horse, was second in the betting, they had an interest in the disappearance of the favourite. Silas Brown, the trainer, is known to have had large bets upon the event, and he was no friend to poor Straker. We have, however, examined the stables, and there is nothing to connect him with the affair."

"And nothing to connect this man Simpson with the interests of the Mapleton stables?"

"Nothing at all."

Holmes leaned back in the carriage and the conversation ceased. A few minutes later our driver pulled up at a neat little red-brick villa with overhanging eaves, which stood by the road. Some distance off, across a paddock, lay a long grey-tiled outbuilding. In every other direction the low curves of the moor, bronze-coloured from the fading ferns, stretched away to the sky-line, broken only by the steeples of Tavistock, and by a cluster of houses away to the westward, which marked the Mapleton stables. We all sprang out with the exception of Holmes, who continued to lean back with his eyes fixed upon the sky in front of him, entirely absorbed in his own thoughts. It was only when I touched his arm that he roused himself with a violent start and stepped out of the carriage.

"Excuse me," said he, turning to Colonel Ross, who had looked at him in some surprise. "I was day-dreaming." There was a gleam in his eyes and a suppressed excitement in his manner which convinced me, used as I was to his ways, that his hand was upon a clue, though I could not imagine where he had found it.

"Perhaps you would prefer at once to go on to the scene of the crime, Mr. Holmes?" said Gregory.

"I think that I should prefer to stay here a little and go into one or two questions of detail. Straker was brought back here, I presume?"

"Yes, he lies upstairs. The inquest is to-morrow."

"He has been in Your service some years, Colonel Ross?"

"I have always found him an excellent servant."

"I presume that you made an inventory of what he had in his pockets at the time of his death, Inspector?"

"I have the things themselves in the sitting-room if you would care to see them."

"I should be very glad."

We all filed into the front room and sat round the central table, while the Inspector unlocked a square tin box and laid a small heap of things before us. There was a box of vestas, two inches of tallow candle, an A.D.P. briar-root pipe, a pouch of sealskin with half an ounce of long-cut Cavendish, a silver watch with a gold chain, five sovereigns in gold, an aluminium pencil-case, a few papers, and an ivory-handled knife with a very delicate inflexible blade marked Weiss and Co., London.

"This is a very singular knife," said Holmes, lifting it up and examining it minutely. "I presume, as I see bloodstains upon it, that it is the one which was found in the dead man's grasp. Watson, this knife is surely in your line."

"It is what we call a cataract knife," said I.

"I thought so. A very delicate blade devised for very delicate work. A strange thing for a man to carry with him upon a rough expedition, especially as it would not shut in his pocket."

"The tip was guarded by a disc of cork which we found beside his body," said the Inspector. "His wife tells us that the knife had lain for some days upon the dressing-table, and that he had picked it up as he left the room. It was a poor weapon, but perhaps the best that he could lay his hand on at the moment."

"Very possibly. How about these papers?"

"Three of them are receipted hay-dealers' accounts. One of them is a letter of instructions from Colonel Ross. This other is a milliner's account for thirty-seven pounds fifteen, made out by Madame Lesurier, of Bond Street, to William Darbyshire. Mrs. Straker tells us that Darbyshire was a friend of her husband's, and that occasionally his letters were addressed here."

"Madame Darbyshire had somewhat expensive tastes," remarked Holmes, glancing down the account. "Twenty-two guineas is rather heavy for a single costume. However, there appears to be nothing more to learn, and we may now go down to the scene of the crime."

As we emerged from the sitting-room a woman who had been waiting in the passage took a step forward and laid her hand upon the Inspector's sleeve. Her face was haggard, and thin, and eager; stamped with the print of a recent horror.

"Have you got them? Have you found them?" she panted.

"No, Mrs. Straker; but Mr. Holmes, here, has come from London to help us, and we shall do all that is possible."

"Surely I met you in Plymouth, at a garden party, some little time ago, Mrs. Straker," said Holmes.

"No, sir; you are mistaken."

"Dear me; why, I could have sworn to it. You wore a costume of dove-coloured silk, with ostrich feather trimming."

"I never had such a dress, sir," answered the lady.

"Ah; that quite settles it," said Holmes; and, with an apology, he followed the Inspector outside. A short walk across the moor took us to the hollow in which the body had a been found. At the brink of it was the furze bush upon which the coat had been hung.

"There was no wind that night, I understand," said Holmes.

"None; but very heavy rain."

"In that case the overcoat was not blown against the furze bushes, but placed there."

"Yes, it was laid across the bush."

"You fill me with interest. I perceive the ground has been trampled up a good deal. No doubt many feet have been there since Monday night."

"A piece of matting has been laid here at the side, and we have all stood upon that."

"Excellent."

"In this bag I have one of the boots which Straker wore, one of Fitzroy Simpson's shoes, and a cast horseshoe of Silver Blaze."

"My dear Inspector, you surpass yourself!" Holmes took the bag, and descending into the hollow he pushed the matting into a more central position. Then stretching himself upon his face and leaning his chin upon his hands he made a careful study of the trampled mud in front of him.

"Halloa!" said he, suddenly, "what's this?"

It was a wax vesta, half burned, which was so coated with mud that it looked at first like a little chip of wood.

"I cannot think how I came to overlook it," said the Inspector, with an expression of annoyance.

"It was invisible, buried in the mud. I only saw it because I was looking for it."

"What! You expected to find it?"

"I thought it not unlikely." He took the boots from the bag and compared the impressions of each of them with marks upon the ground. Then he clambered up to the rim of the hollow and crawled about among the ferns and bushes.

"I am afraid that there are no more tracks," said the Inspector. "I have examined the ground very carefully for a hundred yards in each direction."

"Indeed!" said Holmes, rising, "I should not have the imper-tinence to do it again after what you say. But I should like to take a little walk over the moor before it grows dark, that I may know my ground to-morrow, and I think that I shall put this horseshoe into my pocket for luck."

Colonel Ross, who had shown some signs of impatience at my companion's quiet and systematic method of work, glanced at his watch.

"I wish you would come back with me, Inspector," said he. "There are several points on which I should like your advice, and especially as to whether we do not owe it to the public to remove our horse's name from the entries for the Cup."

"Certainly not," cried Holmes, with decision: "I should let the name stand."

The Colonel bowed. "I am very glad to have had your opinion, sir," said he. "You will find us at poor Straker's house when you have finished your walk, and we can drive together into Tavistock."

He turned back with the Inspector, while Holmes and I walked slowly across the moor. The sun was beginning to sink behind the stables of Mapleton, and the long sloping plain in front of us was tinged with gold, deepening into rich, ruddy brown where the faded ferns and brambles caught the evening light. But the glories of the landscape were all wasted upon my companion, who was sunk in the deepest thought.

"It's this way, Watson," he said at last. "We may leave the question of who killed John Straker for the instant, and confine ourselves to finding out what has become of the horse. Now, supposing that he broke away during or after the tragedy, where could he have gone to? The horse is a very gregarious creature. If left to himself his instincts would have been either to return to King's Pyland, or go over to Mapleton. Why should he run wild upon the moor? He would surely have been seen by now. And why should gipsies kidnap him? These people always clear out when they hear of trouble, for they do not wish to be pestered by the police. They could not hope to sell such a horse. They would run a great risk and gain nothing by taking him. Surely that is clear."

"Where is he, then?"

"I have already said that he must have gone to King's Pyland or to Mapleton. He is not at King's Pyland, therefore he is at Mapleton. Let us take that as a working hypothesis and see what it leads us to. This part of the moor, as the Inspector remarked, is very hard and dry. But it falls away towards Mapleton, and you can see from here that there is a long hollow over yonder, which must have been very wet on Monday night. If our supposition is correct, then the horse must have crossed that, and there is the point where we should look for his tracks."

We had been walking briskly during this conversation, and a few more minutes brought us to the hollow in question. At Holmes' request I walked down the bank to the right and he to the left, but I had not taken fifty paces before I heard him give a shout, and saw him waving his hand to me. The track of a horse was plainly outlined in the soft earth in front of him, and the shoe which he took from his pocket exactly fitted the impression.

"See the value of imagination," said Holmes. "It is the one quality which Gregory lacks. We imagined what might have happened, acted upon the supposition, and find ourselves justified. Let us proceed."

We crossed the marshy bottom and passed over a quarter of a mile of dry, hard turf. Again the ground sloped and again we came on the tracks. Then we lost them for half a mile, but only to pick them up once more quite close to Mapleton. It was Holmes who saw them first, and he stood pointing with a look of triumph upon his face. A man's track was visible beside the horse's.

"The horse was alone before," I cried.

"Quite so. It was alone before. Halloa, what is this?"

The double track turned sharp off and took the direction of King's Pyland. Holmes whistled, and we both followed along after it. His eyes were on the trail, but I happened to look a little to one side, and saw to my surprise the same tracks coming back again in the opposite direction.

"One for you, Watson," said Holmes, when I pointed it out; "you have saved us a long walk which would have brought us back on our own traces. I let us follow the return track."

We had not to go far. It ended at the paving of asphalt which led up to the gates of the Mapleton stables. As we approached a groom ran out from them.

"We don't want any loiterers about here," said he.

"I only wished to ask a question," said Holmes, with his finger and thumb in his waistcoat pocket. "Should I be too early to see your master, Mr. Silas Brown, if I were to call at five o'clock to-morrow morning?"

"Bless you, sir, if anyone is about he will be, for he is always the first stirring. But here he is, sir, to answer your questions for himself. No, sir, no; it's as much as my place is worth to let him see me touch your money. Afterwards, if you like."

As Sherlock Holmes replaced the half-crown which he had drawn from his pocket, a fierce-looking, elderly man strode out from the gate with a hunting-crop swinging in his hand.

"What's this, Dawson?" he cried. "No gossiping! Go about your business! And you—what the devil do you want here?"

"Ten minutes talk with you, my good sir," said Holmes, in the sweetest of voices.

"I've no time to talk to every gadabout. We want no strangers here. Be off, or you may find a dog at your heels."

Holmes leaned forward and whispered something in the trainer's ear. He started violently and flushed to the temples.

"It's a lie!" he shouted. "An infernal lie!"

"Very good! Shall we argue about it here in public, or talk it over in your parlour?"

"Oh, come in if you wish to."

Holmes smiled. " I shall not keep you more than a few minutes, Watson," he said. "Now, Mr. Brown, I am quite at your disposal."

It was quite twenty minutes, and the reds had all faded into greys before Holmes and the trainer reappeared. Never have I seen such a change as had been brought about in Silas Brown in that short time. His face was ashy pale, beads of perspiration shone upon his brow, and his hands shook until the hunting-crop wagged like a branch in the wind. His bullying, over-bearing manner was all gone too, and he cringed along at my companion's side like a dog with its master.

"Your instructions will be done. It shall be done," said he.

"There must be no mistake," said Holmes looking round at him. The other winced as he read the menace in his eyes.

"Oh, no, there shall be no mistake. It shall be there. Should I change it first or not?"

Holmes thought a little and then burst out laughing. "No, don't," said he. "I shall write to you about it. No tricks now or—"

"Oh, you can trust me, you can trust me!"

"Yes, I think I can. Well, you shall hear from me to-morrow." He turned upon his heel, disregarding the trembling hand which the other held out to him, and we set off for King's Pyland.

"A more perfect compound of the bully, coward and sneak than Master Silas Brown I have seldom met with," remarked Holmes, as we trudged along together.

"He has the horse, then?"

"He tried to bluster out of it, but I described to him so exactly what his actions had been upon that morning, that he is con-vinced that I was watching him. Of course, you observed the peculiarly square toes in the impressions, and that his own boots exactly corresponded to them. Again, of course no subordinate would have dared to have done such a thing. I described to him how when, according to his custom, he was the first down, he perceived a strange horse wandering over the moor; how he went out to it, and his astonishment at recognising from the white forehead which has given the favourite its name that chance had put in his power the only horse which could beat the one upon which he had put his money. Then I described how his first impulse had been to lead him back to King's Pyland, and how the devil had shown him how he could hide the horse until the race was over and how he had led it back and concealed it at Mapleton. When I told him every detail he gave it up, and thought only of saving his own skin."

"But his stables had been searched."

"Oh, an old horse-faker like him has many a dodge."

"But are you not afraid to leave the horse in his power now, since he has every interest in injuring it?"

"My dear fellow, he will guard it as the apple of his eye. He knows that his only hope of mercy is to produce it safe."

"Colonel Ross did not impress me as a man who would be likely to show much mercy in any case."

"The matter does not rest with Colonel Ross. I follow my own methods, and tell as much or as little as I choose. That is the advantage of being unofficial. I don't know whether you observed it, Watson, but the Colonel's manner has been just a trifle cavalier to me. I am inclined now to have a little amusement at his expense. Say nothing to him about the horse."

"Certainly not, without your permission."

"And, of course, this is all quite a minor point compared to the question of who killed John Straker."

"And you will devote yourself to that?"

"On the contrary, we both go back to London by the night train."

I was thunderstruck by my friend's words. We had only been a few hours in Devonshire, and that he should give up an investigation which he had begun so brilliantly was quite incomprehensible to me. Not a word more could I draw from him until we were back at the trainer's house. The Colonel and the Inspector were awaiting us in the parlour.

"My friend and I return to town by the midnight express," said Holmes. "We have had a charming little breath of your beautiful Dartmoor air."

The Inspector opened his eyes, and the Colonel's lip curled in a sneer.

"So you despair of arresting the murderer of poor Straker," said he.

Holmes shrugged his shoulders. "There are certainly grave difficulties in the way," said he. "I have every hope, however, that your horse will start upon Tuesday, and I beg that you will have your jockey in readiness. Might I ask for a photograph of Mr. John Straker?"

The Inspector took one from an envelope in his pocket and handed it to him.

"My dear Gregory, you anticipate all my wants. If I might ask you to wait here for an instant, I have a question which I should like to put to the maid."

"I must say that I am rather disappointed in our London consultant," said Colonel Ross, bluntly, as my friend left the room. "I do not see that we are any further than when he came."

"At least, you have his assurance that your horse will run," said I.

"Yes, I have his assurance," said the Colonel, with a shrug of his shoulders. "I should prefer to have the horse."

I was about to make some reply in defence of my friend, when he entered the room again.

"Now, gentlemen," said he, "I am quite ready for Tavistock."

As we stepped into the carriage one of the stable-lads held the door open for us. A sudden idea seemed to occur to Holmes, for he leaned forward and touched the lad upon the sleeve.

"You have a few sheep in the paddock," he said. "Who attends to them?"

"I do, sir."

"Have you noticed anything amiss with them of late?"

"Well, sir, not of much account; but three of them have gone lame, sir."

I could see that Holmes was extremely pleased, for he chuckled and rubbed his hands together.

"A long shot, Watson; a very long shot!" said he, pinching my arm. "Gregory, let me recommend to your attention this singular epidemic among the sheep. Drive on, coachman!"

Colonel Ross still wore an expression which showed the poor opinion which he had formed of my companion's ability, but I saw by the Inspector's face that his attention had been keenly aroused.

"You consider that to be important?" he asked.

"Exceedingly so."

"Is there any other point to which you would wish to draw my attention?"

"To the curious incident of the dog in the night-time."

"The dog did nothing in the night-time."

"That was the curious incident," remarked Sherlock Holmes.

Four days later Holmes and I were again in the train bound for Winchester to see the race for the Wessex Cup. Colonel Ross met us, by appointment, outside the station and we drove in his drag to the course beyond the town. His face was grave and his manner was cold in the extreme.

"I have seen nothing of my horse," said he.

"I suppose that you would know him when you saw him?" asked Holmes.

The Colonel was very angry. "I have been on the turf for twenty years, and never was asked such a question as that before," said he. "A child would know Silver Blaze with his white forehead and his mottled off fore leg."

"How is the betting?"

"Well, that is the curious part of it. You could have got fifteen to one yesterday, but the price has become shorter and shorter, until you can hardly get three to one now."

"Hum!" said Holmes. "Somebody knows something, that is clear!"

As the drag drew up in the inclosure near the grand stand, I glanced at the card to see the entries. It ran:—

Wessex Plate. 50 sovs. each, h ft, with 1,000 sovs. added, for four and five-year olds. Second £300. Third £200. New course (one mile and five furlongs).

1. Mr. Heath Newton's The Negro (red cap, cinnamon jacket).

2. Colonel Wardlaw's Pugilist (pink cap, blue and black jacket).

3. Lord Backwater's Desborough (yellow cap and sleeves).
4. Colonel Ross's Silver Blaze (black cap, red jacket).
5. Duke of Balmoral's Iris (yellow and black stripes).
6. Lord Singleford's Rasper (purple cap, black sleeves).

"We scratched our other one and put all hopes on your word," said the Colonel. "Why, what is that? Silver Blaze favourite?"

"Five to four against Silver Blaze!" roared the ring. "Five to four against Silver Blaze! Fifteen to five against Desborough! Five to four on the field!"

"There are the numbers up," I cried. "They are all six there."

"All six there! Then my horse is running," cried the Colonel, in great agitation. "But I don't see him. My colours have not passed."

"Only five have passed. This must be he."

As I spoke a powerful bay horse swept out from the weighing inclosure and cantered past us, bearing on its back the well-known black and red of the Colonel.

"That's not my horse," cried the owner. "That beast has not a white hair upon its body. What is this that you have done, Mr. Holmes?"

"Well, well, let us see how he gets on," said my friend, imperturbably. For a few minutes he gazed through my field-glass. "Capital! An excellent start!" he cried suddenly. "There they are, coming round the curve!"

From our drag we had a superb view as they came up the straight. The six horses were so close together that a carpet could have covered them, but half way up the yellow of the Mapleton stable showed to the front. Before they reached us, however, Desborough's bolt was shot, and the Colonel's horse, coming away with a rush, passed the post a good six lengths before its rival, the Duke of Balmoral's Iris making a bad third.

"It's my race anyhow," gasped the Colonel, passing his hand over his eyes. "I confess that I can make neither head nor tail of it. Don't you think that you have kept up your mystery long enough, Mr. Holmes?"

"Certainly, Colonel. You shall know everything. Let us all go round and have a look at the horse together. Here he is," he continued, as we made our way into the weighing inclosure where only owners and their friends find admittance. "You have only to wash his face and his leg in spirits of wine and you will find that he is the same old Silver Blaze as ever."

"You take my breath away!"

"I found him in the hands of a faker, and took the liberty of running him just as he was sent over."

"My dear sir, you have done wonders. The horse looks very fit and well. It never went better in its life. I owe you a thousand apologies for having doubted your ability. You have done me a great service by recovering my horse. You would do me a greater still if you could lay your hands on the murderer of John Straker."

"I have done so," said Holmes, quietly.

The Colonel and I stared at him in amazement. "You have got him! Where is he, then?"

"He is here."

"Here! Where?"

"In my company at the present moment."

The Colonel flushed angrily. "I quite recognise that I am under obligations to you, Mr. Holmes," said he, "but I must regard what you have just said as either a very bad joke or an insult."

Sherlock Holmes laughed. "I assure you that I have not associated you with the crime, Colonel," said he; "the real murderer is standing immediately behind you!"

He stepped past and laid his hand upon the glossy neck of the thoroughbred.

"The horse!" cried both the Colonel and myself.

"Yes, the horse. And it may lessen his guilt if I say that it was done in self-defence, and that John Straker was a man who was entirely unworthy of your confidence. But there goes the bell; and as I stand to win a little on this next race, I shall defer a more lengthy explanation until a more fitting time."

We had the corner of a Pullman car to ourselves that evening as we whirled back to London, and I fancy that the journey was a short one to Colonel Ross as well as to myself, as we listened to our companion's narrative of the events which had occurred at the Dartmoor training stables upon that Monday night, and the means by which he had unravelled them.

"I confess," said he, "that any theories which I had formed from the newspaper reports were entirely erroneous. And yet there were indications there, had they not been overlaid by other details which concealed their true import. I went to Devonshire with the conviction that Fitzroy Simpson was the true culprit, although, of course, I saw that the evidence against him was by no means complete.

"It was while I was in the carriage, just as we reached the trainer's house, that the immense significance of the curried mutton occurred to me. You may remember that I was distrait, and remained sitting after you had all alighted. I was marvelling in my own mind how I could possibly have overlooked so obvious a clue."

"I confess," said the Colonel, "that even now I cannot see how it helps us."

"It was the first link in my chain of reasoning. Powdered opium is by no means tasteless. The flavour is not disagreeable, but it is perceptible. Were it mixed with any ordinary dish, the eater would undoubtedly detect it, and would probably eat no more. A curry was exactly the medium which would disguise this taste. By no possible supposition could this stranger, Fitzroy Simpson, have caused curry to be served in the trainer's family that night, and it is surely too monstrous a coincidence to suppose that he happened to come along with powdered opium upon the very night when a dish happened to be served which would disguise the flavour. That is unthinkable. Therefore Simpson becomes eliminated from the case and our attention centres upon Straker and his wife, the only two people who could have chosen curried mutton for supper that night. The opium was added after the dish was set aside for the stable-boy, for the others had the same for supper with no ill effects. Which of them, then, had access to that dish without the maid seeing them?

"Before deciding that question I had grasped the significance of the silence of the dog, for one true inference invariably suggests others. The Simpson incident had shown me that a dog was kept in the stables, and yet, though someone had been in and had fetched out a horse, he had not barked enough to arouse the two lads in the loft. Obviously the midnight visitor was someone whom the dog knew well.

"I was already convinced, or almost convinced, that John Straker went down to the stables in the dead of the night and took out Silver Blaze. For what purpose? For a dishonest one, obviously, or why should he drug his own stable-boy? And yet I was at a loss to know why. There have been cases before now where trainers have made sure of great sums of money by laying against their own horses, through agents, and then preventing them from winning by fraud. Sometimes it is a pulling jockey. Sometimes it is some surer and subtler means. What was it here? I hoped that the contents of his pockets might help me to form a conclusion.

"And they did so. You cannot have forgotten the singular knife which was found in the dead man's hand, a knife which certainly no sane man would choose for a weapon. It was, as Dr. Watson told us, a form of knife which is used for the most delicate operations known in surgery. And it was to be used for a delicate operation that night. You must know, with your wide experience of turf matters, Colonel Ross, that it is possible to make a slight nick upon the tendons of a horse's ham, and to do it subcutaneously so as to leave absolutely no trace. A horse so treated would develop a slight lameness which would be put down to a strain in exercise or a touch of rheumatism, but never to foul play."

"Villain! Scoundrel!" cried the Colonel.

"We have here the explanation of why John Straker wished to take the horse out on to the moor. So spirited a creature would have certainly roused the soundest of sleepers when it felt the prick of the knife. It was absolutely necessary to do it in the open air."

"I have been blind!" cried the Colonel. "Of course, that was why he needed the candle, and struck the match."

"Undoubtedly. But in examining his belongings, I was fortunate enough to discover, not only the method of the crime, but even its motives. As a man of the world, Colonel, you know that men do not carry other people's bills about in their pockets. We have most of us quite enough to do to settle our own. I at once concluded that Straker was leading a double life, and keeping a second establishment. The nature of the bill showed that there was a lady in the case, and one who had expensive tastes. Liberal as you are with your servants, one hardly expects that they can buy twenty-guinea walking dresses for their women. I questioned Mrs. Straker as to the dress without her knowing it, and having satisfied myself that it had never reached her, I made a note of the milliner's address, and felt that by calling there with Straker's photograph, I could easily dispose of the mythical Darbyshire.

"From that time on all was plain. Straker had led out the horse to a hollow where his light would be invisible. Simpson, in his flight, had dropped his cravat, and Straker had picked it up with some idea, perhaps, that he might use it in securing the horse's leg. Once in the hollow he had got behind the horse, and had struck a light, but the creature, frightened at the sudden glare, and with the strange instinct of animals feeling that some mischief was intended, had lashed out, and the steel shoe had struck Straker full on the forehead. He had already, in spite of the rain, taken off his overcoat in order to do his delicate task, and so, as he fell, his knife gashed his thigh. Do I make it clear?"

"Wonderful!" cried the Colonel. "Wonderful! You might have been there."

"My final shot was, I confess, a very long one. It struck me that so astute a man as Straker would not undertake this delicate tendon-nicking without a little practice. What could he practise on? My eyes fell upon the sheep, and I asked a question which, rather to my surprise, showed that my surmise was correct."

"You have made it perfectly clear, Mr. Holmes."

"When I returned to London I called upon the milliner, who at once recognised Straker as an excellent customer, of the name of Darbyshire, who had a very dashing wife with a strong partiality for expensive dresses. I have no doubt that this woman had plunged him over head and ears in debt, and so led him into this miserable plot."

"You have explained all but one thing," cried the Colonel. "Where was the horse?"

"Ah, it bolted and was cared for by one of your neighbours. We must have an amnesty in that direction, I think. This is Clapham Junction, if I am not mistaken, and we shall be in Victoria in less than ten minutes. If you care to smoke a cigar in our rooms, Colonel, I shall be happy to give you any other details which might interest you."

The Brogue

Saki (H. H. Munro)

THE hunting season had come to an end, and the Mullets had not succeeded in selling the Brogue. There had been a kind of tradition in the family for the past three or four years, a sort of fatalistic hope, that the Brogue would find a purchaser before the hunting was over; but seasons came and went without anything happening to justify such ill-founded optimism. The animal had been named Berserker in the earlier stages of its career; it had been rechristened the Brogue later on, in recognition of the fact that, once acquired, it was extremely difficult to get rid of. The unkinder wits of the neighbourhood had been known to suggest that the first letter of its name was superfluous. The Brogue had been variously described in sale catalogues as a light-weight hunter, a lady's hack, and, more simply, but still with a touch of imagination, as a useful brown gelding, standing 15.1. Toby Mullet had ridden him for four seasons with the West Wessex; you can ride almost any sort of horse with the West Wessex as long as it is an animal that knows the country. The Brogue knew the country intimately, having personally created most of the gaps that were to be met with in banks and hedges for many miles round. His manners and characteristics were not ideal in the hunting field, but he was probably rather safer to ride to hounds than he was as a hack on country roads. According to the Mullet family, he was not really road-shy, but there were one or two objects of dislike that brought on sudden attacks of what Toby called the swerving sickness. Motors and cycles he treated with tolerant disregard, but pigs, wheelbarrows, piles of stones by the roadside, perambulators in a village street, gates painted too aggressively white, and sometimes, but not always, the newer kind of beehives, turned him aside from his tracks in vivid imitation of the zigzag course of forked lightning. If a pheasant rose noisily from the other side of a hedgerow the Brogue would spring into the air at the same moment, but this may have been due to a desire to be companionable. The Mullet family contradicted the widely prevalent report that the horse was a confirmed crib-biter.

It was about the third week in May that Mrs. Mullet, relict of the late Sylvester Mullet, and mother of Toby and a bunch of daughters, assailed Clovis Sangrail on the outskirts of the village with a breathless catalogue of local happenings.

"You know our new neighbour, Mr. Penricarde?" she vociferated; "awfully rich, owns tin mines in Cornwall, middle-aged and rather quiet. He's taken the Red House on a long lease and spent a lot of money on alterations and improvements. Well, Toby's sold him the Brogue!"

Clovis spent a moment or two in assimilating the astonishing news; then he broke out into unstinted congratulation. If he had belonged to a more emotional race he would probably have kissed Mrs. Mullet.

"How wonderfully lucky to have pulled it off at last! Now you can buy a decent animal. I've always said that Toby was clever. Ever so many congratulations."

"Don't congratulate me. It's the most unfortunate thing that could have happened!" said Mrs. Mullet dramatically.

Clovis stared at her in amazement.

"Mr. Penricarde," said Mrs. Mullet, sinking her voice to what she imagined to be an impressive whisper, though it rather resembled a hoarse, excited squeak, "Mr. Penricarde has just begun to pay attentions to Jessie. Slight at first, but now unmistakable. I was a fool not to have seen it sooner. Yesterday, at the Rectory garden party, he asked her what her favourite flowers were, and she told him carnations, and to-day a whole stack of carnations has arrived, clove and malmaison and lovely dark red ones, regular exhibition blooms, and a box of chocolates that he must have got on purpose from London. And he's asked her to go round the links with him to-morrow. And now, just at this critical moment, Toby has sold him that animal. It's a calamity!"

"But you've been trying to get the horse off your hands for years," said Clovis.

"I've got a houseful of daughters," said Mrs. Mullet, "and I've been trying—well, not to get them off my hands, of course, but a husband or two wouldn't be amiss among the lot of them; there are six of them, you know."

"I don't know," said Clovis, "I've never counted, but I expect you're right as to the number; mothers generally know these things."

"And now," continued Mrs. Mullet, in her tragic whisper, "when there's a rich husband-in-prospect imminent on the horizon Toby goes and sells him that miserable animal. It will probably kill him if he tries to ride it; anyway it will kill any affection he might have felt towards any member of our family. What is to be done? We can't very well ask to have the horse back; you see, we praised it up like anything when we thought there was a chance of his buying it, and said it was just the animal to suit him."

"Couldn't you steal it out of his stable and send it to grass at some farm miles away?" suggested Clovis; "write 'Votes for Women' on the stable door, and the thing would pass for a Suffragette outrage. No one who knew the horse could possibly suspect you of wanting to get it back again."

"Every newspaper in the country would ring with the affair," said Mrs. Mullet; "can't you imagine the headline, 'Valuable Hunter Stolen by Suffragettes'? The police would scour the countryside till they found the animal."

"Well, Jessie must try and get it back from Penricarde on the plea that it's an old favourite. She can say it was only sold because the stable had to be pulled down under the terms of an old repairing lease, and that now it has been arranged that the stable is to stand for a couple of years longer."

"It sounds a queer proceeding to ask for a horse back when you've just sold him," said Mrs. Mullet, "but something must be done, and done at once. The man is not used to horses, and I believe I told him it was as quiet as a lamb. After all, lambs go kicking and twisting about as if they were demented, don't they?"

"The lamb has an entirely unmerited character for sedateness," agreed Clovis.

Jessie came back from the golf links next day in a state of mingled elation and concern.

"It's all right about the proposal," she announced; "he came out with it at the sixth hole. I said I must have time to think it over. I accepted him at the seventh."

"My dear," said her mother, "I think a little more maidenly reserve and hesitation would have been advisable, as you've known him so short a time. You might have waited till the ninth hole."

"The seventh is a very long hole," said Jessie; "besides, the tension was putting us both off our game. By the time we'd got to the ninth hole we'd settled lots of things. The honeymoon is to be spent in Corsica, with perhaps a flying visit to Naples if we feel like it, and a week in London to wind up with. Two of his nieces are to be asked to be bridesmaids, so with our lot there will be seven, which is rather a lucky number. You are to wear your pearl grey, with any amount of Honiton lace jabbed into it. By the way, he's coming over this evening to ask your consent to the whole affair. So far all's well, but about the Brogue it's a different matter. I told him the legend about the stable, and how keen we were about buying the horse back, but he seems equally keen on keeping it. He said he must have horse exercise now that he's living in the country, and he's going to start riding to-morrow. He's ridden a few times in the Row, on an animal that was accustomed to carry octogenarians and people undergoing rest cures, and that's about all his experience in the saddle—oh, and he rode a pony once in Norfolk, when he was fifteen and the pony twenty-four; and to-morrow he's going to ride the Brogue! I shall be a widow before I'm married, and I do so want to see what Corsica's like; it looks so silly on the map."

Clovis was sent for in haste, and the developments of the situation put before him.

"Nobody can ride that animal with any safety," said Mrs. Mullet, "except Toby, and he knows by long experience what it is going to shy at, and manages to swerve at the same time."

"I did hint to Mr. Penricarde—to Vincent, I should say—that the Brogue didn't like white gates," said Jessie.

"White gates!" exclaimed Mrs. Mullet; "did you mention what effect a pig has on him? He'll have to go past Lockyer's farm to get to the high road, and there's sure to be a pig or two grunting about in the lane."

"He's taken rather a dislike to turkeys lately," said Toby.

"It's obvious that Penricarde mustn't be allowed to go out on that animal," said Clovis, "at least not till Jessie has married him, and tired of him. I tell you what: ask him to a picnic to-morrow, starting at an early hour; he's not the sort to go out for a ride before breakfast. The day after I'll get the rector to drive him over to Crowleigh before lunch, to see the new cottage hospital they're building there. The Brogue will be standing idle in the stable and Toby can offer to exercise it; then it can pick up a stone or something of the sort and go conveniently lame. If you hurry on the wedding a bit the lameness fiction can be kept up till the ceremony is safely over."

Mrs. Mullet belonged to an emotional race, and she kissed Clovis.

It was nobody's fault that the rain came down in torrents the next morning, making a picnic a fantastic impossibility. It was also nobody's fault, but sheer ill-luck, that the weather cleared up sufficiently in the afternoon to tempt Mr. Penricarde to make his first essay with the Brogue. They did not get as far as the pigs at Lockyer's farm; the rectory gate was painted a dull unobtrusive green, but it had been white a year or two ago, and the Brogue never forgot that he had been in the habit of making a violent curtsey, a back-pedal and a swerve at this particular point of the road. Subsequently, there being apparently no further call on his services, he broke his way into the rectory orchard, where he found a hen turkey in a coop; later visitors to the orchard found the coop almost intact, but very little left of the turkey.

Mr. Penricarde, a little stunned and shaken, and suffering from a bruised knee and some minor damages, good-naturedly ascribed the accident to his own inexperience with horses and country roads, and allowed Jessie to nurse him back into complete recovery and golf-fitness within something less than a week.

In the list of wedding presents which the local newspaper published a fortnight or so later appeared the following item:

"Brown saddle-horse, 'The Brogue,' bridegroom's gift to bride."

"Which shows," said Toby Mullet, "that he knew nothing."

"Or else," said Clovis, "that he has a very pleasing wit."

The Maltese Cat

Rudyard Kipling

THEY had good reason to be proud, and better reason to be afraid, all twelve of them; for though they had fought their way, game by game, up the teams entered for the polo tournament, they were meeting the Archangels that afternoon in the final match; and the Archangels men were playing with half a dozen ponies apiece. As the game was divided into six quarters of eight minutes each, that meant a fresh pony after every halt. The Skidars' team, even supposing there were no accidents, could only supply one pony for every other change; and two to one is heavy odds. Again, as Shiraz, the grey Syrian, pointed out, they were meeting the pink and pick of the polo-ponies of Upper India, ponies that had cost from a thousand rupees each, while they themselves were a cheap lot gathered, often from country-carts, by their masters, who belonged to a poor but honest native infantry regiment.

"Money means pace and weight," said Shiraz, rubbing his black-silk nose dolefully along his neat-fitting boot, "and by the maxims of the game as I know it—"

"Ah, but we aren't playing the maxims," said The Maltese Cat. "We're playing the game; and we've the great advantage of knowing the game. Just think a stride, Shiraz! We've pulled up from bottom to second place in two weeks against all those fellows on the ground here. That's because we play with our heads as well as our feet."

"It makes me feel undersized and unhappy all the same," said Kittiwynk, a mouse-coloured mare with a red brow-band and the cleanest pair of legs that ever an aged pony owned. "They've twice our style, these others."

Kittiwynk looked at the gathering and sighed. The hard, dusty polo-ground was lined with thousands of soldiers, black and white, not counting hundreds and hundreds of carriages and drags and dogcarts, and ladies with brilliant-coloured parasols, and officers in uniform and out of it, and crowds of natives behind them; and orderlies on camels, who had halted to watch the game, instead of carrying letters up and down the station; and native horse-dealers running about on thin-eared Biluchi mares, looking for a chance to sell a few first-class polo-ponies. Then there were the ponies of thirty teams that had entered for the Upper India Free-for-All Cup—nearly every pony of worth and dignity, from Mhow to Peshawar, from Allahabad to Multan; prize ponies, Arabs, Syrian, Barb, country-bred, Deccanee, Waziri, and Kabul ponies of every colour and shape and temper that you could imagine. Some of them were in mat-roofed stables, close to the polo-ground, but most were under saddle, while their masters, who had been defeated in the earlier games, trotted in and out and told the world exactly how the game should be played.

It was a glorious sight, and the come and go of the little, quick hooves, and the incessant salutations of ponies that had met before on other polo-grounds or race-courses were enough to drive a four-footed thing wild.

But the Skidars' team were careful not to know their neighbours, though half the ponies on the ground were anxious to scrape acquaintance with the little fellows that had come from the North, and, so far, had swept the board.

"Let's see," said a soft gold-coloured Arab, who had been playing very badly the day before, to The Maltese Cat; "didn't we meet in Abdul Rahman's stable in Bombay, four seasons ago? I won the Paikpattan Cup next season, you may remember?"

"Not me," said The Maltese Cat, politely. "I was at Malta then, pulling a vegetable-cart. I don't race. I play the game."

"Oh!" said the Arab, cocking his tail and swaggering off.

"Keep yourselves to yourselves," said The Maltese Cat to his companions. "We don't want to rub noses with all those goose-rumped half-breeds of Upper India. When we've won this Cup they'll give their shoes to know us."

"We sha'n't win the Cup," said Shiraz. "How do you feel?"

"Stale as last night's feed when a muskrat has run over it," said Polaris, a rather heavy-shouldered grey; and the rest of the team agreed with him.

"The sooner you forget that the better," said The Maltese Cat, cheerfully. "They've finished tiffin in the big tent. We shall be wanted now. If your saddles are not comfy, kick. If your bits aren't easy, rear, and let the saises know whether your boots are tight."

Each pony had his sais, his groom, who lived and ate and slept with the animal, and had betted a good deal more than he could afford on the result of the game. There was no chance of anything going wrong, but to make sure, each sais was shampooing the legs of his pony to the last minute. Behind the saises sat as many of the Skidars' regiment as had leave to attend the match—about half the native officers, and a hundred or two dark, black-bearded men with the regimental pipers nervously fingering the big, beribboned bagpipes. The Skidars were what they call a Pioneer regiment, and the bagpipes made the national music of half their men. The native officers held bundles of polo-sticks, long cane-handled mallets, and as the grand stand filled after lunch they arranged themselves by ones and twos at different points round the ground, so that if a stick were broken the player would not have far to ride for a new one. An impatient British Cavalry Band struck up "If you want to know the time, ask a p'leeceman!" and the two umpires in light dust-coats danced out on two little excited ponies. The four players of the Archangels' team followed, and the sight of their beautiful mounts made Shiraz groan again.

"Wait till we know," said The Maltese Cat. "Two of 'em are playing in blinkers, and that means they can't see to get out of the way of their own side, or they may shy at the umpires' ponies. They've all got white web-reins that are sure to stretch or slip!"

"And," said Kittiwynk, dancing to take the stiffness out of her, "they carry their whips in their hands instead of on their wrists. Hah!"

"True enough. No man can manage his stick and his reins and his whip that way," said The Maltese Cat. "I've fallen over every square yard of the Malta ground, and I ought to know."

He quivered his little, flea-bitten withers just to show how satisfied he felt; but his heart was not so light. Ever since he had drifted into India on a troop-ship, taken, with an old rifle, as part payment for a racing debt, The Maltese Cat had played and preached polo to the Skidars' team on the Skidars' stony polo-ground. Now a polo-pony is like a poet. If he is born with a love for the game, he can be made. The Maltese Cat knew that bamboos grew solely in order that poloballs might be turned from their roots, that grain was given to ponies to keep them in hard condition, and that ponies were shod to prevent them slipping on a turn. But, besides all these things, he knew every trick and device of the finest game in the world, and for two seasons had been teaching the others all he knew or guessed.

"Remember," he said for the hundredth time, as the riders came up, "you must play together, and you must play with your heads. Whatever happens, follow the ball. Who goes out first?"

Kittiwynk, Shiraz, Polaris, and a short high little bay fellow with tremendous hocks and no withers worth speaking of (he was called Corks) were being girthed up, and the soldiers in the background stared with all their eyes.

"I want you men to keep quiet," said Lutyens, the captain of the team, "and especially not to blow your pipes."

"Not if we win, Captain Sahib?" asked the piper.

"If we win you can do what you please," said Lutyens, with a smile, as he slipped the loop of his stick over his wrist, and wheeled to canter to his place. The Archangels' ponies were a little bit above themselves on account of the many-coloured crowd so close to the ground. Their riders were excellent players, but they were a team of crack players instead of a crack team; and that made all the difference in the world. They honestly meant to play together, but it is very hard for four men, each the best of the team he is picked from, to remember that in polo no brilliancy in hitting or riding makes up for playing alone. Their captain shouted his orders to them by name, and it is a curious thing that if you call his name aloud in public after an Englishman you make him hot and fretty. Lutyens said nothing to his men, because it had all been said before. He pulled up Shiraz, for he was playing "back," to guard the goal. Powell on Polaris was half-back, and Macnamara and Hughes on Corks and Kittiwynk were forwards. The tough, bamboo ball was set in the middle of the ground, one hundred and fifty yards from the ends, and Hughes crossed sticks, heads up, with the Captain of the Archangels, who saw fit to play forward; that is a place from which you cannot easily control your team. The little click as the cane-shafts met was heard all over the ground, and then Hughes made some sort of quick wrist-stroke that just dribbled the ball a few yards. Kittiwynk knew that stroke of old, and followed as a cat follows a mouse. While the Captain of the Archangels was wrenching his pony round, Hughes struck with all his strength, and next instant Kittiwynk was away, Corks following close behind her, their little feet pattering like raindrops on glass.

"Pull out to the left," said Kittiwynk between her teeth; "it's coming your way, Corks!"

The back and half-back of the Archangels were tearing down on her just as she was within reach of the ball. Hughes leaned forward with a loose rein, and cut it away to the left almost under Kittiwynk's foot, and it hopped and skipped off to Corks, who saw that, if he was not quick it would run beyond the boundaries. That long bouncing drive gave the Archangels time to wheel and send three men across the ground to head off Corks. Kittiwynk stayed where she was; for she knew the game. Corks was on the ball half a fraction of a second before the others came up, and Macnamara, with a backhanded stroke, sent it back across the ground to Hughes, who saw the way clear to the Archangels' goal, and smacked the ball in before any one quite knew what had happened.

"That's luck," said Corks, as they changed ends. "A goal in three minutes for three hits, and no riding to speak of."

"'Don't know," said Polaris. "We've made 'em angry too soon. Shouldn't wonder if they tried to rush us off our feet next time."

"Keep the ball hanging, then," said Shiraz. "That wears out every pony that is not used to it."

Next time there was no easy galloping across the ground. All the Archangels closed up as one man, but there they stayed, for Corks, Kittiwynk, and Polaris were somewhere on the top of the ball, marking time among the rattling sticks, while Shiraz circled about outside, waiting for a chance.

"We can do this all day," said Polaris, ramming his quarters into the side of another pony. "Where do you think you're shoving to?"

"I'll—I'll be driven in an ekka if I know," was the gasping reply, "and I'd give a week's feed to get my blinkers off. I can't see anything."

"The dust is rather bad. Whew! That was one for my off-hock. Where's the ball, Corks?"

"Under my tail. At least, the man's looking for it there! This is beautiful. They can't use their sticks, and it's driving 'em wild. Give old Blinkers a push and then he'll go over."

"Here, don't touch me! I can't see. I'll—I'll back out, I think," said the pony in blinkers, who knew that if you can't see all round your head, you cannot prop yourself against the shock.

Corks was watching the ball where it lay in the dust, close to his near fore-leg, with Macnamara's shortened stick tap-tapping it from time to time. Kittiwynk was edging her way out of the scrimmage, whisking her stump of a tail with nervous excitement.

"Ho! They've got it," she snorted. "Let me out!" and she galloped like a rifle-bullet just behind a tall lanky pony of the Archangels, whose rider was swinging up his stick for a stroke.

"Not to-day, thank you," said Hughes, as the blow slid off his raised stick, and Kittiwynk laid her shoulder to the tall pony's quarters, and shoved him aside just as Lutyens on Shiraz sent

the ball where it had come from, and the tall pony went skating
and slipping away to the left. Kittiwynk, seeing that Polaris had
joined Corks in the chase for the ball up the ground, dropped
into Polaris' place, and then "time" was called.

The Skidars' ponies wasted no time in kicking or fuming.
They knew that each minute's rest meant so much gain, and
trotted off to the rails, and their saises began to scrape and blanket and rub them at once.

"Whew!" said Corks, stiffening up to get all the tickle of the
big vulcanite scraper. "If we were playing pony for pony, we
would bend those Archangels double in half an hour. But they'll
bring up fresh ones and fresh ones and fresh ones after that—
you see."

"Who cares?" said Polaris. "We've drawn first blood. Is my
hock swelling?"

"Looks puffy," said Corks. "You must have had rather a wipe.
Don't let it stiffen. You'll be wanted again in half an hour."

"What's the game like?" said The Maltese Cat.

"Ground's like your shoe, except where they put too much
water on it," said Kittiwynk. "Then it's slippery. Don't play in the
centre. There's a bog there. I don't know how their next four are
going to behave, but we kept the ball hanging, and made 'em
lather for nothing. Who goes out? Two Arabs and a couple of
country-breds! That's bad. What a comfort it is to wash your
mouth out!"

Kitty was talking with a neck of a lather-covered soda-water
bottle between her teeth, and trying to look over her withers at
the same time. This gave her a very coquettish air.

"What's bad?" said Grey Dawn, giving to the girth and admiring his well-set shoulders.

"You Arabs can't gallop fast enough to keep yourselves
warm—that's what Kitty means," said Polaris, limping to show
that his hock needed attention. "Are you playing back, Grey
Dawn?"

"'Looks like it," said Grey Dawn, as Lutyens swung himself
up. Powell mounted The Rabbit, a plain bay country-bred much
like Corks, but with mulish ears. Macnamara took Faiz-Ullah, a

handy, short-backed little red Arab with a long tail, and Hughes mounted Benami, an old and sullen brown beast, who stood over in front more than a polo-pony should.

"Benami looks like business," said Shiraz. "How's your temper, Ben?" The old campaigner hobbled off without answering, and The Maltese Cat looked at the new Archangel ponies prancing about on the ground. They were four beautiful blacks, and they saddled big enough and strong enough to eat the Skidars' team and gallop away with the meal inside them.

"Blinkers again," said The Maltese Cat. "Good enough!"

"They're chargers-cavalry chargers!" said Kittiwynk, indignantly. "They'll never see thirteen-three again."

"They've all been fairly measured, and they've all got their certificates," said The Maltese Cat, "or they wouldn't be here. We must take things as they come along, and keep your eyes on the ball."

The game began, but this time the Skidars were penned to their own end of the ground, and the watching ponies did not approve of that.

"Faiz-Ullah is shirking—as usual," said Polaris, with a scornful grunt.

"Faiz-Ullah is eating whip," said Corks. They could hear the leather-thonged polo-quirt lacing the little fellow's well-rounded barrel. Then The Rabbit's shrill neigh came across the ground.

"I can't do all the work," he cried, desperately.

"Play the game—don't talk," The Maltese Cat whickered; and all the ponies wriggled with excitement, and the soldiers and the grooms gripped the railings and shouted. A black pony with blinkers had singled out old Benami, and was interfering with him in every possible way. They could see Benami shaking his head up and down, and flapping his under lip.

"There'll be a fall in a minute," said Polaris. "Benami is getting stuffy."

The game flickered up and down between goal-post and goal-post, and the black ponies were getting more confident as they felt they had the legs of the others. The ball was hit out of a little scrimmage, and Benami and The Rabbit followed it, Faiz-Ullah only too glad to be quiet for an instant.

The blinkered black pony came up like a hawk, with two of his own side behind him, and Benami's eye glittered as he raced. The question was which pony should make way for the other, for each rider was perfectly willing to risk a fall in a good cause. The black, who had been driven nearly crazy by his blinkers, trusted to his weight and his temper; but Benami knew how to apply his weight and how to keep his temper. They met, and there was a cloud of dust. The black was lying on his side, all the breath knocked out of his body. The Rabbit was a hundred yards up the ground with the ball, and Benami was sitting down. He had slid nearly ten yards on his tail, but he had had his revenge, and sat cracking his nostrils till the black pony rose.

"That's what you get for interfering. Do you want any more?" said Benami, and he plunged into the game. Nothing was done that quarter, because Faiz-Ullah would not gallop, though Macnamara beat him whenever he could spare a second. The fall of the black pony had impressed his companions tremendously, and so the Archangels could not profit by Faiz-Ullah's bad behaviour.

But as The Maltese Cat said when "time" was called, and the four came back blowing and dripping, Faiz-Ullah ought to have been kicked all round Umballa. If he did not behave better next time The Maltese Cat promised to pull out his Arab tail by the roots and—eat it.

There was no time to talk, for the third four were ordered out.

The third quarter of a game is generally the hottest, for each side thinks that the others must be pumped; and most of the winning play in a game is made about that time.

Lutyens took over The Maltese Cat with a pat and a hug, for Lutyens valued him more than anything else in the world; Powell had Shikast, a little grey rat with no pedigree and no manners outside polo; Macnamara mounted Bamboo, the largest of the team; and Hughes Who's Who, alias The Animal. He was supposed to have Australian blood in his veins, but he looked like a clothes-horse, and you could whack his legs with an iron crow-bar without hurting him.

They went out to meet the very flower of the Archangels' team; and when Who's Who saw their elegantly booted legs and their beautiful satin skins, he grinned a grin through his light, well-worn bridle.

"My word!" said Who's Who. "We must give 'em a little football. These gentlemen need a rubbing down."

"No biting," said The Maltese Cat, warningly; for once or twice in his career Who's Who had been known to forget himself in that way.

"Who said anything about biting? I'm not playing tiddly-winks. I'm playing the game."

The Archangels came down like a wolf on the fold, for they were tired of football, and they wanted polo. They got it more and more. Just after the game began, Lutyens hit a ball that was coming towards him rapidly, and it rolled in the air, as a ball sometimes will, with the whirl of a frightened partridge. Shikast heard, but could not see it for the minute, though he looked everywhere and up into the air as The Maltese Cat had taught him. When he saw it ahead and overhead he went forward with Powell as fast as he could put foot to ground. It was then that Powell, a quiet and level-headed man, as a rule, became inspired, and played a stroke that sometimes comes off successfully after long practice. He took his stick in both hands, and, standing up in his stirrups, swiped at the ball in the air, Munipore fashion. There was one second of paralysed astonishment, and then all four sides of the ground went up in a yell of applause and delight as the ball flew true (you could see the amazed Archangels ducking in their saddles to dodge the line of flight, and looking at it with open mouths), and the regimental pipes of the Skidars squealed from the railings as long as the pipers had breath. Shikast heard the stroke; but he heard the head of the stick fly off at the same time. Nine hundred and ninety-nine ponies out of a thousand would have gone tearing on after the ball with a useless player pulling at their heads; but Powell knew him, and he knew Powell; and the instant he felt Powell's right leg shift a trifle on the saddle-flap, he headed to the boundary, where a native officer was frantically waving a new stick. Before the shouts had ended, Powell was armed again.

Once before in his life The Maltese Cat had heard that very same stroke played off his own back, and had profited by the confusion it wrought. This time he acted on experience, and leaving Bamboo to guard the goal in case of accidents, came through the others like a flash, head and tail low—Lutyens standing up to ease him—swept on and on before the other side knew what was the matter, and nearly pitched on his head between the Archangels' goal-post as Lutyens kicked the ball in after a straight scurry of a hundred and fifty yards. If there was one thing more than another upon which The Maltese Cat prided himself, it was on this quick, streaking kind of run half across the ground. He did not believe in taking balls round the field unless you were clearly overmatched. After this they gave the Archangels five-minuted football; and an expensive fast pony hates football because it rumples his temper. Who's Who showed himself even better than Polaris in this game. He did not permit any wriggling away, but bored joyfully into the scrimmage as if he had his nose in a feed-box and was looking for something nice. Little Shikast jumped on the ball the minute it got clear, and every time an Archangel pony followed it, he found Shikast standing over it, asking what was the matter.

"If we can live through this quarter," said The Maltese Cat, "I sha'n't care. Don't take it out of yourselves. Let them do the lathering."

So the ponies, as their riders explained afterwards, "shut-up." The Archangels kept them tied fast in front of their goal, but it cost the Archangels' ponies all that was left of their tempers; and ponies began to kick, and men began to repeat compliments, and they chopped at the legs of Who's Who, and he set his teeth and stayed where he was, and the dust stood up like a tree over the scrimmage until that hot quarter ended.

They found the ponies very excited and confident when they went to their saises; and The Maltese Cat had to warn them that the worst of the game was coming.

"Now we are all going in for the second time," said he, "and they are trotting out fresh ponies. You think you can gallop, but you'll find you can't; and then you'll be sorry."

"But two goals to nothing is a halter-long lead," said Kittiwynk, prancing.

"How long does it take to get a goal?" The Maltese Cat answered. "For pity's sake, don't run away with a notion that the game is half-won just because we happen to be in luck now! They'll ride you into the grand stand, if they can; you must not give 'em a chance. Follow the ball."

"Football, as usual?" said Polaris. "My hock's half as big as a nose-bag."

"Don't let them have a look at the ball, if you can help it. Now leave me alone. I must get all the rest I can before the last quarter."

He hung down his head and let all his muscles go slack, Shikast, Bamboo, and Who's Who copying his example.

"Better not watch the game," he said. "We aren't playing, and we shall only take it out of ourselves if we grow anxious. Look at the ground and pretend it's fly-time."

They did their best, but it was hard advice to follow. The hooves were drumming and the sticks were rattling all up and down the ground, and yells of applause from the English troops told that the Archangels were pressing the Skidars hard. The native soldiers behind the ponies groaned and grunted, and said things in undertones, and presently they heard a long-drawn shout and a clatter of hurrahs!

"One to the Archangels," said Shikast, without raising his head. "Time's nearly up. Oh, my sire and dam!"

"Faiz-Ullah," said The Maltese Cat, "if you don't play to the last nail in your shoes this time, I'll kick you on the ground before all the other ponies."

"I'll do my best when my time comes," said the little Arab, sturdily.

The saises looked at each other gravely as they rubbed their ponies' legs. This was the time when long purses began to tell, and everybody knew it. Kittiwynk and the others came back, the sweat dripping over their hooves and their tails telling sad stories.

"They're better than we are," said Shiraz. "I knew how it would be."

"Shut your big head," said The Maltese Cat; "we've one goal to the good yet."

"Yes; but it's two Arabs and two country-breds to play now," said Corks. "Faiz-Ullah, remember!" He spoke in a biting voice.

As Lutyens mounted Grey Dawn he looked at his men, and they did not look pretty. They were covered with dust and sweat in streaks. Their yellow boots were almost black, their wrists were red and lumpy, and their eyes seemed two inches deep in their heads; but the expression in the eyes was satisfactory.

"Did you take anything at tiffin?" said Lutyens; and the team shook their heads. They were too dry to talk.

"All right. The Archangels did. They are worse pumped than we are."

"They've got the better ponies," said Powell. "I sha'n't be sorry when this business is over."

That fifth quarter was a painful one in every way. Faiz-Ullah played like a little red demon, and The Rabbit seemed to be everywhere at once, and Benami rode straight at anything and everything that came in his way; while the umpires on their ponies wheeled like gulls outside the shifting game. But the Archangels had the better mounts,—they had kept their racers till late in the game,—and never allowed the Skidars to play football. They hit the ball up and down the width of the ground till Benami and the rest were outpaced. Then they went forward, and time and again Lutyens and Grey Dawn were just, and only just, able to send the ball away with a long, spitting backhander. Grey Dawn forgot that he was an Arab; and turned from grey to blue as he galloped. Indeed, he forgot too well, for he did not keep his eyes on the ground as an Arab should, but stuck out his nose and scuttled for the dear honour of the game. They had watered the ground once or twice between the quarters, and a careless waterman had emptied the last of his skinful all in one place near the Skidars' goal. It was close to the end of the play, and for the tenth time Grey Dawn was bolting after the ball, when his near hind-foot slipped on the greasy mud, and he rolled over and over, pitching Lutyens just clear of the goal-post; and the triumphant Archangels made their goal. Then "time" was called—two goals all; but Lutyens had to be helped up, and Grey Dawn rose with his near hind-leg strained somewhere.

"What's the damage?" said Powell, his arm around Lutyens.

"Collar-bone, of course," said Lutyens, between his teeth. It was the third time he had broken it in two years, and it hurt him.

Powell and the others whistled.

"Game's up," said Hughes.

"Hold on. We've five good minutes yet, and it isn't my right hand. We'll stick it out."

"I say," said the Captain of the Archangels, trotting up, "are you hurt, Lutyens? We'll wait if you care to put in a substitute. I wish—I mean—the fact is, you fellows deserve this game if any team does. Wish we could give you a man, or some of our ponies—or something."

"You're awfully good, but we'll play it to a finish, I think."

The Captain of the Archangels stared for a little. "That's not half bad," he said, and went back to his own side, while Lutyens borrowed a scarf from one of his native officers and made a sling of it. Then an Archangel galloped up with a big bath-sponge, and advised Lutyens to put it under his armpit to ease his shoulder, and between them they tied up his left arm scientifically; and one of the native officers leaped forward with four long glasses that fizzed and bubbled.

The team looked at Lutyens piteously, and he nodded. It was the last quarter, and nothing would matter after that. They drank out the dark golden drink, and wiped their moustaches, and things looked more hopeful.

The Maltese Cat had put his nose into the front of Lutyens' shirt and was trying to say how sorry he was.

"He knows," said Lutyens, proudly. "The beggar knows. I've played him without a bridle before now—for fun."

"It's no fun now," said Powell. "But we haven't a decent substitute."

"No," said Lutyens. "It's the last quarter, and we've got to make our goal and win. I'll trust The Cat."

"If you fall this time, you'll suffer a little," said Macnamara.

"I'll trust The Cat," said Lutyens.

"You hear that?" said The Maltese Cat, proudly, to the others. "It's worth while playing polo for ten years to have that said of you. Now then, my sons, come along. We'll kick up a little bit, just to show the Archangels this team haven't suffered."

And, sure enough, as they went on to the ground, The Maltese Cat, after satisfying himself that Lutyens was home in the saddle, kicked out three or four times, and Lutyens laughed. The reins were caught up anyhow in the tips of his strapped left hand, and he never pretended to rely on them. He knew The Cat would answer to the least pressure of the leg, and by way of showing off—for his shoulder hurt him very much—he bent the little fellow in a close figure-of-eight in and out between the goal-posts. There was a roar from the native officers and men, who dearly loved a piece of dugabashi (horse-trick work), as they called it, and the pipes very quietly and scornfully droned out the first bars of a common bazaar tune called "Freshly Fresh and Newly New," just as a warning to the other regiments that the Skidars were fit. All the natives laughed.

"And now," said The Maltese Cat, as they took their place, "remember that this is the last quarter, and follow the ball!"

"Don't need to be told," said Who's Who.

"Let me go on. All those people on all four sides will begin to crowd in—just as they did at Malta. You'll hear people calling out, and moving forward and being pushed back; and that is going to make the Archangel ponies very unhappy. But if a ball is struck to the boundary, you go after it, and let the people get out of your way. I went over the pole of a four-in-hand once, and picked a game out of the dust by it. Back me up when I run, and follow the ball."

There was a sort of an all-round sound of sympathy and wonder as the last quarter opened, and then there began exactly what The Maltese Cat had foreseen. People crowded in close to the boundaries, and the Archangels' ponies kept looking sideways at the narrowing space. If you know how a man feels to be cramped at tennis—not because he wants to run out of the court, but because he likes to know that he can at a pinch—you will guess how ponies must feel when they are playing in a box of human beings.

"I'll bend some of those men if I can get away," said Who's Who, as he rocketed behind the ball; and Bamboo nodded without speaking. They were playing the last ounce in them, and The Maltese Cat had left the goal undefended to join them. Lutyens gave him every order that he could to bring him back, but this was the first time in his career that the little wise grey had ever played polo on his own responsibility, and he was going to make the most of it.

"What are you doing here?" said Hughes, as The Cat crossed in front of him and rode off an Archangel.

"The Cat's in charge—mind the goal!" shouted Lutyens, and bowing forward hit the ball full, and followed on, forcing the Archangels towards their own goal.

"No football," said The Maltese Cat. "Keep the ball by the boundaries and cramp 'em. Play open order, and drive 'em to the boundaries."

Across and across the ground in big diagonals flew the ball, and whenever it came to a flying rush and a stroke close to the boundaries the Archangel ponies moved stiffly. They did not care to go headlong at a wall of men and carriages, though if the ground had been open they could have turned on a sixpence.

"Wriggle her up the sides," said The Cat. "Keep her close to the crowd. They hate the carriages. Shikast, keep her up this side."

Shikast and Powell lay left and right behind the uneasy scuffle of an open scrimmage, and every time the ball was hit away Shikast galloped on it at such an angle that Powell was forced to hit it towards the boundary; and when the crowd had been driven away from that side, Lutyens would send the ball over to the other, and Shikast would slide desperately after it till his friends came down to help. It was billiards, and no football, this time—billiards in a corner pocket; and the cues were not well chalked.

"If they get us out in the middle of the ground they'll walk away from us. Dribble her along the sides," cried The Maltese Cat.

So they dribbled all along the boundary, where a pony could not come on their right-hand side; and the Archangels were furious, and the umpires had to neglect the game to shout at the people to get back, and several blundering mounted policemen tried to restore order, all close to the scrimmage, and the nerves of the Archangels' ponies stretched and broke like cob-webs.

Five or six times an Archangel hit the ball up into the middle of the ground, and each time the watchful Shikast gave Powell his chance to send it back, and after each return, when the dust had settled, men could see that the Skidars had gained a few yards.

Every now and again there were shouts of "Side! Off side!" from the spectators; but the teams were too busy to care, and the umpires had all they could do to keep their maddened ponies clear of the scuffle.

At last Lutyens missed a short easy stroke, and the Skidars had to fly back helter-skelter to protect their own goal, Shikast leading. Powell stopped the ball with a backhander when it was not fifty yards from the goalposts, and Shikast spun round with a wrench that nearly hoisted Powell out of his saddle.

"Now's our last chance," said The Cat, wheeling like a cockchafer on a pin. "We've got to ride it out. Come along."

Lutyens felt the little chap take a deep breath, and, as it were, crouch under his rider. The ball was hopping towards the right-hand boundary, an Archangel riding for it with both spurs and a whip; but neither spur nor whip would make his pony stretch himself as he neared the crowd. The Maltese Cat glided under his very nose, picking up his hind legs sharp, for there was not a foot to spare between his quarters and the other pony's bit. It was as neat an exhibition as fancy figure-skating. Lutyens hit with all the strength he had left, but the stick slipped a little in his hand, and the ball flew off to the left instead of keeping close to the boundary. Who's Who was far across the ground, thinking hard as he galloped. He repeated stride for stride The Cat's manoeuvres with another Archangel pony, nipping the ball away from under his bridle, and clearing his opponent by half a fraction of an inch, for Who's Who was clumsy behind. Then he drove away towards the right as The Maltese Cat came up from the left; and Bamboo held a middle course exactly between them. The three were making a sort of Government-broad-arrow-shaped attack; and there was only the Archangels' back to guard the goal; but immediately behind them were three Archangels racing all they knew, and mixed up with them was Powell sending Shikast along on what he felt was their last hope. It takes a very good man to stand up to the rush of seven crazy ponies in the last quarters of a Cup game, when men are riding with their necks for sale, and the ponies are delirious. The Archangels' back missed his stroke and pulled aside just in time to let the rush go by. Bamboo and Who's Who shortened stride to give The Cat room, and Lutyens got the goal with a clean, smooth, smacking stroke that was heard all over the field. But there was no stopping the ponies. They poured through the goalposts in one mixed mob, winners and losers together, for the pace had been terrific. The Maltese Cat knew by experience what would happen, and, to save Lutyens, turned to the right with one last effort, that strained a back-sinew beyond hope of repair. As he did so he heard the right-hand goalpost crack as a pony cannoned into it—crack, splinter and fall like a mast. It had been sawed three parts through in case of accidents, but it upset the pony nevertheless, and he blundered into another, who blundered into the left-hand post, and then there was confusion and dust and wood. Bamboo was lying on the ground, seeing stars; an Archangel pony rolled beside him, breathless and angry; Shikast had sat down dog-fashion to avoid falling over the others, and was sliding along on his little bobtail in a cloud of dust; and Powell was sitting on the ground, hammering with his stick and trying to cheer. All the others were shouting at the top of what was left of their voices, and the men who had been spilt were shouting too. As soon as the people saw no one was hurt, ten thousand native and English shouted and clapped and yelled, and before any one could stop them the pipers of the Skidars broke on to the ground, with all the native officers and men behind them, and marched up and down, playing a wild Northern tune called "Zakhme Began," and through the insolent blaring of the pipes and the high-pitched native yells you could hear the Archangels' band hammering, "For they are all jolly good fellows," and then reproachfully to the losing team, "Ooh, Kafoozalum! Kafoozalum! Kafoozalum!"

Besides all these things and many more, there was a Commander-in-chief, and an Inspector-General of Cavalry, and the principal veterinary officer of all India standing on the top of a regimental coach, yelling like school-boys; and brigadiers and colonels and commissioners, and hundreds of pretty ladies joined the chorus. But The Maltese Cat stood with his head down, wondering how many legs were left to him; and Lutyens watched the men and ponies pick themselves out of the wreck of the two goal-posts, and he patted The Maltese Cat very tenderly.

"I say," said the Captain of the Archangels, spitting a pebble out of his mouth, "will you take three thousand for that pony—as he stands?"

"No thank you. I've an idea he's saved my life," said Lutyens, getting off and lying down at full length. Both teams were on the ground too, waving their boots in the air, and coughing and drawing deep breaths, as the saises ran up to take away the ponies, and an officious water-carrier sprinkled the players with dirty water till they sat up.

"My aunt!" said Powell, rubbing his back, and looking at the stumps of the goal-posts, "That was a game!"

They played it over again, every stroke of it, that night at the big dinner, when the Free-for-All Cup was filled and passed down the table, and emptied and filled again, and everybody made most eloquent speeches. About two in the morning, when there might have been some singing, a wise little, plain little, grey little head looked in through the open door.

"Hurrah! Bring him in," said the Archangels; and his sais, who was very happy indeed, patted The Maltese Cat on the flank, and he limped in to the blaze of light and the glittering uniforms, looking for Lutyens. He was used to messes, and men's bedrooms, and places where ponies are not usually encouraged, and in his youth had jumped on and off a mess-table for a bet. So he behaved himself very politely, and ate bread dipped in salt, and was petted all round the table, moving gingerly; and they drank his health, because he had done more to win the Cup than any man or horse on the ground.

That was glory and honour enough for the rest of his days, and The Maltese Cat did not complain much when the veterinary surgeon said that he would be no good for polo any more. When Lutyens married, his wife did not allow him to play, so he was forced to be an umpire; and his pony on these occasions was a flea-bitten grey with a neat polo-tail, lame all round, but desperately quick on his feet, and, as everybody knew, Past Pluperfect Prestissimo Player of the Game.

The Doctor's Horse

Mary E. Wilkins Freeman

THE horse was a colt when he was purchased with the money paid by the heirs of one of the doctor's patients, and those were his days of fire. At first it was opined that the horse would never do for the doctor: he was too nervous, and his nerves beyond the reach of the doctor's drugs. He shied at every wayside bush and stone; he ran away several times; he was loath to stand, and many a time the doctor in those days was forced to rush from the bedsides of patients to seize his refractory horse by the bridle and soothe and compel him to quiet. The horse in that untamed youth of his was like a furnace of fierce animal fire; when he was given rein on a frosty morning the pound of his iron-bound hoofs on the rigid roads cleared them of the slow-plodding country teams. A current as of the very freedom and invincibility of life seemed to pass through the taut reins to the doctor's hands. But the doctor was the master of his horse, as of all other things with which he came in contact. He was a firm and hard man in the pursuance of his duty, never yielding to it with love, but unswervingly stanch. He was never cruel to his horse; he seldom whipped him, but he never petted him; he simply mastered him, and after a while the fiery animal began to go the doctor's gait, and not his own.

When the doctor was sent for in a hurry, to an emergency case, the horse stretched his legs at a gallop, no matter how little inclined he felt for it, perhaps on a burning day of summer. When there was no haste, and the doctor disposed to take his time, the horse went at a gentle amble, even though the frosts

113

of a winter morning were firing his blood and every one of his iron nerves and muscles was strained with that awful strain of repressed motion. Even on those mornings the horse would stand at the door of the patient who was ill with old-fashioned consumption or chronic liver disease, his four legs planted widely, his head and neck describing a long downward curve, so expressive of submission and dejection that it might have served as a hieroglyphic for them, and no more thought of letting those bounding impulses of his have their way than if the doctor's will had verily bound his every foot to the ground with unbreakable chains of servitude. He had become the doctor's horse. He was the will of the doctor, embodied in a perfect compliance of action and motion. People remarked how the horse had sobered down, what a splendid animal he was for the doctor, and they had thought that he would never be able to keep him and employ him in his profession.

Now and then the horse used to look around at the empty buggy as he stood at the gate of a patient's house, to see if the doctor were there, but the will which held the reins, being still evident to his consciousness, even when its owner was absent, kept him in his place. He would have no thought of taking advantage of his freedom; he would turn his head and droop it in that curve of utter submission, shift his weight slightly to another foot, make a sound which was like a human sigh of patience, and wait again. When the doctor, carrying his little medicine-chest, came forth, he would sometimes look at him, sometimes not; but he would set every muscle into an attitude of readiness for progress at the feel of the taut lines and the sound of the masterly human voice behind him.

Then he would proceed to the house of the next patient, and the story would be repeated. The horse seemed to live his life in a perfect monotony of identical chapters. His waiting was scarcely cheered or stimulated by the vision and anticipation of his stall and his supper, so unvarying was it. The same stall, the same measure of oats, the same allotment of hay. He was never put out to pasture, for the doctor was a poor man, and unable to buy another horse and to spare him. All the variation which came to his experience was the uncertainty as to the night calls. Sometimes he would feel a slight revival of spirit and rebellion when led forth on a bitter winter night from his stolidity of repose, broken only by the shifting of his weight for bodily comfort, never by any perturbation of his inner life. The horse had no disturbing memories, and no anticipations, but he was still somewhat sensitive to surprises. When the flare of the lantern came athwart his stall, and he felt the doctor's hand at his halter in the deep silence of a midnight, he would sometimes feel himself as a separate consciousness from the doctor, and experience the individualizing of contrary desires.

Now and then he pulled back, planting his four feet firmly, but he always yielded in a second before the masterly will of the man. Sometimes he started with a vicious emphasis, but it was never more than momentary. In the end he fell back into his state of utter submission. The horse was not unhappy. He was well cared for. His work, though considerable, was not beyond his strength. He had lost something, undoubtedly, in this complete surrender of his own will, but a loss of which one is unconscious tends only to the degradation of an animal, not to his misery.

The doctor often remarked with pride that his horse was a well-broken animal, somewhat stupid, but faithful. All the timid women folk in the village looked upon him with favor; the doctor's wife, who was nervous, loved to drive with her husband behind this docile horse, and was not afraid even to sit, while the doctor was visiting his patients, with the reins over the animal's back. The horse had become to her a piece of mechanism absolutely under the control of her husband, and he was, in truth, little more. Still, a furnace is a furnace, even when the fire runs low, and there is always the possibility of a blaze.

The doctor had owned the horse several years, though he was still young, when a young woman came to live in the family. She was the doctor's niece, a fragile thing, so exposed as to her net-work of supersensitive nerves to all the winds of life that she was always in a quiver of reciprocation or repulsion. She feared everything unknown, and all strength. She was innately suspicious of the latter. She knew its power to work her harm, and believed in its desire to do so. Especially was she afraid of that rampant and uncertain strength of a horse. Never did she ride behind one but she watched his every motion; she herself shied in spirit at every wayside stone. She watched for him to do his worst. She had no faith when she was told by her uncle that this horse was so steady that she herself could drive him. She had been told that so many times, and her confidence had been betrayed. But the doctor, since she was like a pale weed grown in the shade, with no stimulus of life except that given at its birth, prescribed fresh air and, to her consternation, daily drives with him. Day after day she went. She dared not refuse, for she was as compliant in her way to a stronger will as the horse. But she went in an agony of terror, of which the doctor had no conception. She sat in the buggy all alone while the doctor visited his patients, and she watched every motion of the horse. If he turned to look at her, her heart stood still.

And at last it came to pass that the horse began in a curious fashion to regain something of his lost spirit, and met her fear of him, and became that which she dreaded. One day as he stood before a gate in late autumn, with a burning gold of maple branches over his head and the wine of the frost in his nostrils, and this timorous thing seated behind him, anticipating that which he could but had forgotten that he could do, the knowledge and the memory of it awoke in him. There was a stiff northwester blowing. The girl was huddled in shawls and robes; her little, pale face looked forth from the midst with wide eyes, with a prospectus of infinite danger from all life in them; her little, thin hands clutched the reins with that consciousness of helplessness and conviction of the horse's power of mischief which is sometimes like an electric current firing the blood of a beast.

Suddenly a piece of paper blew under the horse's nose. He had been unmoved by fire-crackers before, but to-day, with that current of terror behind him firing his blood, that paper put him in a sudden fury of panic, of self-assertion, of rage, of all three combined. He snorted; the girl screamed wildly. He started; the girl gave the reins a frantic pull. He stopped. Then the paper blew under his nose again, and he started again. The girl fairly gasped with terror; she pulled the reins, and the terror in her hands was like a whip of stimulus to the evil freedom in the horse. She screamed again, and the sound of that scream was the climax. The horse knew all at once what he was—not the doctor, but a horse, with a great power of blood and muscle which made him not only his own master, but the master of all weaker things. He gave a great plunge that was rapture, the assertion of freedom—freedom itself—and was off. The faint screams of the frightened creature behind him stimulated him to madder progress. At last he knew, by her terrified recognition of it, his own sovereignty of liberty.

He thundered along the road; he had no more thought of his pitiful encumbrance of servitude, the buggy, than a free soul of its mortal coil. The country road was cleared before him; plodding teams were pulled frantically to the side; women scuttled into door-yards; pale faces peered after him from windows. Now and then an adventurous man rushed into his path with wild halloos and a mad swinging of arms, then fled precipitately before his resistless might of advance. At first the horse had heard the doctor's shouts behind him, and had laughed within himself, then he left them far behind. He leaped, he plunged, his iron-shod heels touched the dashboard of the buggy. He heard splintering wood. He gave another lunging plunge, then he swerved and leaped a wall. Finally he had cleared himself of everything except a remnant of his harness. The buggy was a wreck, strewn piecemeal over a meadow. The girl was lying unhurt, but as still as if she were dead; but the horse which her fear had fired to new life was away in a mad gallop over the autumn fields, and his youth had returned. He was again himself—what he had been when he first awoke to a consciousness of existence and the joy of bounding motion in his mighty nerves and muscles. He was no longer the doctor's horse, but his own.

The doctor had to sell him. After that his reputation was gone, and, indeed, he was never safe. He ran away with the doctor. He would not stand a moment unless tied, and then pawed and pulled madly at the halter, and rent the air with impatient whinnies. So the doctor sold him, and made a good bargain. The horse was formed for speed, and his lapse from virtue had increased his financial value. The man who bought him had a good eye for horse-flesh, and had no wish to stand at doors on his road to success, but to take a bee-line for the winning-post. The horse was well cared for, but for the first time he felt the lash and heard curses; however, they only served to stimulate to a fiercer glow the fire which had awakened within him. He was never his new master's horse as he had been the doctor's. He gained the reputation of speed, but also of vicious nervousness. He was put on the race-course. He made a record at the county fair. Once he killed his jockey. He used to speed along the road drawing a man crouched in a tilting gig. Few other horses could pass him. Then he began to grow old.

At last, when the horse was old, he came into his first master's hands again. The doctor had grown old, older than the horse, and he did not know him at first, though he did say to his old wife that he looked something like that horse which he had owned which ran away and nearly killed his niece. After he said that, nothing could induce the doctor's wife to ride behind him; but the doctor, even in his feeble old age, had no fear, and the sidelong fire in the old horse's eye, and the proud cant of his neck, and his haughty resentment at unfamiliar sights on the road pleased him. He felt a confidence in his ability to tame this untamed thing, and the old man seemed to grow younger after he had bought the horse. He had given up his practice after a severe illness, and a young man had taken it, but he began to have dreams of work again. He never knew that he had bought his own old horse until after he had owned him some weeks. He was driving him along the country road one day in October when the oaks were a ruddy blaze, and the sumacs like torches along the walls, and the air like wine with the smell of grapes and apples. Then suddenly, while the doctor was sitting in the buggy with loose reins, speeding along the familiar road, the horse stopped; and he stopped before the house where had used to dwell the man afflicted with old-fashioned consumption, and

the window which had once framed his haggard, coughing vis-
age reflected the western sunlight like a blank page of gold.
There the horse stood, his head and long neck bent in the old
curve. He was ready to wait until the consumptive arose from
his grave in the churchyard, if so ordered. The doctor stared at
him. Then he got out and went to the animal's head, and man
and horse recognized each other. The light of youth was again in
the man's eyes as he looked at his own spiritual handiwork. He
was once more the master, in the presence of that which he had
mastered. But the horse was expressed in body and spirit only
by the lines of utter yielding and patience and submission. He
was again the doctor's horse.

The Horses of Bostil's Ford

Zane Grey

I

BOSTIL himself was half horse. The half of him that was human he divided between love of his fleet racers and his daughter, Lucy.

He had seen ten years of hard riding on that wild Utah border, where a horse meant all the world to a man; and then lucky strikes of water and gold on the vast plateau wilderness north of the Rio Virgin had made him richer than he knew. His ranges beyond Bostil's Ford were practically boundless, his cattle numberless, and, many as were his riders, he always had need of more.

In those border days every rider loved his horse as a part of himself. If there was a difference between any rider of the sage and Bostil, it was that, as Bostil had more horses, so he had more love.

If he had any unhappiness, it was because he could not buy Wildfire and Nagger, thoroughbreds belonging to one Lamar, a poor daredevil rider who would not have parted with them for all the gold in the uplands. And Lamar had dared to cast longing eyes at Lucy. When he clashed with Bostil he avowed his love, and offered to stake his horses and his life against the girl's hand, deciding the wager by a race between Wildfire and the rancher's great gray, Sage King.

Among the riders, when they sat around their campfires, there had been much speculation regarding the outcome of such a race. There never had been a race, and never would be, so the riders gossiped, unless Lamar were to ride off with Lucy.

In that case there would be the grandest race ever run on the uplands, with the odds against Wildfire only if he carried double.

If Lamar put Lucy up on Wildfire, and he rode Nagger, there would be another story. Lucy was a slip of a girl, born on a horse, and could ride like a burr sticking in a horse's mane. With Wildfire she would run away from anyone on Sage King—which for Bostil would be a double tragedy, equally in the loss of his daughter and the beating of his favorite. Then such a race was likely to end in heartbreak for all concerned, because the Sage King would outrun Nagger, and that would bring riders within gunshot.

Bostil swore by all the gods that the King was the swiftest horse in the wild upland of wonderful horses. He swore that the gray could look back over his shoulder and run away from Nagger, and that he could kill Wildfire on his feet. That poor beggar Lamar's opinion of his steeds was as preposterous as his love for Lucy!

Now, Bostil had a great fear which made him ever restless, ever watchful. That fear was of Cordts, the rustler. Cordts hid back in the untrodden ways. He had fast horses, faithful followers, gold for the digging, cattle by the thousand, and women when he chose to ride off with them. He had always had what he wanted—except one thing. That was a horse. That horse was the Sage King.

Cordts was a gunman, outlaw, rustler, a lord over the free ranges; but, more than all else, he was a rider. He knew a horse. He was as much horse as Bostil. He was a prince of rustlers, who thought a horse thief worse than a dog; but he intended to become a horse thief. He had openly declared it. The passion he had conceived for the Sage King was the passion of a man for an unattainable woman. He swore that he would never rest—that he would not die till he owned the King; so Bostil had reason for his great fear.

One morning, as was sometimes the rancher's custom, he ordered the racers to be brought from the corrals and turned loose in the alfalfa fields near the house. Bostil loved to watch them graze; but ever he saw that the riders were close at hand, and that the horses did not graze too close to the sage.

He sat back and gloried in the sight. He owned a thousand horses; near at hand was a field full of them, fine and mettlesome and racy; but Bostil had eyes only for the six blooded favorites. There was Plume, a superb mare that got her name from the way her mane swept in the wind when she was on the run; there were Bullet, huge, rangy, leaden in color, and Two-Face, sleek and glossy and cunning; there was the black stallion Sarchedon, and close to him the bay Dusty Ben; and lastly Sage King, the color of the upland sage, a horse proud and wild and beautiful.

"Where's Lucy?" presently asked Bostil. As he divided his love, so he divided his anxiety.

Some rider had seen Lucy riding off, with her golden hair flying in the breeze.

"She's got to keep out of the sage," growled Bostil. "Where's my glass? I want to take a look out there. Where's my glass?"

The glass could not be found.

"What're those specks in the sage? Antelope?"

"I reckon that's a bunch of hosses," replied a hawk-eyed rider.

"Huh! I don't like it. Lucy oughtn't to be ridin' round alone. If she meets Lamar again, I'll rope her in a corral!"

Another rider drew Bostil's attention from the gray waste of rolling sage.

"Bostil, look! Look at the King! He smells somethin'—he's lookin' for somethin'! So does Sarch.'"

"Yes," replied the rancher. "Better drive them up. They're too close to the sage."

Sage King whistled shrilly and began to prance.

"What in the—" muttered Bostil.

Suddenly up out of the alfalfa sprang a dark form. Like a panther it leaped at the horse and caught his mane. Snorting wildly, Sage King reared aloft and plunged. The dark form swung up. It was a rider, and cruelly he spurred the racer.

Other dark forms rose almost as swiftly, and leaped upon the other plunging horses. There was a violent, pounding shock of frightened horses bunching into action. With a magnificent bound, Sage King got clear of the tangle and led the way.

Like Indians, the riders hung low and spurred. In a single swift moment they had the horses tearing into the sage.

"Rustlers! *Cordts! Cordts!*" screamed Bostil. "He sneaked up in the sage! Quick, men—rifles, rifles! No! No! Don't shoot! *You might kill a horse!* Let them go. They'll get the girl, too—there must be more rustlers in the sage—they've got her now! There they go! Gone! Gone! All that I loved!"

II

A T almost the exact hour of the rustling of the racers, Lucy Bostil was with Jim Lamar at their well-hidden rendezvous on a high, cedared slope some eight or ten miles from the ranch. From an opening in the cedars they could see down across the gray sage to the alfalfa fields, the corrals, and the house. In Lucy's lap, with her gauntlets, lay the field glass that Bostil's riders could not find; and close by, halted under a cedar, Lucy's pinto tossed his spotted head at Lamar's magnificent horses.

"You unhappy boy!" Lucy was saying. "Of course I love you; but, Jim, I can't meet you any more like this. It's not playing square with Dad."

"Lucy, if you give it up, you don't love me," he protested.

"I *do* love you."

"Well, then—"

He leaned over her. Lucy's long lashes drooped and warm color flushed her face as she shyly lifted it to give the proof exacted by her lover.

They were silent a moment, and she lay with her head on his breast. A soft wind moaned through the cedars, and bees hummed in the patches of pale lavender daisies. The still air was heavily laden with the fragrance of the sage.

Lamar gently released her, got up, and seemed to be shaking off a kind of spell.

"Lucy, I know you mustn't meet me any more. But oh, Lord, Lord, I do love you so! I had nothing in the world but the hope of seeing you, and now that'll be gone. I'll be such a miserable beggar!"

Lucy demurely eyed him.

"Jim, your clothes are pretty ragged, and you look a little in need of some good food, but it strikes me you're a splendid-looking beggar. You suit me. You oughtn't say you have nothing. Look at your horses!"

Lamar's keen gray eyes softened. Indeed, he was immeasurably rich, and he gazed at his horses as if that were the first moment he had ever laid eyes on them.

Both were of tremendous build. Nagger was dark and shaggy, with arched neck and noble head that suggested race, loyalty, and speed. Wildfire was so finely pointed, so perfectly balanced, that he appeared smaller than Nagger; but he was as high, as long, and he had the same great breadth of chest; and though not so heavy, he had the same wonderful look of power. As red as fire, with sweeping mane and tail, like dark tinged flames, and holding himself with a strange alert wildness, he looked his name.

"Jimmy, you have those grand horses," went on Lucy. "And look at *me*!"

Lamar did look at her, yearningly. She was as lithe as a young panther. Her rider's suit, like a boy's, rather emphasized than hid the graceful roundness of her slender form. Lamar thought her hair the gold of the sage at sunset, her eyes the blue of the deep haze in the distance, her mouth the sweet red of the upland rose.

"Jimmy, you've got me corralled," she continued archly, "and I'm Dad's only child."

"But, Lucy, I *haven't* got you!" he passionately burst out.

"Yes, you have. All you need is patience. Keep hanging round the Ford till Dad gives in. He hasn't one thing against you, except that you wouldn't sell him your horses. Dad's crazy about horses. Jim, he wasn't so angry because you wanted to race Wildfire against the King *for me*; he was furious because you were so sure you'd win. And see here, Jim dear—if ever you and Dad race the red and the gray, you let the gray win, if you love me and want me! Else you'll *never* get me in this world."

"Lucy! I wouldn't pull Wildfire— I wouldn't break that horse's heart even to—to get you!"

"That's the rider in you, Jim. I like you better for it; but all the same, I know you would."

"I wouldn't!"

"You don't love me!"

"I do love you."

"Well, then!" she mocked, and lifted her face.

"Oh, child, you could make me do anything," went on Lamar presently. "But, Lucy, you've ridden the King, and you're the only person besides me who was ever up on Wildfire. Tell me, isn't Wildfire the better horse?"

"Jim, you've asked me that a thousand times."

"Have I? Well, tell me."

"Yes, Jim, if you can compare two such horses, Wildfire is the better."

"You darling! Lucy, did Bostil ever ask you that?"

"About seven million times."

"And what did you tell him?" asked Lamar, laughing, yet earnest withal.

"I wouldn't dare tell Dad anything but the Sage King could run Wildfire off his legs."

"You—you little hypocrite! Which of us were you really lying to?"

"I reckon it was Dad," replied Lucy seriously. "Jim, I can ride, but I haven't much horse sense. So what I think mayn't be right. I love the King and Wildfire—all horses. Really I love Nagger best of all. He's so faithful. Why, it's because he loves you that he nags you. Wildfire's no horse for a woman. He's wild. I don't think he's actually any faster than the King; only he's a desert stallion, and has killed many horses. His spirit would break the

King. It's in the King to outrun a horse; it's in Wildfire to kill him. What a shame ever to let those great horses race!"

"They never will, Lucy, dear. And now I'll see if the sage is clear; for you must be going."

III

LAMAR'S eye swept the gray expanse. A few miles out he saw a funnel-shaped dust cloud rising behind a bunch of dark horses, and farther on toward the ranch more puffs of dust and moving black specks.

"Lucy, something's wrong," he said quietly. "Take your glass. Look there!"

"Oh, dear, I'm afraid Dad has put the boys on my trail," rejoined Lucy, as she readjusted the glass and leveled it. Instantly she cried: "Three riders and three led horses—unsaddled. I don't know the riders. Jim! I see Sarchedon and Bullet, if ever I saw them in my life!"

"Rustlers! I knew it before you looked," said Jim, with compressed lips. "Give me the glass." He looked, and while he held the glass leveled he spoke: "Yes, Sarch and Bullet—there's Two-Face. The three unsaddled horses I don't know. They're dark bays—rustlers' horses. That second bunch I can't make out so well for dust, but it's the same kind of a bunch—three riders, three led horses. Lucy, there's the King. Cordts has got him!"

"Oh, Jim, it will ruin Dad!" cried Lucy, wringing her hands.

Lamar appeared suddenly to become obsessed by a strange excitement.

"Why, Jim, we're safe hidden here," said Lucy, in surprise.

"Girl! Do you think me afraid? It's only that I'm—" His face grew tense, his eyes burned, his hands trembled. "What a chance for me! Lucy, listen. Cordts and his men—picked men, probably—sneaked up in the sage to the ranch, and run off bareback on the racers. They've had their horses hidden, and then changed saddles. They're traveling light. There's not a long gun among them. *I've got my rifle.* I can stop that bunch—kill some of them, or maybe all—get the horses back. If I only had more shells for my rifle! I've only ten in the magazine. I'm so poor I can't buy shells for my rifle."

"Dear Jim, don't risk it, then," said Lucy, trembling.

"I will risk it," he cried. "It's the chance of my life. Dearest, think—think what it'd mean to Bostil if I killed Cordts and got back the King! Think what it'd mean for me! Cordts is the bane of the uplands. He's a murderer, a stealer of women. Bostil can't sleep for fear of him. I will risk it. I can do it. Little girl, watch, and you'll have something to tell your father!"

With his mind made up and action begun, Jim grew cold and deliberate. Freeing Lucy's pinto, he put her saddle on Nagger, muttering:

"If we have to run for it, you'll be safe on him."

As he tightened the cinches on Wildfire, he spoke low to the red stallion. A twitching ripple quivered over the horse, and he pounded the ground and champed his bit.

"S-sh! Quiet there!" Jim called, louder, and put a hand on the horse.

Wildfire seemed to turn to stone. Next Lamar drew the long rifle from its sheath and carefully examined it. "Come," he said to Lucy. "We'll go down and hide in the edge of the cedars. That bunch'll pass on the trail within a hundred paces."

Lamar led the way down the slope, and took up a position in a clump of cedars. The cover was not so dense as he had thought it would be. There was not, however, any time to hunt for better.

"Lucy, hold the horses here. Look at Wildfire's ears! Already he's seen that bunch. Dear, you're not afraid—for once we've got the best of the rustlers. If only Cordts comes up in time!"

As the rustlers approached, Lamar, peering from his covert, felt himself grow colder and grimmer. Presently he knew that the two groups were too far apart for them both to pass near him at the same time. He formed a resolve to let the first party go by. It was Cordts he wanted—and the King.

Lamar lay low while moments passed. The breeze brought the sharp sound of iron-shod hooves. Lamar heard also a coarse laugh—gruff voices—the jingle of spurs. There came a silence—then the piercing whistle of a frightened horse.

Lamar raised himself to see that the rustlers had halted within pistol-shot. The rider on Two-Face was in the lead, and the cunning mare had given the alarm. Jim thought what a fool he had been to imagine that he could ambush rustlers when they had Two-Face. She had squared away, head high, ears up, and she looked straight at the hiding place.

It appeared as if all the rustlers pulled guns at the same instant, and a hail of bullets pattered around Lamar. Leaping up, he shot once—twice—three times. Riderless horses leaped, wildly plunged, and sheered off into the sage.

Lamar shifted his gaze to Cordts and his followers. At sound of the shots, the rustlers had halted, now scarcely a quarter of a mile distant.

"Are y-you all right, Jim?" whispered Lucy.

Lamar turned, to see the girl standing with eyes tight shut.

"Yes, I'm all right, but I'm stumped now. Cordts heard the shots from my rifle. He and his men won't ride any closer. There, they've started again—they've left the trail!"

Lucy opened her eyes.

"Jim, they're cutting across to head off Sarch. He's leading. If they ever catch the other racers, it'll be too late for you.'

"Too late?"

"They'll be able to change mounts—you can't catch them then"

"Lucy!"

"Get up on Wildfire—go after Cordts!" cried the girl breathlessly.

"Great Scott, I hadn't thought of that! Lucy, it's Wildfire against the King. That race *will* be run! Climb up on Nagger. girl, you're going with me. You'll be safer trailing after me than hiding here. If they turn on us, I can drop them all."

He had to lift her up on Nagger; but once in the saddle, when the huge black began to show how he wanted to run, her father's blood began to throb and burn in the girl, and she looked down upon her lover with a darkening fire in her eyes.

"Girl, it'll be the race we've dreamed of! It's for your father. It's Wildfire against the King!"

"I'll stay with you—as long as Nagger lasts," she said.

IV

LAMAR leaped astride Wildfire, and ducked low under the cedars as the horse bolted. He heard Nagger crash through close behind him. Cordts and his companions were riding off toward the racers. Sarch was leading Bullet and Two-Face around in the direction of the ranch. The three unsaddled mounts were riding off to the left.

One rustler turned to look back, then another. When Cordts turned, he wheeled the King, and stopped as if in surprise. Probably he thought that his men had been ambushed by a company of riders. Not improbably, the idea of actual pursuit had scarcely dawned upon them; and the possibility of any one running them down, now that they were astride Bostil's swift horses, had never occurred to them at all. Motionless they sat, evidently trying to make out their pursuers.

When Lamar stood up in his stirrups, and waved his long rifle at them, it was probably at that instant they recognized him. The effect was significant. They dropped the halters of the three unsaddled horses, and headed their mounts to the left, toward the trail.

Which way they went was of no moment to Lamar. Wildfire and Nagger could run low, stretched out at length, in brush or in the open. It was evident, however, that Cordts preferred open running, and as he cut across the trail, Lamar gained. This trail was one long used by the rustlers in driving cattle, and it was a wide, hard-packed road. Lamar knew if for ten miles, until it turned into the rugged and broken passes. He believed the race would be ended before Cordts had a chance to take to the canyons.

Nagger had his nose even with Wildfire's flank. Lucy rode with both hands at strong tension on the bridle. Her face was pale, her eyes were gleaming darker, and wisps of her bound hair whipped in the wind. Lamar's one pride, after what he felt for his horses, was in Lucy, and in the fact that she could ride them. She was a sweetheart for a rider!

"Pull him, Lucy, pull him!" he shouted. "Don't let him get going on you. Wait till Plume and Ben are out of it!"

As for himself, he drew an iron arm on Wildfire's bridle. The grimness passed from Lamar's mood, taking with it the cold, sickening sense of death already administered, and of impending fight and blood.

Lucy was close behind on the thundering Nagger, and he had no fear for her, only a wild joy in her, that she was a girl capable of riding this race with him. So, as the sage flashed by, and the wind bit sweet, and the quick, rhythmic music of Wildfire's hooves rang in his ears, Lamar began to live the sweetest thing in a rider's career—the glory of the one running race wherein he staked pride in his horse, love of a girl, and life.

Wildfire was not really running yet; he had not lengthened out of his gallop. He had himself in control, as if the spirit in him awaited the call of his master. As for the speed of the moment, it was enough for Lamar to see the space between him and Cordts gradually grow less and less. He wanted to revel in that ride while he could. He saw, and was somehow glad, that Cordts was holding in the King.

His sweeping gaze caught a glimpse of Bullet and Two-Face and Sarchedon dotting the blue horizon line; and he thrilled with the thought of the consternation and joy and excitement there would be at Bostil's ranch when the riderless horses trooped in. He looked back at Lucy to smile into her face, to feel his heart swell at the beauty and wonder of her. With a rider's keen scrutiny, he glanced at her saddle and stirrups, and at the saddle girths.

He helped Wildfire to choose the going, and at the turns of the trail he guided him across curves that might gain a yard in the race. And this caution seemed ordered in the fringe of Lamar's thought, with most of his mind given to the sheer sensations of the ride—the flashing colored sage, the speeding white trail, the sharp bittersweetness of the air, the tang and sting of the wind, the feel of Wildfire under him, a wonderful, quivering, restrained muscular force, ready at a call to launch itself into a thunderbolt. For the moment with Lamar it was the ride—the ride!

As he lived it to the full, the miles sped by. He gained on Dusty Ben and Plume; the King slowly cut out ahead; and the first part of the race neared an end, whatever that was to be.

The two nearer rustlers whirled in their saddles to fire at Lamar. Bullets sped wildly and low, kicking up little puffs of dust. They were harmless, but they quickened Lamar's pulse, and the cold, grim mood returned to him. He loosened the bridle. Wildfire sank a little and lengthened; his speed increased, and his action grew smoother. Lamar turned to the girl and yelled:

"Let him go!"

Nagger shot forward, once more with his great black head at Wildfire's flank.

Then Lamar began to return the fire of the rustlers, aiming carefully and high, so as to be sure not to hit one of the racers. As he gained upon them, the bullets from their revolvers skipped uncomfortably close past Wildfire's legs.

Lamar, warming to the fight, shot four times before he remembered how careful he must be of his ammunition. He must get closer!

Soon the rustlers pulled Ben and Plume, half lifting them in the air, and, leaping off the breaking horses, they dashed into the sage, one on each side of the trail. The move startled Lamar; he might have pulled Wildfire in time, but Lucy could never stop Nagger in such short distance. Lamar's quick decision was that it would be better to risk shots as they sped on. He yelled to Lucy to hug the saddle, and watched for the hiding rustlers.

He saw spouts of red—puffs of smoke—then a dark from behind a sage bush. Firing, he thought he heard a cry. Then, whirling to the other side, he felt the wind of bullets near his face—saw another dark form—and fired as he rode by.

Over his shoulder he saw Lucy hunched low in her saddle, and the big black running as if the peril had spurred him. Lamar sent out a wild and exulting cry. Ben and Plume were now off the trail, speeding in line, and they would not stop soon; and out in front, perhaps a hundred yards, ran the Sage King in beautiful action. Cordts fitted the horse. If the King was greater than Wildfire, Cordts was the rider to bring it out.

"Jim! Jim!" suddenly pealed in Lamar's ears. He turned with a tightening round his heart. *"Nagger! He was hit! He was hit!"* screamed Lucy.

The great black was off his stride.

"Pull him! Pull him! Get off! Hide in the sage!" yelled Lamar.

Lucy made no move to comply with his order. Her face was white. Was she weakening? He saw no change of her poise in the saddle; but her right arm hung limp. She had been hit!

Lamar's heart seemed to freeze in the suspension of its beat, and the clogging of icy blood. He saw her sway.

"Lucy, hang on! Hang on!" he cried, and began to pull the red stallion.

To pull him out of that stride took all Lamar's strength, and then he only pulled him enough to let Nagger come up abreast. Lamar circled Lucy with his arm and lifted her out of her saddle.

"Jim, I'm not hurt much. If I hadn't seen Nagger was hit, I'd never squealed."

"Oh, Lucy!" Lamar choked with the release of his fear and the rush of pride and passion.

"Don't pull Wildfire! He'll catch the King yet!"

Lamar swung the girl behind him. The way she wrapped her uninjured arm about him and clung showed the stuff of which Lucy Bostil was made. Wildfire snorted as if in fierce anger that added weight had been given him, as if he knew it was no fault of his that Sage King had increased the lead.

Lamar bent forward and now called to the stallion—called to him with the wild call of the upland rider to his horse. It was the call that let Wildfire know he was free to choose his going and his pace—free to run—free to run down a rival—free to kill.

And the wild stallion responded. He did not break; he wore into a run that had slow increase. The demon's spirit in him seemed to gather mighty forces, so that every magnificent stride was a little lower, a little longer, a little faster, till the horse had attained a terrible celerity. He was almost flying; and the white space narrowed between him and the Sage King.

Lamar vaguely heard the howling of the wind in his ears, the continuous ringing sound of Wildfire's hooves. He vaguely noticed the blurring of the sage and the swift fleeting of the trail under him. He scarcely saw the rustler Cordts; he forgot Lucy. All his senses that retained keenness were centered in the running of the Sage King. It was so swift, so beautiful, so worthy of the gray's frame and name, that a pang numbed the rider's breast because Bostil's great horse was doomed to lose the race, if not his life.

For long the gray ran even with his red pursuer. Then, by imperceptible degrees, Wildfire began to gain. He was a desert stallion, born with the desert's ferocity of strife, the desert's imperious will; he never had love for any horse; it was in him to rule and to kill. Lamar felt Wildfire grow wet and hot, felt the marvelous ease of the horse's action gradually wearing to strain.

Another mile, and the trail turned among ridges of rock, along deep washes, at length to enter the broken country of crags and canyons. Cordts bent round in the saddle to shoot at Lamar. The bullet whistled perilously close; but Lamar withheld his fire. He had one shell left in his rifle; he would not risk that till he was sure.

He watched for a break in the King's stride, for the plunge that meant that the gray was finished. Still the race went on and on. And in the lather that flew back to wet Lamar's lips he tasted the hot blood of his horse. If it had been his own blood, the last drops spilled from his heart, he could not have felt more agony.

At last Sage King broke strangely, slowed in a few jumps, and, plunging down, threw Cordts over his head. The rustler leaped up and began to run, seeking cover.

Wildfire thundered on beyond the prostrate King. Then, with terrible muscular convulsion, as of internal collapse, he, too, broke and pounded slow, slower—to a stop.

Lamar slipped down and lifted Lucy from the saddle. Wildfire was white except where he was red, and that red was not his glossy, flaming skin. He groaned and began to sag. On one knee and then the other he knelt, gave a long heave, and lay at length.

Lamar darted back in pursuit of Cordts. He descried the rustler running along the edge of a canyon. Lamar realized that he must be quick; but the rifle wavered because of his terrible eagerness. He was shaken by the intensity of the moment. With tragic earnestness he fought for coolness, for control.

Cordts reached a corner of cliff where he had to go slowly, to cling to the rock. It was then that Lamar felt himself again chilled through and through with that strange, grim power. He pulled trigger. Cordts paused as if to rest. He leaned against the fact of the cliff, his hands up, and he kept that posture for a long moment. Then his hands began to slip. Slowly he swayed out over the canyon. His dark face flashed. Headlong he fell, to vanish below the rim.

Lamar hurriedly ran back and saw that the King was a beaten, broken horse, but he would live to run another race. Up the trail Lucy was kneeling beside Wildfire, and before Lamar got there he heard her sobbing. As if he were being dragged to execution, the rider went on, and then he was looking down upon his horse and crying:

"Wildfire! Wildfire!"

Choked, blinded, killed on his feet, Wildfire heard the voice of his master.

"Jim! Oh, Jim!" moaned Lucy.

"He beat the King! And he carried double!" whispered Lamar.

While they knelt there, the crippled Nagger came limping up the trail, followed by Dusty Ben and Plume.

Again the rider called to his horse, with a cry now piercing, thrilling; but this time Wildfire did not respond.

V

THE westering sun glanced brightly over the rippling sage, which rolled away from the Ford like a gray sea. Bostil sat on his porch, a stricken man. He faced the blue haze of the West, where, some hours before, all that he loved had vanished. His riders were grouped near him, silent, awed by his face, awaiting orders that did not come.

From behind a ridge puffed up a thin cloud of dust. Bostil saw it, and gave a start. Above the sage appeared a bobbing black dot—the head of a horse.

"Sarch!" exclaimed Bostil.

With spurs clinking, his riders ran and trooped behind him.

"There's Bullet!" cried one.

"An' Two-Face!" added another.

"Saddled an' riderless!"

Then all were tensely quiet, watching the racers come trotting in single file down the ridge. Sarchedon's shrill neigh, like a whistle blast, pealed in from the sage. From fields and corrals clamored the answer, attended by the clattering of hundreds of hooves.

Sarchedon and his followers broke from trot to canter—canter to gallop—and soon were cracking their iron shoes on the stony road. Then, like a swarm of bees, the riders surrounded the racers and led them up to Bostil.

On Sarchedon's neck showed a dry, dust-caked stain of reddish tinge. Bostil's right-hand man, the hawk-eyed rider, gray as the sage from long service, carefully examined the stain.

"Wall, the rustler that was up on Sarch got plugged, an' in fallin' forrard he spilled some blood on the hoss's neck."

"Who shot him?" demanded Bostil.

"I reckon there's only one rider on the sage thet could ever hev got close enough to shoot a rustler up on Sarch."

Bostil wheeled to face the West. His brow was lowering; his hands were clenched. Riders led away the tired racers, and returned to engage with the others in whispered speculation.

The afternoon wore on; the sun lost its brightness, and burned low and red. Again dust clouds, now like reddened smoke, puffed over the ridge. Four horses, two carrying riders, appeared above the sage.

"Is that—a gray horse—or am I blind?" asked Bostil unsteadily.

The old rider shaded the hawk eyes with his hand.

"Gray he is—gray as the sage, Bostil—an' so help me if he ain't the King!"

Bostil stared, rubbed his eyes as if his sight was dimmed, and stared again.

"Do I see Lucy?"

"Shore—shore!" replied the old rider. "I seen her long ago. Why, sir, I can see thet gold hair of hers a mile across the sage. She's up on Ben."

The light of joy on Bostil's face slowly shaded, and the change was one that silenced his riders. Abruptly he left them, to enter the house.

When he came forth again, brought out by the stamp of hooves on the stones, his riders were escorting Lucy and Lamar into the courtyard. A wan smile flitted across Lucy's haggard face as she saw her father, and she held out one arm to him. The other was bound in a bloody scarf.

Cursing deep, like the muttering of thunder, Bostil ran out.

"Lucy! For Heaven's sake! You're not bad hurt?"

"Only a little, Dad," she said, and slipped down into his arms.

He kissed her pale face, and, carrying her to the door, roared for the women of his household.

When he reappeared, the crowd of riders scattered from around Lamar. Bostil looked at the King. The horse was caked with dusty lather, scratched and disheveled, weary and broken, yet somehow he was still beautiful. He raised his drooping head, and reached for his master with a look as soft and dark and eloquent as a woman's.

No rider there but felt Bostil's grief. He loved the King. He believed the King had been beaten; and his rider's glory and pride were battling with love. Mighty as that was in Bostil, it did not at once overcome his hatred of defeat.

Slowly the gaze of the rancher moved from the King to tired Ben and Plume, over the bleeding Nagger, at last to rest on the white-faced Lamar. But Bostil was not looking for Lamar. His hard eyes veered to and fro. Among those horses there was not the horse he sought.

"Where's the red stallion?" he asked.

Lamar raised eyes dark with pain, yet they flashed as he looked straight into Bostil"s face.

"Wildfire's dead."

"Shot?"

"No."

"What killed him?" Bostil's voice had a vibrating ring.

"The King, sir; killed him on his feet."

Bostil's lean jaw bulged and quivered. His hand shook a little as he laid it on the King's tangled mane.

"Jim—what the—" he said brokenly, with voice strangely softened.

"Mr. Bostil, we've had some fighting and running. Lucy was hit—so was Nagger. And the King killed Wildfire on his feet. But I got Cordts and three of his men—maybe four. I've no more to say, sir."

Bostil put his arm round the young man's shoulder.

"Lamar, you've said enough. If I don't know how you feel about the loss of that grand horse, no rider on earth knows. But let me say I reckon I never knew your real worth. You can lead my riders. You can have the girl—God bless you both! And you can have anything else on this ranch—except the King!"

The Old Jim Horse

J. Lincoln Steffens

THE Superintendent of Horses in the New York Fire Department sent a substitute to Thirty-three Engine one day a year or two ago, and took away a big roan horse which had served there for eighteen years and nine months. "Horse registered No. 60, unfit," is the way this act was reported officially. But the men, passing the news around the house, and thence from company to company all over town, said:

"They've taken the old Jim horse. They're going to sell Thirty-three's old Jim."

Now the firemen all knew that the old Jim horse was unfit for duty. Captain Nash, the foreman of Thirty-three, had been watching secretly for two or three years the growth of a film over the animal's big, intelligent eyes. No expert superintendent of firehorses was needed to see that Jim was going blind. But what of that? There wasn't a horse in the service that knew the business so well as Jim. There wasn't a fireman who loved a big fire more than the roan that ran in the middle of Thirty-three's team of three.

"He learned what he had to do in five minutes after he was bought and delivered here," said Captain Nash. "He caught on the first time they showed him. We never locked him in a stall. It wasn't necessary; for he never left it without permission, except to get a drink or to respond to an alarm of fire. At the first tap of the gong, he sprang forward to his place. Sometimes he came so fast that he had to slide to stop himself under the harness; and when we let him out in the street to

139

wander around, he'd run at the call of the gong, stop on the sidewalk, turn about, and back into his place at the pole. Why, we used to put boxes and chairs in his way from the stall, but he jumped over them and would still be first in the collar. They oughtn't to have condemned Jim. He never cost the city a cent for doctor's bills. Once he fell down on the way to a fire and was dragged a block over the Broadway cobbles; but he got up without our stopping, and though he was pretty sore, we never reported him, and he got over it. Sometimes a hose would burst, but Jim didn't care if only he could turn his head out of the way. Many a shower of falling glass he has stood without flinching, as the scars on his back show, but he was never laid off a day. Half a dozen horses that were mated to him have lived their day and died, trying to pull up even with old Jim. It isn't so long ago they sent us up a spare horse to take the place of one of Jim's mates that was off being shod. There was one run, and Jim chewed the young horse's neck to make him keep up his end, afraid we'd lose first water. He was a great firehorse, was Jim. The only trouble he gave was at mealtimes, which he knew like a clock; and if his feed wasn't set down before him on the minute, he made a fuss, pawing at the side of his stall and starting all the other horses to kicking."

Possibly Captain Nash was prejudiced. He and Jim had served together in the same house for eleven years. But if there was anything so very wrong in concealing Jim's aging weaknesses, the captain was not the only one to blame. Hugh Bonner, the Chief of the Department, had his downtown quarters in Thirty-three's house, and he knew all about Jim, and all about Captain Nash, too, for that matter. Yet he kept mum. Then there was the Superintendent of Horses: why didn't he do something before? It is true he had condemned Jim five years ago. This, however, is the way he did it. After inspecting the horse, he walked up to the captain and said:

"Nash, the old Jim horse is getting unfit. I guess I'll have to send you a substitute."

Captain Nash did not say anything. The substitute came, and he accepted the new horse, but he didn't send Jim away. He handed over another horse. Now the stableman did not know the difference, perhaps, but the Superintendent did. He must have found that he had been fooled; and the captain, liable to punishment for disobeying orders, worried for a week. But nothing came of it. Possibly the Superintendent reported the case to the Chief. If he did, it is curious the Chief never mentioned the matter to Captain Nash. At any rate, the Chief must have known that the Jim horse had been condemned, and he certainly saw the Jim horse afterward first at many a fire.

A year or two later, the Superintendent condemned Jim again, and he did it rather sharply this time. He did not say, "Nash, the old Jim horse," and so on. He commanded Captain Nash to deliver "registered horse No. 60"; but after he was out of the door, he paused, turned half around, and said:

"He isn't fit to run to fires, Nash. You better trade him off to me for a good, strong, young horse. Anyhow, I'm going to do my duty, and if you want—"

The rest was nothing but a grumble which no one could be expected to understand. The new horse arrived. The Captain hesitated, till at last he thumped on his desk, and shouted down to the man on watch to transfer to the training stables the worst horse in the house. The fireman who received the order grinned, and delivered the next-to-the-oldest horse, an animal that "never was no good, nohow." And when the trampling of the departing hooves had died away, the men upstairs who heard the order stopped the game of cards while one of them went below. He walked, around the engine to Jim's stall, told him to get back, though the horse was not more than half a foot over the line, then returned to the game. He did not report anything verbally, but the others looked in his face, and resumed the play in great good humor. Just as they were forgetting the incident, the Captain came out of his room and passed downstairs. He had to get something out of the feed room, which is back of the horses. Old Jim tried to attract the Captain's attention, but the Captain wouldn't notice him.

The third time the Superintendent acted, he did not give the Captain a chance for any of his tricky horse-trading. He had "registered horse No. 60" removed without talking about it, and Captain Nash was at a loss.

"I knew what it meant," said the Captain afterward. "We had a horse here once, the Buck horse. He was a good fire-horse, too; nothing like Jim, but he served faithful for years, and then went lame in his off hind leg. We did what we could for him till the inspector got onto it and took him away and sold him at auction. About a year after that, when we were all standing out in front of the house one day, an old, broken-down, lame horse came along the street, pulling one of those carts that go around collecting clamshells. He balked right opposite the door. We thought at first he was tired, and I guess he was. Maybe some of the younger firemen laughed when the crazy old driver licked his horse. But all of a sudden we took notice of the horse's sore leg, and somebody said:

"'It's the old Buck horse, boys.'

"And it was. He had stopped because he wanted to come in home, the old Buck horse did. And his leg was worse."

So Captain Nash remembered the Buck horse when they took away the Jim horse. He waited till the Chief came to the house.

Then he told him. "Chief," he said, "they've come and got the old Jim horse at last."

The Chief did not answer.

"I'd just as lief keep him, Chief," the Captain continued. "He's the best horse I had. A little film over his eyes, and pretty old, but he's—he's the old Jim horse, Chief."

Another pause.

"They'll sell him into some old ash cart or to a Polish peddler. And Jim's served long enough to have a pension."

Then the Chief answered:

"Why don't you write his record up to the Board? I'll endorse it."

"I ain't much on the write," said Nash, "but I'll try it, if you say so."

That was on a Saturday. Captain Nash took Sunday for the job, and here is his formal report to the Board of Fire Commissioners:

> I respectfully forward a brief history of the roan team of horses formerly used in the engine of this company. Of the original Jack horse I have not much to write, he being killed while responding to an alarm for fire at station 236 on May 30, 1881, by colliding with the shaft of Engine 13 tender. The point of the shaft entered his breast. . . . As to the horse Jim, who was received at these quarters on January 14, 1879, and performed duty therein until November 4, 1897, a period of eighteen years and nine months, the first eleven years of which Jim and his mate had to draw a heavy first-class engine, when the runs were more frequent and much longer than those of the present day, when the same identical engine is drawn by three horses. The Jim horse, in the opinion of all the officers and members ever connected with this company, and the many distinguished persons who visited these quarters, was such that they expressed the belief that there never was a horse that showed more intelligence than the Jim horse.

Here followed a recital of Jim's distinguishing traits in much the same language as that already quoted from Captain Nash. Chief Bonner wrote something, too:

> I take great pleasure in transmitting for your consideration the history of the Jim horse of Engine Thirty-three, for a period of nearly twenty years. . . . He was about seven years old when purchased, which would make him nearly twenty-seven years of age. I appeal to the Board in behalf of this faithful animal, that he be retained in the service of the department, and assigned to some company where the duties will be light, and that the Superintendent of Horses be directed to not include in his sale registered No. 60, which is the number assigned to this faithful animal.

"This worked," said the Captain. When these communications were read at the Board meeting, the commissioners were silent a moment. Then the president said that he thought Jim had earned his pension and should be retired. No one objected; so the Superintendent of Horses was directed to keep Jim for such light work as might turn up, if there was any such. At any rate, he was not to be sold. This was the first time in the history of the department that a horse was retired like a fireman; but it paid. For example, it put a stop to Captain Nash's grumbling about the new middle horse that runs now with Thirty-three Engine.

Carved in Sand

Erle Stanley Gardner

I. Tenderfoot Contraption

WHEN a man lives a great deal in the open, little things sometimes stick in his mind. That was the way with the remark the college professor made to me.

"Everything in nature," he said, "has two points of manifestation."

"Meaning positive and negative?" I asked him, just to let him know that he wasn't going to spring any theory on me that I couldn't at least talk about.

"Not exactly that," he said. "It's something a little more subtle."

I swept my hand in a half circle, including in the gesture the sweep of sun-glittering sand and cacti-studded desert. "What would be the double manifestation of that?" I asked him.

"I don't know," he said. "I'm not enough of a desert man to know its manifestations. But you know it. If you'll only watch it, you'll find that it does have a dual manifestation."

It was only a little thing perhaps, but somehow it stuck in my mind; and it seemed that I'd found the answer in Pete Ayers. Pete was desert born and desert bred, and the shifting sands had got into his blood. He was as restless as a swirl of loose sand in the embrace of a desert wind. Of course the desert leaves its mark on everybody who lives in it. Most of the men who have lived in the desert have gray eyes, firm lips, a slow, deliberate way of moving about that is deceptive to a man who doesn't know the breed. When occasion requires they are as fast as greased lightning, and as deadly as a cornered lion. Ayers was different. He was just a happy-go-lucky kid who was forever rolling into mischief and stumbling out. He was always in trouble, always getting out of it by some fluke.

Now he lay stretched out beside me on the edge of the rim rock, the hot desert sun beating down on our backs. He handed me the binoculars.

"Brother," he said, "watch where the bullet strikes. I'm betting even money that I don't miss him by more than two inches, and I'll bet on a direct hit for reasonable odds."

That was the way with Pete; always making a bet, always willing to wager his shirt on the outcome of whatever he happened to be doing.

"Wait a minute, Pete," I said as he cocked the rifle. "Let's make certain that it's a coyote. He's acting sort of funny for a coyote."

"He's going to act a lot funnier," said Pete as he nestled his cheek against the stock of the rifle, "in just about one minute."

I focused the binoculars on the slope across the long dry canyon. Ordinarily I don't go in much for binoculars in the desert, because a desert man cannot afford to be cluttered up with a lot of weight. The tenderfoot always carries a camera, binoculars, hunting knife, and compass. They're things that are all right in their way, but the real desert man starts out with a six-gun, a canteen, a pocket knife, a box of matches, and a sack of tobacco. That's about all he needs.

The binoculars were good ones that Pete had won from a tenderfoot in a poker game the night before. They brought up the opposite slope of the canyon with a clearness that made the black shadows transparent.

"Hold everything, Pete!" I said. "It's a police dog!"

I heard Pete's grunt of incredulity, but he lowered the rifle and turned startled blue eyes to me.

"Hell," he said, "you're crazy! There aren't any police dogs out here. Them's tenderfoot binoculars and there's mebbe a sort of tenderfoot influence about 'em."

"Take a look yourself," I said.

Pete put down the rifle and reached for the binoculars. He focused them to his eyes, and then gave a low whistle.

"Hell!" he said. "And I'll bet I'd have hit him!"

I said nothing. We watched the animal for several seconds.

"What the hell's he doing here?" asked Pete.

I didn't know any more than he did—not as much, in fact, so I couldn't say anything. We lay there in silence, with the desert sun beating down on the glittering expanse of waste, making the black rim rock on the other side of the canyon twist and writhe in the heat waves.

After a while Pete passed the binoculars across to me. I found the dog again, steadied my elbows on the hot rock, and watched closely.

"He's running around in little circles, looking for a scent of some kind," I said. "Now it looks as though he's found it. He runs along straight for ten or fifteen yards, then stops and circles, and then starts going straight. Now, he's found what he wants. He's running close to the ground—and making time."

"Hell," said Pete dryly, "you don't need to tell me everything he's doin', I got eyes, even if they don't magnify eight diameters."

The police dog fascinated me. I couldn't understand what he was doing out here in the desert. I kept the binoculars on him and watched him as he angled down the slope. He was running rapidly now, wagging his tail as he ran, and apparently following the scent without difficulty. He ran down around the edge of the slope, rounded an outcropping of rock, crossed the canyon, and vanished behind a ledge of the rim rock on our side of the canyon.

"Well," said Pete, "the show's over."

"No," I told him, "I'm going to find out what that dog's doing out here."

"That's just the way with you," he said. "Filled full of curiosity."

But I could see from the light in his blue eyes that he was curious, and that he also favored giving the dog a break. A police dog can't live long in the desert. A coyote can get by nicely, but not a dog, no matter how big or how strong he is. It's a question of generations of training, and the coyote has something that no dog has: a certain toughness that enables him to get by.

We moved along the rim rock. I was holding the binoculars by the strap when we reached the next little peak from which we could look down in the canyon.

Pete's exclamation at my elbow showed me that he had seen the camp. I raised the binoculars, and through them saw an automobile, rather battered and dilapidated; a white tent; a canteen; a cot; a box of provisions. Then I saw a woman's bare arm reach out around the edge of the tent and pick something from the box.

"Looks like a woman down there," I said.

"What the devil would anybody want to camp in that canyon for?" asked Pete.

"Prospector maybe," I told him.

"A woman prospector?" he asked.

"Maybe. She had a white arm. Looked like she was city-bred."

"Just the arm shows?" asked Pete.

"That was all," I said.

"All right," he said. "Keep the binoculars then."

Suddenly the woman came out from around the edge of the tent. I could see at once that she was city-bred. The cut of her clothes, the delicacy of her complexion, the angry red sunburn on the backs of her forearms, all told the story. But the thing that interested me and held me breathlessly watching was the expression on her face. It was an expression of sheer terror.

The police dog had evidently been out with her and had lost her. He had been smelling along the dry sand of the desert, trying to pick up her trail; and now he was trotting along at her side, wagging his tail. Yet the woman's face was twisted and distorted with terror.

She was carrying something in her hand, and she ran twenty or thirty yards back up the slope to the roots of a sagebrush and started digging with her left hand. Her right hand pushed something into the little hole, and then she patted the sand over it, got to her feet, and walked back toward the camp.

I handed the binoculars to Pete, and as my eyes focused on the camp I saw two dots moving from around the slope of the canyon. I saw the police dog grow rigid, and after a few seconds I could hear the sound of his bark.

"Hell," said Pete, "she looks scared."

"She is," I said. "Look at the two dots coming around the slope there, about half a mile down the canyon, Pete."

He raised the glasses and grunted as his eyes took in the two dots. "Two men," he said, "with rifles and six-guns. They've got cartridges in the belts of the six-guns, and they look as though they were getting ready to shoot."

"Are they coming toward the camp?" I asked.

"Toward the camp," he said. "Hell, Bob, after this I think I'm going to carry these tenderfoot contraptions all the time. In the meantime, I'm going down and cut in on that deal."

"Count me in," I told him.

He snapped the binoculars back into the case.

"Going back to get the burros?" I asked him.

"They'll wait," he told me. "Let's go."

The rim rock was a good ten feet in a straight drop. Then there was some loose sand, and the sheer slope of the side of the canyon.

Pete went over the rim rock without hesitation, lit in the sand, threw up a flurry of dust, made two jumps, and started sliding down the ridge. I didn't make quite so clean a leap, and I felt the impact as I struck the sand. My feet went out from under me, I rolled over a couple of times, got to my feet, and started sprinting down the slope, digging my heels into the soil, grabbing at the little clumps of sagebrush and taking long jumps to avoid the patches of rock.

Pete kept gaining on me. I don't know why he didn't go down head over heels, but he managed to bound down as lightly as a mountain goat.

II. Manners in the Desert

APPARENTLY the girl didn't see or hear us. She was looking at two men who were approaching.

The police dog heard us, however, and whirled, starting to bark. With that the woman turned and saw us, of course. She called the dog back and stood staring at us, and once more I caught the expression of terror on her face.

Pete's bronze hand went to his sombrero, swept it off in a bow, and he said, "Pardon me, ma'am, we just dropped in."

There was a ghost of a smile on her face, but it still held that expression of terror.

"It was almost a drop," she said, looking back up the slope where the dust clouds were still drifting about in the hot sun. "Who are you and what do you want?"

Pete jerked his head toward the direction of the approaching figures. "Just thought," he said, "that we'd see if you needed any assistance."

I saw her mouth tighten. "No," she said, "you can't be of any assistance to me."

I didn't beat about the bush at all. "Do you know the men who are coming?" I asked.

"I think so," she said.

"What do they want?" I asked.

"Me," she said.

I waited for an explanation, but there wasn't any. The dog was growling in his throat, but he was lying on the ground where she had ordered him to stay, his yellow eyes glinting from us to the men who were coming up the dry wash.

The two men came up with the tense, watchful attitude of men who are expecting to engage in gunplay at almost any minute. They looked us over and they looked the girl over. One of them stepped off to one side and said to the girl. "You're Margaret Blake?"

She nodded her head.

"You know who we are and why we are here?" he said.

She said nothing.

He looked from her over to us. "Who are these men?" he asked.

"I don't know," she said.

The man shifted his attention to Pete. "What's your connection with this?" he asked.

Pete grinned at him, a cold, frosty grin. "Don't you know who I am?" he asked.

"No," said the other man, his eyes narrowing, "who are you?"

"I'm the guy,' said Pete, "who is going to see that the young woman here gets a square deal."

"This woman," said the man, "is under arrest."

"Arrest for what?" asked Pete.

"As an accessory," said the man.

"To what?"

"Murder."

Pete laughed. "She don't look like she'd be good at murder,' he said.

"You can't always tell by looks," said one of the men. "Now, you two fellows get started out of here. I don't like the way you horned in on this party."

"Don't you, now?" said Pete.

The other man said in a low voice, "Make them give up their guns, Charlie. We can't let them go out in the desert with their guns. They might ambush us."

"Yes," said Charlie. "You fellows will have to leave your guns here."

"Now *I'll* tell one," I told him.

I saw grinning devils appear at the corners of Pete's mouth, caught the glint of his blue eyes as he reached slowly to his gun, pulled it out of the holster, and looked at it almost meditatively.

"You don't want me to give *this* gun up?" he asked.

"That's what we want," said Charlie.

"This gun," said Pete, "is a funny gun. It goes off accidentally, every once in a while."

"Pete!" I cautioned him.

The warning came too late. There was a spurt of flame from Pete's gun. I heard the impact of the heavy bullet as it struck the stock of the rifle in the hands of the man nearest Pete.

There was nothing to do but back his play, and so I made what speed I could snaking my six-gun from its holster.

The two men were taken completely by surprise. They had thought that their rifles were sufficient to command the situation. As a matter of fact, at close quarters a rifle is very likely to prove a cumbersome weapon, particularly when a man tries to take in too much territory with it.

"Drop it!" I told the man.

His eyes looked into the barrel of my Colt, and there was a minute when I didn't know exactly what was going to happen. Then the gun thudded to the sand. The bullet had jerked the other's gun from his grasp.

"All right, Bob," said Pete, "they'll get their hands in the air, and you can unbuckle the belts and let their six-guns slip off."

"First, let's make sure they've got their hands in the air," I told him.

Two pairs of hands came up slowly.

"You boys are making the mistake of your lives," said Charlie. "You're going to find yourselves in the pen for this."

"Please don't," the girl pleaded with us. "I'll go with them. It's inevitable."

"No," said Pete, "I don't like their manners—and I always play my hunches."

I unbuckled the guns, let them drop to the ground.

"We're officers," Charlie started to explain, "and you—"

"Sure," said Pete. "I knew you were officers as soon as I saw you. You've got that look about you—and your manners are so rotten. Now turn around and start walking back the way you came. I suppose you've got an automobile staked out around the edge of the slope, haven't you?"

They didn't say anything.

Pete shook his head. "Rotten manners," he said, "You don't answer courteous questions."

"Please!" said the girl. "Don't do this for me. He's right in what he says. You're going to get into serious trouble."

"Miss," said Pete, "getting into serious trouble is something that I'm accustomed to. I get into a new kind of trouble every day. Come on you two, let's march."

We turned them around, but it took a prod with the muzzle of my six-gun to get Charlie started. After they had started they moved along doggedly and steadily.

We rounded the slope and found their car parked in a little draw. Pete's gun pointed the road to town.

"I'm going to be standing here," he said, "until that car is just a little black spot in the middle of a dust cloud, way over on the desert there. And if you should hesitate or turn around and start back, something tells me that you'll have tire trouble right away."

The men didn't say a word. They climbed into the automobile. The starting motor whirred, the engine responded, and the car crept along the sandy wash, struck the harder road, and rattled into speed. Pete and I stood there until the machine had vanished in the distance, leaving behind it nothing but a wisp of dust.

Pete looked at me and grinned. "Sore, Bob?" he asked.

"No," I told him. "I had to back your play, but I wish you'd use a little discretion sometimes."

"Discretion, hell!" he said. "There's no fun in discretion. Let's go back and talk with the woman. You can figure it out for yourself, Bob. She's okay. Those men were on the wrong track, that's all."

I wasn't so certain, but I holstered my weapon. We started trudging back through the sand. When we rounded the edge of the slope and could look up the canyon, I could see dust settling in the afternoon sunlight.

"Two dust clouds," I told him grimly.

Sure enough, the camp was still there; but the automobile, the young woman, and the police dog had gone.

Pete looked at me, and his face was ludicrous in its crestfallen surprise. "Hell!" he said.

"It's going to take them about two hours to get to town," I said. "Then they'll get some more guns, a couple of others to help them, and start back. The next question is, where can we be in two hours?"

Pete's eyes started to twinkle once more. "I know a swell bunch of country where there's an old cabin," he said, "and I don't think the burros would leave much of a trail getting up there."

"How far can we be on that trail in two hours?" I wanted to know.

"We can be pretty near there."

"Okay," I told him. "Let's go."

We climbed back up to the burros, got the string lined up, and started plodding up the slope toward the old cabin that Pete knew about.

After about an hour the country changed, and we began to run into stunted cedar, glimpsing pines up on the high slopes of the mountain country beyond. Another half hour, and we were well up in the mountains, from where we could look back over the desert.

I paused and pointed back toward the place where I knew the little desert town was situated. "Pete," I said, "you've got those binoculars. Take a look and see if you can see anything that looks like pursuit."

He was focusing the binoculars on the road when I heard a peculiar throbbing sound which grew in volume. I raised my eyes and picked out a little speck against the blue sky—a speck that might have been a buzzard, except that it was moving forward across the sky with steady purpose.

I tapped Pete on the shoulder and pointed with my finger. He raised the binoculars, looked for a minute, and then twisted his face into a grimace.

"They'll pick her up with that," I said, "before she's gone thirty miles."

"There's lots of places she could go inside of thirty miles," Pete said.

"Not with that automobile," I told him, "and not in this country."

Pete shrugged his shoulders. "How the hell did we know they were going to get an airplane to chase her with?"

"How the hell did I know that you were going to start gunplay?" I told him, with some irritation in my voice.

"You should have been able to tell that," said Pete, "by looking at the woman. She was too pretty."

I sighed. "Well," I told him, "I always wanted to know what it felt like to be a fugitive from justice."

"Hell!" said Pete from the depths of his experience. "There ain't no novelty to it—not after the first time or two. It feels just like anything else."

I didn't say anything more. I merely watched the airplane as it diminished in the distance. I was still looking at it when I saw two other planes coming from the west. The plane I had seen first tilted from side to side, making signaling motions, and the other two planes swung in behind it. I focused the binoculars on them and saw them fly in formation, until suddenly they started down toward the desert.

The sun was just setting. The valley was filled with deep purple shadows. In the high places was the hush of coming twilight.

"What did you see?" asked Pete.

"Two more planes," I told him, snapping the binoculars into the leather case.

Pete grinned at me. "That," he said, "isn't going to keep us from eating, is it?"

"Not this meal," I told him, "but I don't know about the next."

III. Accessories to the Crime

PETE had his blankets spread out on the other side of a little ridge. I was careful not to disturb him as I got up and sat there in the moonlight, looking down on the dark mystery of the shadow-filled valleys below. It was cold up here, but I had a blanket wrapped around me, Indian fashion.

Down below, as far as the eye could reach, stretched the desert; a great waste of level spaces, broken by jagged mountain spurs—mountains that were still a part of the desert, dry, arid, covered with juniper, stunted cedar, and an occasional pine. There were no tumbling streams, no dense underbrush—just barren rock and dry trees that rustled in the wind which was blowing from the desert.

Looking down into the black splotches of darkness in the valleys, I knew what was going on in the desert. The wind was stirring the sand into soft whispers, typifying the restlessness of the desert. For the desert is ever restless, ever changing. Its moods change as frequently as the appearance of the desert mountains is changed by sunlight and shadow.

Even up here in this cold, high place the desert seemed to be whispering its mysterious messages; the noise made by drifting sand as it scours against the soft desert rocks, carving them into weird structures, polishing, cutting, drifting, changing, ever changing.

I sat there for three or four hours, watching the moon climb over the eastern rim of the mountains, watching the black pools of mysterious shadow in the canyons gradually recede until the golden surface of the desert glinted up at me from below. Several times I listened to hear Pete's snores, but no sound came from his direction.

After a while I felt somewhat relaxed, and rolled back into my blankets, where it was warmer. In fifteen or twenty minutes I began to feel drowsy, and drifted off to sleep. After all, as Pete had remarked, being a fugitive from justice didn't feel particularly unique, once one had become accustomed to it.

I woke early in the morning and watched the east taking on a brassy hue. It was still and cold. There was not a sound, not a breath. The stars, which had blazed steadily during the night, had now receded to mere needle points of light; and soon they became invisible.

I kicked back the blankets, put on my boots and leather jacket, stamped my feet to get the circulation in them, and walked around the little ledge, to the place where Pete had spread his blankets. The blankets were there, but Pete wasn't.

I looked over the ground, and felt of the blankets. There was frost on the inside of them, where they had been turned back when Pete slipped out. I studied the tracks as well as I could, and then I knew that Pete had slipped one over on me. He had pulled out long before I had got up to watch the moonlight.

Fifty yards from camp I found a piece of paper stuck on a bush. When he had to be, Pete was glib with his tongue, and glib with a pencil if he couldn't talk. He was one of those fellows who expressed himself well.

I unfolded the note and read:

Dear Bob:
 I got you into this, and there's no reason why I shouldn't take the blame. You didn't do anything except follow my lead. I don't know how serious it is, but I'm going to find out. You sit tight until I come back.
                                            (Signed) Pete

I should have known that Pete would have done something like that, and I felt irritated that I hadn't guessed it in advance and guarded against it.

It was all right for Pete to claim that I had been blameless and that he was going to take the responsibility. I probably wouldn't have started things if Pete hadn't been there—and then again I might have. But I didn't need a nurse or a guardian, and when I pulled a gun on an officer it was my own free and voluntary act. I didn't like the way Pete was trying to shield me, as though I were a child, instead of a man ten years his senior.

I got some firewood together, got the coffee to boiling, and sat crouched by the fire, warming my hands and waiting for a while before I drank the coffee, hoping that Pete would show up. When he didn't show up, I drank a couple of cups of coffee, but kept the pot hot so that he could have some when he came in.

The sun climbed slowly up the blue-black of the desert sky, and there was still no sign of Pete. I went out on a projecting rock where I could look down into the valley, and kept watch on what was going on. Toward ten o'clock I heard the sound of automobiles, and I could make them out through the glasses, two carloads of men jolting their way along the floor of the valley.

An hour later, I heard them coming back; and the glasses showed me that which I had dreaded to see, yet expected. In the rear seat of the first automobile was a man and a woman. At that distance I couldn't make out their features, but I didn't have much doubt who they were.

I waited until the machines had gone the length of the valley and turned through the pass into the level desert, then I threw packs on the burros and started back down the mountain. Pete knew exactly where I had been camped, and he also knew that I had the binoculars. I figured that he probably would have a chance to use his pencil once more.

I hit the trail of the automobiles and started following along, keeping my eyes pretty much on the ground. Within half a mile I found what I was looking for, a folded piece of paper lying by the side of the road, catching the glint of the hot desert sun. I unfolded the paper. It was a note from Pete, all right. He hadn't put any heading on it at all, so that if the officers discovered it, it wouldn't give them any clue which would lead to me. The note read simply:

> They caught me. I put up a fight, but they got me, and I guess they got me dead to rights. The woman is the daughter of Sam Blake. Blake killed a prospector named Skinner who had a cabin over in Sidewinder Canyon. They jailed him, and the woman helped him escape. They caught him again and are holding her as an accessory. I don't know what they're going to put against me. I told them you didn't know anything about it and had backed my play with an empty gun. I don't think they're going to look for you.

I knew Bob Skinner, and I also knew the place over in Sidewinder Canyon. It was fifteen or twenty miles over the mountains.

There was nothing much to be done except trail along behind the automobiles, so I plugged along doggedly through the desert sunshine. All the time, I kept thinking about the stuff the woman had buried at the foot of the sagebrush when she saw the two men coming from the direction of the road. When I got near that first camp of hers, I made a detour and went into it. The officers had been all through it, probably looking for evidence.

I climbed back into the shade cast by a spur of rock, and got out the tenderfoot's binoculars again. When I was sure that I had the desert all to myself, I went over to the clump of sagebrush and dug in the sand.

I found a package done up in a newspaper. The package had hacksaw blades and a gun. The hacksaw blades had been used, and I figured that was how Sam Blake had managed to slip out of jail. As far as I could tell, the gun hadn't been fired.

It was a .45 single-action Colt, and it had been carried around quite a bit in a holster.

I looked at the newspaper. It was an extra edition, hurriedly thrown together; one of those little hand-printed efforts put out in small desert towns, usually once a week or once every two weeks.

Ordinarily they contained nothing more exciting than a chronicle of the comings and goings of people who live in a small community.

But this paper was different. Across the top, in big blotchy headlines, black type announced:

BLAKE BREAKS JAIL

Down below:

OFFICERS SUSPECT WOMAN ACCOMPLICE

I sat down on my heels in the sand, and read everything that the paper contained. It was an account of the jailbreak, which didn't interest me particularly, and an account of the crime, which interested me more.

Sam Blake charged that Bob Skinner had jumped a claim which Blake had staked, stripping the claim of the valuable gold that was in a pocket and then skipping out.

I knew Skinner. He was the sort of customer who would be likely to do that very thing. Blake asserted that Skinner had picked up more than five thousand dollars in gold from the pocket, and so Blake had taken his gun and gone down into Sidewinder Canyon.

A lunger by the name of Ernest Peterman had seen him going down toward Skinner's cabin. Peterman had a little cabin up on the summit of a ridge on the east side of Sidewinder Canyon. He'd seen Blake coming along the trail which led to the canyon, and had recognized him. He'd watched him go down to Skinner's cabin. It had been about two-thirty in the afternoon, and Peterman said he knew that Skinner was alive at the time because there was a lot of smoke coming out of the chimney of Skinner's shack. He hadn't paid any particular attention to it, however; he'd just given the scene a casual glance and then gone out to take his afternoon sunbath.

It happened that a ranger had dropped in to see Skinner sometime the next day. He'd found Skinner dead, with a bullet hole in his forehead and a knife wound in his heart. He'd found horse tracks in the trail, and had been able to mark them because of a broken shoe on the right hind foot. He'd trailed the horse into the little settlement, had found it, identified it as belonging to Blake, and had finally forced Blake to admit that he'd been to the cabin.

At first Blake denied it. Later on, he admitted that he'd gone down to have a settlement with Skinner, but he claimed that Skinner was dead when he got there. Things looked black for him because he hadn't reported the murder, and because at first he'd denied that he'd gone down to see Skinner at all. But the thing that clinched the case against him was the testimony of the lunger. If smoke had been coming out of the chimney at the time Blake hit the shack, it was a cinch Skinner had been alive then. Nobody doubted the good faith of the lunger.

I read the paper and frowned. I could see that Pete Ayers had acted on impulse, and the impulse had led him into trouble. We were going to be hooked as accessories, along with the girl. The authorities didn't like the idea of Blake sawing the bars of the jail window and slipping out into the night.

I led the burros over to a nearby spring, saw that they had water, and then started on the long journey over the mountains to Sidewinder Canyon. I didn't dare to strike the main trails. On the other hand, with burros I could keep moving over the desert mountains, particularly after the moon came up.

IV. The Desert Whispers

IT was well past daylight when I came out of the jagged mountain formation on the west and into Sidewinder Canyon. I could look down the twisting canyon and see the roof of the prospector's shack. I staked out the burros, and went down on foot.

I could see where the officers and the curious ones had been tramping around the shack. I sat out on a little sandy plateau, and there had been a desert wind in the night which had wiped out most of the tracks; yet they showed as confused indentations in the sand.

It looked as though at least ten or a dozen people had milled around the shack, tracking down the ground.

I went into the cabin. The door was open, of course, as is customary in mountain or desert cabins. There was the damp, musty smell of places which are shaded from the purifying effect of direct sunlight. There was also another musty smell which was more ominous and unforgettable; the smell of death.

I found the bed where Skinner had been sleeping. I found red stains, dry and crusted, on the blankets; stains also on the floor. Lazy flies buzzed in circles over the red stains. It was not a pleasant place to be.

I made but a casual inspection. I knew that others had been there before, and that every inch of the cabin had been searched. Doubtless some of the searchers had been desert men.

I walked out into the sunlight and took a great breath of fresh air, looking up into the clear blue of the cloudless sky, then over at the glittering expanse of jagged, barren ranges which hemmed in the canyon. Everything was still and silent.

Far up in the heavens a black dot marked a circling buzzard. I started to look around.

It was ten minutes later that I saw something I couldn't explain. That was a fresh break in the little corral back of the house. It was a crazy structure of weather-beaten lumber, held together by rusted nails and supported by posts set into the soft sand at various angles. It was the place where Bob Skinner had kept his prospecting burros; and I could see that a horse had been in the corral recently, and it looked to me as though the break in the corral had been done recently. In one place a board had been splintered, and the splinters hadn't as yet become dulled by the desert sunlight. The clean board showed out from beneath its weather-beaten veneer.

I looked over the stretch of sand around the corral. Useless to look for tracks there. The wind had leveled the sand out and made it into miniature drifts. It was right in line with the opening of a little canyon, down which the night wind would sweep with concentrated force.

I rolled a cigarette and sat looking at that break in the corral fence. After a while I started up the canyon. By the time I had gone a hundred yards I came to a little sheltered place, where there was some soft sand that hadn't been blown by the wind. I saw the tracks of a horse, and to one side the print of a booted foot.

The sun was climbing higher now, and the walls of the little canyon began to radiate heat. I plugged my way along over the rocks, searching for the faintest sign of tracks. A little later on I found more tracks. Then I struck a little trail that ran along the side of the canyon, and in this trail it was easy to follow the tracks. They were the tracks of a horse, and behind the horse, the tracks of a man.

I worked along the little dry canyon, and struck a level place. The horse was running here, and the tracks of the man were heavy on the toes and lighter on the heels.

After a while I got into country that didn't have much sand, but I could follow the tracks better because there hadn't been anything to drift with the desert night wind. I saw the tracks of the horse climb up a ridge, and I followed them.

Near the top of the ridge I struck horse tracks again, and farther on I struck horse tracks and no man tracks. I followed the horse tracks off and on for three or four hundred yards, looking for man tracks. There weren't any.

I went back and tried to pick up the man tracks. I couldn't find them again. They had gone to the top of the ridge and then vanished.

I sat down on my heels, rolled another cigarette, and thought for a while.

There was a spring down the ridge, and three or four miles over toward the head of Sidewinder Canyon. It wasn't a particularly good spring—just a trickle of brackish water, thick with alkali—but it was a spring just the same. I started working down toward that spring.

I didn't see any man tracks until I was within fifty yards of the spring; then I picked up the tracks of booted feet again. As nearly as I could tell, they were the same tracks that I had seen following along behind the horse tracks.

I searched around the spring, and found horse tracks. These didn't look like the same horse tracks that I had seen earlier in the day. They were the tracks of a bigger horse, and they seemed to be fresher. I went over to the trail which led into the spring, and I could see where the horse had come in along this trail and gone out along it.

I kept poking along, looking in the sagebrush, and finally I found a hole dug in the side of the mountain. It was about a foot deep by two feet long. I poked around in the hole. It wasn't a hole that had been dug with a shovel, but something that had been scooped in the side of the mountain, and half filled in with slag from the side of the bank above. There wasn't anything in the hole.

I went down and followed the tracks of the horse. They went down the trail, evenly spaced and at regular intervals.

I turned back from that trail and went back up the ridges the way I had come into the spring. It was hot now, and the sun was beating down with steady, eye-dazzling fury.

I managed to get back up to the last place where I had found the horse tracks, and started tracking the horse. That was comparatively easy. The horse had worked over toward the west and north, following down a ridge which wasn't quite so rocky, and on which there was a more dusty soil to hold the tracks.

I knew that my burros were trained in the ways of the desert and could shift for themselves until I got back; but I was in need of food, and the inside of my mouth felt raw from drinking the alkali water at the little spring. Nevertheless I kept pushing on, working against time, and at length I found where the horse had started wandering back and forth from a direct line, as though looking for something to graze on.

I followed the tracks until it got dark, and then I built a little fire and huddled over it, keeping warm until the moon came up. Then I began my tracking once more. It was slow work, but I took no chances of getting off the trail. I just worked slowly along the trail, following it along the sides of the ridges; and finally I came to something black lying on the ground.

I saw that it was a saddle, and feeling the tie in the latigo, I could tell that the saddle had been bucked off. The horn was smashed, and there were places where the iron hooves had cut the leather of the saddle. The horse had evidently bucked and twisted, and had walked out from under the saddle. The blankets were off to one side. Rocks were pushed loose from the indentations in the earth which had held them, as though the horse had been standing on his head and striking out with all four feet.

I marked the place where the saddle was, and kept on working down the slope.

It was still dark when I heard a horse whinny.

I called to him. Then I heard his shod feet ringing on the rocks as he came up to me. He was glad to see me. Right then, a man represented food and water to him, and he was eager for human companionship. There wasn't any rope around his neck, but I didn't need any. I twisted my fingers in his mane, and he followed along with me like a dog. When I came back to the place where the saddle lay, I got it back on him, and climbed into it.

He had lost his bridle, but I cut off the strings from the saddle, roped them together, and made a rough hackamore.

The horse was weak, thirsty, and tired; but he was glad to yield to human direction once more, and he carried me back over the ridges.

It was two hours past daylight when I came to the spring, where the horse drank greedily. I let him rest for half or three quarters of an hour, and gave him a chance to browse on some of the greenery which grew around the edges of the water. Then I sent him down the trail and found my burros, standing with full stomachs and closed eyes, their long ears drooping forward.

I got a rope from my pack, slipped it around the neck of the horse, and started along the trail which led up the east slope of the mountains on the side of the canyon. When I got to the top I poked around, looking for a camp, and after a while I saw the glint of the sun on something white. A man rolled over in the sunlight, pulled a blanket around his nude figure, and got to his feet. He stood grinning at me sheepishly.

I rode over to him, "You're Ernest Peterman?" I asked.

He nodded. He was getting back his health there in the high places of the desert, I knew. That much could be seen in the bronzed skin, the clear eye, and the poise of his head.

Man has devised many different methods for combating various ills, but he has never yet devised anything which is superior to the healing hand of nature in the desert. Let a man get into the high places of the dry desert atmosphere, where the sun beats down from a cloudless sky; let him live a simple life, bathing in sunshine, and resting with the cold night air fresh in his nostrils, and there is nothing which is incurable.

"I wanted you to take a little ride with me," I told him.

"How far?" he asked.

"Just up to the top of the ridge."

"All right, In an hour or so?"

"No," I told him. "Now. I want to get there about a certain time in the afternoon."

"What time?" he asked.

"The same time that you saw Sam Blake go down into Sidewinder Canyon," I told him.

He shrugged his shoulders and shook his head, as though trying to shake loose some disagreeable memory.

"I didn't want to do it," he said.

"Do what?" I asked.

"Testify," he told me.

"I didn't say you did."

"I know," he said. "It isn't that. It's just the thoughts that have been worrying me lately. Have you seen his daughter?"

I nodded.

"A wonderful girl," he said. "I don't think her father could be a murderer."

"He went down there with a gun, didn't he?" I asked.

"Yes."

"You don't suppose he just went down there to pay a social call, do you?"

"I don't know. He'd been robbed. Everybody seems to think that Skinner really robbed him."

"Did you know Skinner at all well?" I asked.

He shook his head.

"Ever get up to the top of the ridge much?"

"I've been up there once or twice in the morning."

"How did you happen to be up there on that particular afternoon?"

"I don't know. I was restless, and I just started walking up there. It was a hot day. I took it easy."

"And the shadows were just beginning to form on the western rim of the mountains?" I asked.

He nodded.

"And you could look down on Skinner's little shack?"

He nodded again.

"All right," I said, "I'd like to have you take a ride up there with me."

I let him ride the horse, and he seemed to feel a lot easier when I had a rope around the horse's neck, leading him. I took it that Peterman was pretty much of a tenderfoot in the desert.

"How did you happen to come to the desert country?" I asked him.

"I've tried everything else."

"Are you afraid of it?"

"Yes," he said, "I was dreadfully afraid at first. And then I got so I wasn't afraid."

"How did that happen?" I wanted to know. "Usually when a man sees the desert he either loves it or he hates it. If he hates it his hatred is founded on fear."

"I know," he said. "I hated it at first, and I hated it because I was afraid of it. I'm willing to admit it."

"What changed you?"

"You'd laugh if I told you," he said.

I looked at him, at the bronzed skin, the clear eye, the steady poise of the head, and I smiled. "Perhaps," I said, "I wouldn't laugh."

"It was the whispers," he said. "The whispers at night."

"You mean the sand whispers?" I asked.

He nodded. "There was something reassuring about them," he said. "At first they frightened me. It seemed as though voices were whispering at me; and then, gradually, I began to see that this was the desert, trying to talk; that it was whispering words of reassurance."

I nodded, and we didn't say anything more until we got to the summit of the ridge. I looked over the ridge, and checked Peterman as he started to look over.

"Not yet," I said. "Wait about fifteen minutes."

He sat and looked at me as though he thought I might be a little bit off in my upper story. But already the desert had begun to put its mark upon him; and so he didn't say anything, merely watched me as I smoked a cigarette.

When I had finished two cigarettes, I nodded my head.

"All right," I said. "Now look over."

He got up and looked over the top of the ridge. He looked around for a moment and said, "I don't see anything."

"Look down at Skinner's cabin."

He looked down, and all of a sudden I heard him give an exclamation, his eyes widening in surprise.

I unstrapped the binoculars and handed them to him. "All right," I said, "take another look."

V. Make Way for a Witness

SUN beat down upon the little desert town with its dusty main street and its unpainted board structures squatting in the gray desert which lined either side of the road. A big pile of tin cans marked the two ends of the main street, and these piled-up tin cans were bordered by a nondescript collection of junk which spread out over the desert, interspersed with clumps of sagebrush.

There were occasional automobiles on the street; automobiles, for the most part, of an ancient vintage, innocent of finish and as weather-beaten and dust-covered as the board structures themselves. There were also horses tied to the hitching rack in front of the general merchandise store, and a couple of sleepy burros rested on three legs at a time, casting black shadows on a dusty street.

We rode toward the building where the preliminary hearing was being held. A crowd of people were jammed into the little structure, despite the intense sunlight which beat down upon the roof. Other people crowded around the outside of the building, blocking the windows, craning their necks to listen. Out in the street little groups, recognizing the futility of trying to hear what was going on inside, formed gabbing centers of gossip to discuss the case.

I climbed from the saddle burro and dropped the rope reins over his head. "Make way for a witness," I said.

Men looked around at men. "Hell! It's Bob Zane," someone said. "Make way, you fellows, here comes Bob Zane."

I pushed my way into the courtroom. The tenderfoot clung to my blue shirt. He was sort of frightened and subdued. The atmosphere of the place reeked with the odor of packed bodies and many breaths. People stared at us with cold, curious eyes.

Abruptly, the little space around the judge's desk opened ahead of us, and the two officers stared with startled eyes into my face. One of them went for his gun.

"There he is now!" shouted Charlie, the deputy.

"Order in the courtroom!" yelled a wizened justice of the peace, whose white goatee quavered with indignation.

The officer pulled out the gun and swung it in my direction. "The man who was the accomplice of Pete Ayers, one of the defendants in this case," he shouted.

The judge banged on the desk. "Order in the court! Order in the court! Order in the court!" he screamed in a high piping voice.

I squared myself and planted my feet, conscious of the business end of the gun that was trained at my middle.

"Just a minute," I said. "I came to surrender myself and demand an immediate hearing. I'm charged with being an accessory in a murder case. I can't be an accessory unless there's been a murder, and unless the person I aided is guilty. I've got a witness with me who wants to change his testimony."

I half turned, and pushed forward the tenderfoot.

Peterman looked about him, gulped, and nodded.

"You can't interrupt proceedings this way!" piped the judge.

"Don't you want to hear the evidence?" I asked.

"Of course," he said, "but you aren't a witness."

I held up my right hand and moved a step forward, holding him with my eyes. "All right," I said, "swear me in."

He hesitated a moment, then his head nodded approvingly as his shrill, falsetto voice intoned the formal oath of a witness.

I moved abruptly toward the witness chair. One of the officers started toward me with handcuffs, but I turned to face the judge. I began to speak rapidly, without waiting to be questioned by anybody.

"The man who killed Bob Skinner," I said, "put a horse in Skinner's corral. When he had finished killing Skinner, there was blood on his hands, and when he tried to catch the horse, the horse smelled the blood, and lunged away from him. The man chased after the horse in a frenzy of haste, and the horse broke through the corral fence and started up the canyon, back of the house. The man followed along behind him, trying to catch the horse.

"A windstorm obliterated the tracks in the sand in front of the corral and around the house, so that the tracks couldn't have been seen unless the officers had appreciated the significance of that break in the corral fence and had gone on up the canyon looking for tracks. I took the course that a horse would naturally have taken, and I picked up the tracks again, up the canyon. And also the tracks of the man who was following."

Having gone that far, I could see that I wasn't going to be interrupted. I looked out over the courtroom and saw eyes that were trained upon me, sparkling with curiosity. I saw that the judge was leaning forward on the edge of his chair. The two officers had ceased their advance and were standing rooted to the spot.

Pete Ayers, who had stared at me with consternation when I pushed my way into the courtroom, was now grinning happily. Damn him! I don't suppose he ever knows what it is to worry over anything. He is as happy-go-lucky as a cloud of drifting sand in the desert. The girl was staring at me with a white face and bloodless lips. She didn't yet appreciate what my coming meant; but Pete knew me, and his face was twisted into that gleeful grin which characterizes him when he is getting out of a tight place.

"All right," snapped the judge in that high, piping voice of his, "go on. What did you find?"

"I followed the horse tracks to the top of the ridge," I said, "and I found where the man had quit chasing the horse. Then I followed the man tracks a way, and lost them. But I figured what a man would do who was out in the desert and hot from chasing a horse he couldn't catch. So I worked on down the ridge to a spring, and once more found the tracks, this time at the spring. I looked around and found where the man had dug a hole and had buried something near the spring. Then I found where he had walked out, secured another horse, ridden back to the spring, pulled whatever had been in the hole out of its place of concealment, and ridden away. He hadn't bothered to look after the horse that had been left in the mountains, figuring that it would die in the desert from lack of water and food.

"I then went back to the place where I had left the horse tracks, and started following the horse. Eventually I found the saddle, and then I found the horse."

There was a commotion in the courtroom. The officers conferred together in whispers, and one of them started toward the door. I quit talking for a little while and watched the officer who was pushing his way through the swirling group of men.

Outside the building a horse whinnied, and the whinny sounded remarkable significant, upon the hot, still air and the sudden silence of that room—a silence broken only by the irregular breathing of men who are packed into the narrow quarter, and who must breathe through their mouths.

"Well?" rasped the judge. "Go on. What happened?"

"I found the saddle," I said, "and I found the horse. I brought the horse back and I brought the saddle back."

"What does all that prove?" asked the judge, curiously.

"It proves," I said, "that the murderer of Bob Skinner wasn't Sam Blake. It proves that Sam Blake came down to call for a showdown with Bob Skinner, but Skinner was dead when he got there. Somebody had murdered Skinner in order to take the gold from his cabin, and the horse had balked at the odor of blood. The murderer had chased the horse for a while, but he couldn't continue to chase him, because he was carrying enough gold to make it difficult for him to keep going after the horse. So he went down to the spring and cached the gold; then he went out to get another horse, and later came back after the gold."

The judge's glittering eyes swung as unerringly as those of a vulture spotting a dead rabbit to the bronzed face of Ernest Peterman, the tenderfoot.

"That man," he said, "swears that he saw smoke coming out of Bob Skinner's cabin just before Sam Blake went in there."

"He *thought* he saw smoke, your honor," I said. "He's a tenderfoot, and new to the desert. He didn't go up on the ridge very often, and he wasn't familiar with Bob Skinner's cabin. Particularly when the afternoon sunlight throws a black shadow from the western ridge."

"What's the shadow got to do with it?" asked the judge.

"It furnishes a black background for the tree that's growing just back of the house, right in line with the chimney on Skinner's cabin."

"A tree?" piped the judge. "What's a tree got to do with it?"

"The tree," I said slowly, "is a blue paloverde tree."

"What's a blue paloverde tree?" the judge inquired petulantly.

"One that you've seen many times, your honor," I said, "in certain sections of the desert. It only grows in a very few places in the desert. It requires a certain type of soil and a certain type of climate. It isn't referred to as a paloverde tree in these parts. Your honor has probably heard it called a smoke tree."

I sat back and let that shot crash home.

The blue paloverde grows in the desert. The Indians called it the smoke tree because it sends up long, lacy branches that are of a bluish-green; and when the sun is just right, seen against a black shadow, the smoke tree looks for all the world like a cloud of smoke rising up out of the desert.

Peterman was a tenderfoot, and he'd climbed up on the ridge just when the western shadows had furnished a black background for the smoke tree behind Skinner's cabin. He had taken a look at the scene and decided that smoke was coming out of the chimney. No one had ever thought to have him go back and take a look at the cabin under similar circumstances. They had been so certain that Sam Blake was guilty of the murder that they hadn't bothered to check the evidence closely.

The judge was staring at me as though I had destroyed some pet hobby of his. "Do you mean to say that a man mistook a smoke tree for smoke coming from a chimney?" he asked.

I nodded. "Keener eyes than his have made the same mistake, your honor," I said, "which is the reason the Indians called the tree the smoke tree."

"Then who owned the horse?" asked the judge. "Who was it that went in there before Sam Blake called at the cabin?"

I pointed my finger dramatically at the place where the officers had been standing.

"I had hoped," I said, "that the guilty man would betray himself by his actions. I notice that one of the men has left the courtroom hurriedly."

As I spoke, there was the sound of a terrific commotion from outside. A shot was fired, a man screamed, a horse gave a shrill squeal of agony; then there was the sound of a heavy, thudding impact, and the stamping of many feet.

Men turned and started pushing toward the narrow exit which led from the place where the hearing was being conducted. They were men who were accustomed to the freedom of the outdoors. When they started to go through a door, they all started at once.

It was a struggling rush of bodies that pulled and jostled. Some men made for the windows, some climbed on the shoulders and heads of others and fought their way over the struggling mass of humanity. Futilely, the judge pounded his gavel again and again. Margaret Blake screamed, and I saw Pete Ayers slip a circling arm around her shoulder and draw her close to him.

I thought it was a good time to explain to the judge.

"That horse I found, your honor," I said, pushing close to him so that I could make my voice heard above the bedlam of sound, "was a nervous bronco. He made up to me all right because he was thirsty and hungry, but he was a high-strung, high-spirited horse. I left him tied to the rack out in front. I thought perhaps the owner of the horse might try to climb on his back and escape, hoping to take that bit of four-legged evidence with him. But horses have long memories. The last time the horse had seen that man, he had smelled the odor of human blood and had gone crazy with fright."

The crowd thinned out of the courtroom. Here and there a man who had been pushed against a wall or trampled underfoot, cursed and ran, doubled over with pain, or limping upon a bad leg; but the courtroom had emptied with startling speed.

I crossed to the window as the judge laid down his gavel. Impelled by curiosity, he crowded to my side. Outside, we saw, the men were circling about a huddled figure on the sidewalk. The horse, his ears laid back, his nostrils showing red, his eyes rolled in his head until the whites were visible, was tugging and pulling against the rope that held him to the hitching rack. I noticed that there were red stains on one forehoof, and a bullet wound in his side.

Lying on the sidewalk, a rude affair of worn boards, was the crumpled body of the deputy who had helped to make the arrest of Margaret Blake that first time we had seen her. The whole top of his head seemed to have been beaten in by an iron hoof.

The judge looked and gasped. He started for the door, then caught himself with an appreciation of the dignity which he, as a magistrate, owed to himself. He walked gravely back to the raised desk which sat on the wooden platform, raised the gavel, and banged it down hard on the desk.

"Court," he said, "is adjourned!"

It wasn't until after Pete Ayers and Margaret Blake had started out in the desert on their honeymoon that I got to thinking of the words of the college professor.

The desert is a funny place. It's hard to know it long without thinking that there's something alive about it. You get to thinking those sand whispers are not just a hissing of dry sand particles against rock or sagebrush, but real whispers from the heart of the desert.

The desert shows itself in two ways. There's the grim cruelty which is really a kindness, because it trains men to rely upon themselves and never to make mistakes. Then there's the other side of the desert, the carefree dust clouds that drift here and there. They're as free as the air itself.

Pete Ayers was a part of the desert. The desert had branded him with the brand of carefree sunlight and the scurrying dust cloud.

The desert had recorded the telltale tracks that had led to the discovery of the real murderer. Every man is entitled to his own thoughts. Mine are that it's all just two sides of the desert, the grim side that holds justice for murderers, and the happy side that leaves its stamp on men like Pete Ayers.

Pete Ayers clapped me on the back. His bride stared at me with starry eyes.

"We owe it all to you, Bob Zane!" she said, her lips quivering.

But I looked out at the desert. The white heat of an afternoon sun had started the horizons to dancing in the heat waves. Mirages glinted in the distance. A gust of wind whipped up a little desert dust-spout, and it scurried along, the sagebrush bending its head as the dust-spout danced over it.

"No," I told her, "you owe it to the desert. The desert is kind to those who love it. She held the evidence, carved in sand, for the righting of a wrong and the betrayal of a real culprit to justice."

Pete Ayers grinned at me and said, "You're getting so you talk just like that swivel-eyed college professor you guided around last month."

But his smiling eyes shifted over my shoulder and caught sight of the swirling dust cloud scampering merrily over the desert. I watched his expression soften as his eyes followed the swirling sand. And then I knew that college professor was right.

Shadow Quest

William F. Nolan

HIS name was striking: John Shadow. Otherwise, he was a very ordinary fellow. No wife. No family. A drifter, making his way through life as best he could. No goals. No ambitions. He gambled some, losing more than he won. He boxed for pocket money in Dodge City, cut timber in Canada, punched cows along the Cimarron, rode the rods west as a road tramp, served as a bouncer in Santa Fe, and played piano at a fancy house in El Paso. That job ended abruptly when Shadow ran off with one of the house ladies (her name was Margie). But they didn't stay together. Margie left him for a buffalo hunter two weeks later.

He was at loose ends. He owned the clothes on his back, a lump-headed mustang, and a new Winchester he'd won in a Kansas poker game. And not much else.

That was when John Shadow decided to ride into the Sierra Madres after Diablo.

He heard about him in the border town of Los Lobos along the American side of the Rio Grande. A wild stallion. El Diablo Blanco—the White Devil. Fast, smart . . . and mean. Two trappers at the bar were talking about the stallion.

"Has he been hunted?" Shadow asked.

"By the best," said the bartender, a beefy man in a stained apron. "With relays of horses. Sometimes they've run him a hundred miles in one day, but he always outsmarts 'em. Disappears like smoke in the wind. Lemme tellya, if a horse can laugh, he's laughing."

"I'm good with horses," Shadow said quietly.

The barman's smile was cynical. "Got a real *way* with 'em, eh?"

"I'd say so," nodded Shadow.

"Well, then, here's your chance." And he exchanged grins with the two trappers. "Just take yourself a little jaunt up into the Sierras an' fetch out the white."

"I need to think on it," Shadow told him.

He returned to the bar later that same afternoon.

"I'm going after him," he said.

It was a full day's ride into the upper foothills of the Sierra Madres. Shadow was following a crude, hand-drawn map provided by the barman after he'd convinced him he was serious in his quest for the white. The barman had indicated the area where the horse had been most often seen—but Shadow had no guarantee that Diablo had remained in this section of the mountains.

He was well aware of the various methods used in the capture of wild horses. Often, a sizable group of riders pursued the target animals, attempting to force them into a circular run, gradually tightening the circle. Sometimes hunters used relays of horses, constantly maintaining fresh mounts in the hope of running down the winded herd.

There was the story of a legendary hunt by a young Cheyenne warrior in which the Indian had traveled on foot for many hundreds of miles over a period of several months in pursuit of a single horse. The natural speed of a wild horse is reduced by its need to graze each day. Whenever the animal stopped to eat, the Indian's tireless, loping stride would close the distance between them. The Cheyenne lived on water and parched corn, eating as he ran, thus constantly forcing the pursuit.

Eventually, so the story went, both hunter and hunted became gaunt and weakened. The long trail ended on the naked slope of a snowcapped peak high above timberline when the Indian managed to lasso his totally exhausted quarry.

Of course, even if this fanciful tale were true, Shadow had no patience for such an arduous pursuit.

When he was within range of the horse, Shadow intended to bring down the animal with a bullet from his Winchester. The shot would require extreme accuracy, since his bullet must crease the nape of the neck at a spot that would jar the animal's spinal column. This would stun the horse, allowing its capture.

Diablo was unusual in that he ran alone. Most wild horses run with others of their kind, in herds numbering up to fifty or more, but the white stallion had always been a loner, staying well clear of the herds ranging the Sierra Madres. He wanted no young colts or laboring mares to slow his swift progress.

Many attempts had been made to capture him. One group of hunters, led by Colonel Matthew Sutton, had plans for Diablo as an Eastern show horse, and ran the stallion for six weeks without letup. Eleven horses had galloped themselves to death during that brutal pursuit, while the proud white drifted ahead of them, beyond their reach, defiant and strong.

One frustrated hunter claimed that the stallion had never truly existed—that he was nothing more than an apparition, a white ghost who galloped like a cloud across the sky.

When John Shadow repeated this last claim to a trapper he'd met in the high mountains, a one-armed veteran named Hatcher, the old man declared: "Oh, he's real enough all right, Diablo is. I've seen him by sun and by moon, in good weather and bad. There was one time I come up on him close enough to near touch that smooth silk hide of his, but then he took off like a streak of white lightning."

The old man cackled at the memory. "A pure wonder, he is. Ain't no horse like him nowhere in these mountains or out of 'em, and that's a fact."

"Then you don't think I can catch him?" asked John Shadow.

"Sure ya can—as easy as you can reach out and catch the wind." And Hatcher cackled again.

There was a great difference between the arid, sterile mountains around El Paso and this lush terrain of the Sierra Madres. Here Shadow found water in abundance, and rich grass, and thickly wooded hills—a veritable paradise that provided Diablo with everything he needed to sustain his wild existence.

Despite the old trapper's firm conviction that the great horse could never be captured, Hatcher had nonetheless provided solid hope. The trapper had agreed that Diablo did indeed frequent this particular section of mountain wilderness.

Luck and a keen eye might well reward him here.

Just a day later, as he was riding out of a shallow draw onto the level of a grassed plateau, John Shadow had his first look at the legendary stallion.

Diablo had been nibbling the green, tender sprouts that tipped a thick stand of juniper and now he raised his head to scent the wind. He nickered softly. Nostrils flaring, he suddenly wheeled about to face the rider at the far end of the plateau.

Shadow had slipped the new Winchester from its scabbard, since the range permitted him to fire, but he slowly lowered the weapon, awed by the animal's size and beauty. Easily seventeen hands tall, deep-chested, sheathed with rippling muscle, and as white as a drift of newly fallen snow, Diablo was truly magnificent.

The horse stood immobile for a long moment, studying his enemy. Then, with a toss of his thick mane and a ringing neigh of defiance, he trotted away, breaking into a smooth-flowing gallop that carried him swiftly out of sight.

Dammit! I could have fired, Shadow told himself; *I could have ended it here and now with a single shot.*

The light had been ideal and he was certain he could have creased the animal's neck. And there had been ample time for the shot. But the sheer power and majesty of the horse had kept him from firing. What if his bullet had missed its mark and struck a vital area? What if he had killed this king of stallions? Many wild horses have been fatally shot by hunters attempting to stun them.

No, he decided, *I need to be closer, a lot closer, to make absolutely* certain *of the shot. And now that he's aware of me, it's not going to be easy.*

That night, after a meal of mountain grouse roasted over his campfire, Shadow spread his blanket across a bed of fragrant pine needles on the forest floor. Lying on his back, hands laced behind his head, under a mass of tall pines that crowded the stars, he considered the meaning of freedom.

He had always thought of himself as a free man, yet through much of his life he'd been bound by the commands of others—when he had served in the war, when he was working in bars and brothels, when he'd been a cowpuncher and lumberman. In Diablo, John Shadow had witnessed true freedom. The great horse owed allegiance to no one. The whole wide world of the mountain wilderness served as his personal playground. He ran at no man's bidding, served no master but himself.

And now I'm trying to take that freedom away from him, thought Shadow. I'm trying to saddle and bridle him, bend his will to mine, feed him oats instead of his wild sweet grass, make him gallop at my command.

Did he have the right? Did *anyone* really have the right to own such a glorious animal?

With these melancholy thoughts drifting through his consciousness, Shadow closed his eyes, breathing deeply of the clean mountain air. The faint whisper of wind, rustling the trees, lulled him to sleep.

He awakened abruptly, shocked and wide-eyed, to an earth-shaking roar.

The morning sun was slanting down in dusty yellow bars through the pine branches, painting the forest floor in shades of brilliant orange. At the edge of the clearing, not twenty-five feet from where John Shadow had been sleeping, a huge, brown-black grizzly had reared up to a full-battle position, its clawed forepaws extended like a boxer's hands. The monstrous jaws gaped wide in anger, yellow fangs gleaming like swords in the wide red cave of its mouth.

The mighty bruin, a full thousand pounds of bone and muscle, was not facing directly toward Shadow, but was angled away from him, in the direction of another enemy.

Diablo!

Incredible as it seemed, the tall white stallion was trotting around the grizzly in a wary half-circle, ears flattened, eyes glaring, prehensile upper lip pulled back from its exposed teeth.

The horse was plainly preparing to attack.

Shadow was amazed. He had never known a horse to challenge a grizzly. Even the scent of an approaching bear was enough to send the fiercest stallion into a gallop for safety—yet here was Diablo, boldly facing this forest mammoth with no trace of fear.

Then an even greater shock struck the hunter: Diablo was defending *him*! The bear had apparently been making his forest rounds, overturning rocks for insects, ripping apart dead logs for grubs and worms, when he'd encountered the sleeping figure of John Shadow. He was about to descend on the hunter when the stallion intervened.

It made no logical sense. Yet, somehow, the white horse had felt protective of the man who had been hunting him. That Diablo had come to his rescue was a fact John Shadow accepted, although he was truly stunned by such an act. The scene seemed to be part of a dream, yet Shadow knew he was fully awake. What was happening, *was* happening.

Now Diablo reared up, with a ringing neigh, to strike at the brute's head with his stone-sharpened forehooves. A hoof connected with the bruin's skull like a dropped hammer, and the bear staggered back, roaring horribly, its eyes like glowing sparks of fire.

Then the grizzly counterattacked, lunging ponderously forward to rake one of its great paws across the stallion's neck. This blow, powerful enough to take a man's head off at the shoulders, buckled Diablo's legs, and the stunned animal toppled backward and down, blood running from an open neck wound.

The bear lumbered forward to finish his opponent, but by now Shadow had his Winchester in hand, and he began firing at the dark-shagged beast.

The giant grizzly seemed impervious to bullets. With a frightful bellow of rage, he charged wildly at the hated manthing.

Shadow stopped firing to roll sideways—barely avoiding the razored claws, which scored the log next to his head. With the huge bruin looming above him like a brown-black mountain, Shadow pumped three more rounds into the beast at heart level.

They did the job.

Like a chopped tree, the monster crashed to the forest floor, expiring with a final, defiant death-growl. It had taken five rifle bullets to kill him.

Diablo lay on his side, only half conscious, breathing heavily, as Shadow tended the stallion's injured shoulder. Using fresh water from his canteen, he cleansed the wound, then treated it with an old Indian remedy: he carefully packed a mix of forest herbs and mud over the wound, and tied it in place with a shirt from his saddle roll.

Amazingly, the animal did not resist these efforts. Diablo seemed to understand that Shadow was trying to help him.

If those claws had gone a half-inch deeper, Shadow knew, the shoulder muscle would have been ruined, crippling the great horse.

He ran his hand soothingly along the stallion's quivering flank, murmuring in a soft voice, "Easy, boy, easy now. You're going to be all right . . . you're going to be fine. . . ."

And Diablo rolled an anxious eye toward John Shadow.

It took more than a week before the white stallion was willing to follow a lead rope. During this entire period Shadow worked night and day to win the gallant animal's trust, talking, stroking, picking lush seed grass for the horse to eat.

The shoulder wound healed rapidly.

On the ninth day after the bear attack, Shadow began his ride back to Los Lobos, with Diablo trotting behind him on the lead rope.

Shadow was smiling as he rode. Now, suddenly, his life held purpose and meaning. Soon he would teach Diablo to accept him as a rider; he would be the first to guide this glorious beast over valley and plain—and riding him, Shadow knew, would be like riding the wind itself. There would be a mutual trust between them. A deep understanding. A bonding of spirits.

Before he had made this trip into the Sierra Madres John Shadow had never believed in miracles.

Now, looking back at the splendor of Diablo, he knew he had been wrong.

Crazy Over Horses

Marion Holland

JANEY'S body sat in civics class, but her mind was far, far away. Automatically her eyes followed the teacher's chalk across the blackboard as he drew three large rectangles and labeled them: *Executive. Legislative. Judicial.*

But Janey was back in the middle of the summer—back in Westhope with her cousins. Again the gravel scrunched under her booted feet as she and her cousins ran down the long drive from the house to the stables. Again she saw Eddie, the stable-boy, leading out the three shining horses, all saddled and ready for the early morning ride. Again she heard Golden Sun, the tall chestnut she had ridden all summer, whicker a soft welcome as he pushed his nose against her shoulder and watched with wise, dark eyes while she reached in her pocket for the bit of apple. She could still feel on the palm of her hand the velvet touch of his soft lips as he nuzzled the tidbit from her hand.

More clearly than the squeak of chalk on the blackboard, Jane could hear the muffled thud of hoofs as the horses picked their way down the narrow path behind the stables, the hollow clup-clup as they crossed the little plank bridge over the stream. "It isn't fair," she thought passionately, "that only very rich people can afford to own horses." She would cheerfully have wiped every automobile from the face of the earth, if only that would bring back the wonderful time when people all had horses of their own.

The teacher's voice droned on and on, but Janey was conscious of it only as a persistent buzzing in the distance, like the

185

large flies that bumbled noisily around the stables she was dreaming about.

". . . And finally, the Supreme Court, whose members are appointed by the President and confirmed by the Senate. Unlike the other judges we have mentioned, these nine men are not called by the title of Judge. They are called—who can tell the class?"

His questioning eye caught Janey's wide, intent gaze. "What do we call the members of the Supreme Court—Jane McGregor?"

"Horses," said Jane dreamily.

After school she paused at the door of the girls' locker room. She could hear the story being passed gleefully around by members of her civics class. Peggy's voice arose above the hubbub.

"Then she looked him right in the eye, and said, 'Horses!' Imagine!"

There were delighted and incredulous shrieks. Jane made her way unobserved to her locker.

"Oh, well," said Carol, in an indulgent tone, "you know Janey. She's crazy about horses."

"Crazy is right," whooped Peggy, "Hoof-and-mouth disease, I call it. Honestly, gals, I'll bet she sleeps standing up and eats out of a nose bag. Every time she opens her mouth I expect to hear her shinny—or whatever it is that horses do! First thing you know, she'll be *looking* like a horse!"

Jane slammed her locker shut and stalked to the door. "I'd rather look like a horse than like some people I know," she said.

Carol would have walked home with her, but Jane brushed by and strode on alone, kicking at the bright leaves on the sidewalk. It was bad enough, she thought resentfully, not to be able to ride all winter long, or even to see any horses except the junkman's poor rickety animal. But she couldn't even talk about horses to any of her friends; either they thought she was bragging about her rich relatives, or they just didn't listen. Except Carol, good old Carol. And even she had finally said plaintively, "Look, let's not talk about horses any more. I'm scared of horses, sort of."

"Oh, *no*," Jane had cried. "Nobody could be scared of horses!"

"*I* could," Carol had replied with feeling. "I was on a horse once—a horse about a mile high! The ground was so far away I could hardly see it, and my teeth were chattering so loud the old horse turned his head around to see what all the noise was. Then he opened his mouth about a yard and a half—you never saw so many teeth in your life! I couldn't decide whether he was laughing at me, or just getting ready to chew my leg off, so I sat there and hollered, 'Get me down off of here, somebody!'"

At home it was just as bad. Her father, she knew, was proud of her horsemanship. She had heard him bragging to his friends about it: "Jane's cousins have been riding all their lives—practically jumped from the cradle into the saddle, but Jane is just about as good on horseback!" But even he hadn't the vaguest idea how she felt about horses. To him, riding was just another athletic skill, like playing tennis, and a good horse was no better than a good tennis racket. When she asked for a horse for her birthday, he threw up his hands.

"It's impossible!" he exclaimed. "Why, do you have any idea what it costs your uncle to keep up that stable? Even aside from the price of a good saddle horse, it would be out of the question for us to keep one."

"Good heavens!" her mother cried in alarm. "I should say so! Oh dear, I do think a horse is so—so . . ."

"So what?" demanded Jane.

"So *large*, dear."

"Well, then, if I can't have a horse for my birthday, I don't want anything."

"But of course you'll have a party, dear. Why, you've always had a party, and it's always been *such* fun, hasn't it?"

"I don't want any old party," replied Jane sulkily. "All I want is a horse."

"And you'll need a new dress," her mother went on brightly, just as if Jane hadn't spoken. "I saw the loveliest dress last week, in Higger's window, I think it was. Just your type. It was rather expensive, but as long as it will do for the Fall Dance, too . . ."

"The Fall Dance?" Jane echoed blankly.

"Why certainly. You're going, aren't you? I thought you said Chuck Ryan had asked you."

"Oh, he *asked* me, all right," mumbled Jane. "But I don't know. Honestly, Mother, Chuck Ryan is an awful dope. Do you know what he said the other day? He said, 'Horses? Why I thought the horse was extinct, like the dodo!' Anyway, I don't want to go to the old Fall Dance."

"*Really*, Jane . . ." began her mother, in exasperation, but Jane had fled to the sanctuary of her own room where she could be alone.

At school she continued to dream her way through classes, doodling little sketches of horses on the margins of her notebooks. One day, in geometry, a piece of paper with a horse sketched on it slipped from her desk to the floor. She reached for it quickly, but not quickly enough. The boy across the aisle picked it up, glanced at it casually.

"Too short in the pastern," he commended.

With scarlet cheeks, Jane snatched the drawing. Short in the pastern, indeed! Well, maybe it was, at that. At least he hadn't said thick in the ankles, as Chuck Ryan certainly would have. She glanced sidewise at him.

His name was Grant Davidson, and that was all she knew about him. He was new in school this year. He was tall and gangling, and she had often stumbled over his big feet in the aisle on her way to her seat. But he must know something about horses. She promptly resolved to get acquainted with him.

This turned out to be harder than she had anticipated. Every time she ran into him around school, she gave him a smile and a cordial greeting, and every time he replied, without enthusiasm, "Hiya." If only she could catch him outside of school and start a conversation—but she never saw him outside of school. He wasn't in the noisy crowd that descended on the corner drugstore at three-thirty. He wasn't out for football, she discovered by hanging around one afternoon and watching the squad practice. Of course Chuck, the big oaf, thought she had come to watch him, but that couldn't be helped. She finally came to the conclusion that Grant must have some kind of a regular job after school. She asked a few cautious questions of people, but nobody seemed to know Grant Davidson.

One morning, about a week before her birthday, she ran into Chuck at the corner, and they bicycled to school together.

"Well, today's the big day!" he exclaimed. Jane looked blank. "Say—don't you know what day this is?" he demanded.

"Why, Friday—isn't it?"

"'Friday,' she says. Listen, dimwit, we play our first game this afternoon, and the coach is starting me at right half. How do you like *that*?"

Suddenly Jane remembered the dogged way Chuck had worked to make the team for three years.

"Oh, how swell!" she exclaimed warmly. "I'm so glad—and you can just bet I'll be out there this afternoon rooting for you!"

"Atta girl," he replied heartily. "Say, this is just like old times, isn't it? I knew you were all right, all the time, Janey. That's what I kept telling the gang—Janey's off the beam, but it's strictly temporary. A regular gal, like Jane McGregor, I kept saying—it stands to reason she isn't going to go on mooning forever about something as sissy as riding around on a horse, in a pair of fancy pants! I knew you'd snap out of it." Jane's eyes began to flash dangerously, but Chuck blundered happily on. "Stick around after the game, huh? We'll go someplace. And remember that date for the Fall Dance."

Jane exploded. "Chuck Ryan, don't you ever dare speak to me again as long as you live! Riding horseback isn't sissy—it takes a lot more brains and nerve and skill than kicking a silly old football around and rolling in the mud! I'd rather go riding any day than watch any old football game that was ever played! In fact, I'm not even going to the game this afternoon, so there. And you can just get yourself another date for the Fall Dance."

Chuck's mouth sagged open. "But you said . . ." "I did not!" she snapped. "Anyway, I've got another date—I'm going with Grant Davidson!"

As she pedaled on alone toward school, Jane wondered, "Now what in the world made me say *that*? I can't even get a civil hello out of the guy—fat chance I have of getting an invitation to the Fall Dance!"

Well, one thing—she wasn't going out to the field and watch Chuck Ryan cover himself with glory. The big gorilla. Right after her last class, she dashed to the bicycle rack, grabbed her bike, and started for home. She took the first corner at breakneck speed, and nearly collided with another bike. The rider was Grant Davidson.

"Hi!" she greeted him, when she had recovered her breath. "Say, do you go home this way, too? It's funny we never ran into each other before, isn't it?"

"Yes," he replied, and rode on in silence.

"Oh, dear," she thought, "this is where I ought to start a perfectly fascinating conversation or something." But he was riding so rapidly that it took all her breath just to keep up with him. Soon they were speeding along a street heading for the edge of town.

"Do you live this far out?" asked Grant finally.

"Well, no. But I'm going this way today," she said casually. "And that's no lie," she thought.

The houses got farther and farther apart, the sidewalks disappeared, fields of ragged goldenrod bordered the road. And still Grant pedaled along in stony silence, and Jane racked her brains for something to say.

Suddenly he slowed down and stopped at a narrow dirt lane. "Well, so long," he said abruptly, and before Jane could open her mouth, he turned off into the lane and disappeared in a cloud of dust.

"Boy! What a brush-off," she muttered, staring after him.

Well, it didn't take a brick house to fall on *her*. But as she wheeled her bike around, she heard a sound she hadn't heard since she left Westhope—the eager nicker of a horse who sees a friend approaching. She wouldn't—she couldn't—go back to town until she had at least seen the horse, even if it was only a farm animal.

She thrust her bike under some bushes and started cautiously up the lane on foot. At the first bend she stopped. There was a farmhouse, old and comfortably ugly with wide, sagging porches, and beyond it a barn, a stable, and scattered out-buildings. A rail

fence surrounded a broad expanse of sloping meadow. Grant
Davidson stood at the fence with his back toward her, rubbing
the ears of a bay horse—a little fellow, hardly more than a colt—
who was playfully nipping his shoulder. In the meadow two
other horses were grazing, a gray and a black. One glance told
Jane that these were no farm animals. They were fine saddle
horses—beauties, all of them.

Grant turned and went into the barn, and the little bay, with
a toss of its head and a flourish of his heels, cantered off to join
the other horses. If only she had an apple or a carrot, she might
coax one of them over to the fence.

"I suppose I'm trespassing, or something," she thought, "but
I don't see how they can do anything more than throw me
out!"

At the corner of the barn, she ran smack into Grant. He was
wearing heavy boots and carrying a rake and a shovel.

"Oh—hello," she said lamely. So this was his after-school job.
"Do you suppose they'd mind if I just went and talked to the
horses?"

"Who?" he asked.

"Why, they . . ." she nodded toward the house. "The people
that own them."

"Oh—I dunno," he answered evasively. "Horses don't much
like being squealed at and pawed over." He turned his back on
her and walked off toward the stable.

Jane stared after him, seething. "Why—why . . ." she sput-
tered. What did he take her for, anyway? Maybe he thought that
if he was rude enough, she would get mad and go away. "Well, I
just won't," she thought grimly, "at least, not until someone
comes out of the house and orders me away." She perched on
the fence and watched Grant clean one of the box stalls, raking
out the old straw and litter. It reminded her pleasantly of the
way she had hung around the stables at Westhope, watching
Eddie putter around with his chores, but Eddie treated her like
a human being.

She tried again. "Do you work here every day?"

He nodded without looking up.

"Do they—do they ever let you ride any of the horses?"

A smile flitted across his face. Then he replied shortly, "Yeah. It's part of my job. The horses need exercise—more than they get."

Jane's words tumbled out. "Oh—do you think—I wonder—I mean, would they ever let me ride? I'd give anything to . . ."

"These aren't livery stable hacks," he replied scornfully. "They're fine horses, with sensitive mouths."

"But I can ride. Honestly, I can . . ." But Grant had disappeared. He returned in a minute with a load of clean straw and began spreading it evenly across the floor of the stall. Jane was almost crying with anger and disappointment. "I can too ride," she repeated.

"That's what a lot of people think," he said rudely, and went on. "You know anything about horses? Ever clean out a stall? Can you saddle a horse? Rub it down properly?"

"No," she said crossly. "The stableman did all that."

"That's what I thought," he replied, and continued his work.

The horses were grazing on the far side of the meadow, and Jane knew there wasn't a chance of coaxing one over to the fence. "Maybe I can get acquainted with the people who live here," she thought desperately. "There must be *some* way! I've just got to ride those horses."

"Oh, Grant!" called a woman's voice from the house. He set down his rake and walked off without a backward glance. Jane sat on the fence and thought, and the more she thought, the madder she got. So Grant Davidson thought if you couldn't muck out a stall, you couldn't ride a horse.

"Of all the pig-headed, bad-tempered dopes!" she muttered, feeling thoroughly pig-headed and bad-tempered herself. "I'll show *him!*" She jumped down from the fence and pushed open the stable door. In a corner of the back room she found a pair of overalls hanging from a nail. They were much too big, but she stepped into them, rolled the pants up around the ankles, and seized the rake. She went to work where Grant had left off, raking out the trampled litter with vicious jabs. Then she scraped and smothed the packed clay of the floor with the square-ended shovel. To her surprise, she found she was beginning to enjoy herself. She spread the clean, shining straw on the floor with as much care and pride as if she were setting a table for a dinner party.

It was not easy work. By the time she had finished the next stall, perspiration was dripping down her face, and there was a brand new blister at the base of her thumb, but she stepped back and surveyed her work with a glow of satisfaction. "What next?" she wondered. The water buckets needed filling. There was one in each stall, set into a bracket to keep the horses from overturning it. She tugged at one, but could not get it out.

"Like this," said Grant at her elbow, and handed her the bucket. "Use the faucet at the corner of the barn. Rinse the bucket well before you refill it." The full buckets were heavy, but she made the trip three times, raising another blister and slopping a good deal of water into her loafers.

"Now what?" she asked. Grant put down the bag of feed he was carrying.

"That's all," he said, grinning. Jane grinned back. "Look, Jane," he said, "I'm sorry I was so nasty, but I was in an awful temper this afternoon. I wanted to stay at school for the game— and I couldn't. So I took it out on you."

"I was in a sort of temper myself," admitted Jane. "So let's call it even. Oh—look!" The horses were crowding around the gate.

"They think it's dinner time," explained Grant. "If I don't let the gray one in, he'll come over the fence in a minute."

"I like the little bay best," said Jane. "Do you ride him much?"

"Sunny? I've handled him a lot. He's used to the feel of a saddle and bridle. He could be broken now by a lightweight, but he won't be up to my weight for another year."

"Oh!" breathed Jane. "I—I weigh ninety-seven pounds."

He look her over appraisingly. "Say—that's an idea. Of course, I'd have to see you ride first. You need light hands for that job. Can you ride in those overalls?"

"I can ride in anything!" she cried.

"O.K. I'll saddle Lady for you, and I want you to watch while I do it, because next time, you're going to do it while *I* watch."

"Next time!" Jane's heart was singing as she vaulted into the saddle.

"Take her around the meadow a couple of times," Grant directed.

At first Jane rode stiffly, acutely conscious of Grant's critical eye on her. Her hands felt wooden, and getting a good knee grip in a pair of baggy overalls was a very different matter from riding in well-tailored breeches. But by the time Lady settled into a smooth canter, Jane had forgotten everything else in the world. Around and around the big meadow they swept. Jane could have gone on forever, but she pulled Lady down to a trot and returned triumphantly to the gate. Then she noticed the tall woman leaning on the fence beside Grant.

"Oh, my!" she thought in a sudden panic. "I bet she's mad at him for letting me ride her horse. Oh, what if he loses his job!"

But Grant was smiling and waving. As Jane jogged through the gate, Grant turned to the woman and said, "Mother, this is Jane McGregor. How about it—shall I let her break Sunny for me?"

Jane blushed and stammered something, as Mrs. Davidson said, "I am very happy to meet you, Jane. I expect you could do a good job on Sunny—if you aren't afraid to take a few spills. Come up to the house, you two, when you're through, and we'll try to find something to eat."

Later, sitting on the porch with Grant and his mother, eating cake and drinking cold milk, Jane blurted out, "I—I thought Grant was the stable-boy."

"I am," he replied, through a large mouthful of cake. "Of course Dad helps on week ends."

"Grant has been in complete charge of the stable ever since we moved here," explained his mother. "It was that or give up the horses and move into an apartment. The only thing that worries me is the fact that he doesn't seem to have gotten acquainted with anyone at school yet."

"Well, gosh," complained Grant. "I have to rush right home after school. And then, most people are such dopes about horses. You can't very well walk up to a perfect stranger and say, 'Come on home with me this afternoon, and we'll have a fine time shoveling out a stable!'"

"I don't see why not!" exclaimed Jane, with spirit. "I'll come and shovel every day—that is, if you'll let me. And as for getting acquainted, *I* know what! You just come to my birthday party a week from tomorrow, and you'll get acquainted with the whole gang! They're a pretty good bunch, too," she added, "even if they are dopes about horses!"

As Jane bicycled home, protesting muscles told her that she would be stiff tomorrow, but she rode in a haze of happiness. She burst into the house, shouting, "Mother! Mother! Say, isn't it about time we did something about my party?"

"Your party?"

"Sure—it's my birthday next week. Don't I *always* have a party?"

Mrs. McGregor beamed. "Why, Jane, darling, I'm so glad you're taking an interest in things at last. I was afraid you'd never stop mooning because you couldn't have a horse."

Jane threw her arms around her mother in a bear hug. "I don't have to moon any more about horses I haven't got," she caroled. "I've *got* horses—or just as good as! I can ride every single day, yes, and mess around the stable all I want. Golly, I've got to dig up my jodhpurs and some overalls that fit. And, jeepers, I'd better get on the phone and start rounding up the gang! How many may I ask? And I'll have to make up with Chuck first. I know, I'll ask him to bring Carol—she hasn't got a date for the Fall Dance yet. And, say, Mother—how about a new dress? Something that will just knock your eye out. There's a new boy coming, and he doesn't know anything about it yet, but I have a date with him for the Fall Dance!"

The Summer of the Beautiful White Horse

William Saroyan

ONE day back there in the good old days when I was nine and the world was full of every imaginable kind of magnificence, and life was still a delightful and mysterious dream, my cousin Mourad, who was considered crazy by everybody who knew him except me, came to my house at four in the morning and woke me up by tapping on the window of my room.

Aram, he said.

I jumped out of bed and looked out the window.

I couldn't believe what I saw.

It wasn't morning yet, but it was summer and with daybreak not many minutes around the corner of the world it was light enough for me to know I wasn't dreaming.

My cousin Mourad was sitting on a beautiful white horse.

I struck my head out of the window and rubbed my eyes.

Yes, he said in Armenian. It's a horse. You're not dreaming. Make it quick if you want a ride.

I knew my cousin Mourad enjoyed being alive more than anybody else who had ever fallen into the world by mistake, but this was more than even I could believe.

In the first place, my earliest memories had been memories of horses and my first longings had been longings to ride.

This was the wonderful part.

In the second place, we were poor.

This was the part that wouldn't permit me to believe what I saw.

197

We were poor. We had no money. Our whole tribe was poverty-stricken. Every branch of the Garoghlanian family was living in the most amazing and comical poverty in the world. Nobody could understand where we ever got money enough to keep us with food in our bellies, not even the old men of the family. Most important of all, though, we were famous for our honesty. We had been famous for our honesty for something like eleven centuries, even when we had been the wealthiest family in what we liked to think was the world. We were proud first, honest next, and after that we believed in right and wrong. None of us would take advantage of anybody in the world, let alone steal.

Consequently, even though I could see the horse, so magnificent; even though I could *smell* it, so lovely; even though I could *hear* it breathing, so exciting; I couldn't *believe* the horse had anything to do with my cousin Mourad or with me or with any of the other members of our family, asleep or awake, because I *knew* my cousin Mourad couldn't have *brought* the horse, and if he couldn't have bought it he must have *stolen* it, and I refused to believe he had stolen it.

No member of the Garoghlanian family could be a thief.

I stared first at my cousin and then at the horse. There was a pious stillness and humor in each of them which on the one hand delighted me and on the other frightened me.

Mourad, I said, where did you steal this horse?

Leap out of the window, he said, if you want a ride.

It was true then. He *had* stolen the horse. There was no question about it. He had come to invite me to ride or not, as I chose.

Well, it seemed to me stealing a horse for a ride was not the same thing as stealing something else, such as money. For all I knew, maybe it wasn't stealing at all. If you were crazy about horses the way my cousin Mourad and I were, it wasn't stealing. It wouldn't become stealing until we offered to sell the horse, which of course I knew we would never do.

Let me put on some clothes, I said.

All right, he said, but hurry.

I leaped into my clothes.

I jumped down to the yard from the window and leaped up onto the horse behind my cousin Mourad.

That year we lived at the edge of town, on Walnut Avenue. Behind our house was the country: vineyards, orchards, irrigation ditches, and country roads. In less than three minutes we were on Olive Avenue, and then the horse began to trot. The air was new and lovely to breathe. The feel of the horse running was wonderful. My cousin Mourad who was considered one of the craziest members of our family began to sing. I mean, he began to roar.

Every family has a crazy streak in it somewhere, and my cousin Mourad was considered the natural descendant of the crazy streak in our tribe. Before him was our uncle Khosrove, an enormous man with a powerful head of black hair and the largest mustache in the San Joaquin Valley, a man so furious in temper, so irritable, so impatient that he stopped anyone from talking by roaring, *It is no harm; pay no attention to it.*

That was all, no matter what anybody happened to be talking about. Once it was his own son Arak running eight blocks to the barber shop where his father was having his mustache trimmed to tell him their house was on fire. The man Khosrove sat up in the chair and roared, It is no harm; pay no attention to it. The barber said, But the boy says your house is on fire. So Khosrove roared, Enough, it is no harm, I say.

My cousin Mourad was considered the natural descendant of this man, although Mourad's father was Zorab, who was practical and nothing else. That's how it was in our tribe. A man could be the father of his son's flesh, but that did not mean that he was also the father of his spirit. The distribution of the various kinds of spirit of our tribe had been from the beginning capricious and vagrant.

We rode and my cousin Mourad sang. For all anybody knew we were still in the old country where, at least according to our neighbors, we belonged. We let the horse run as long as it felt like running.

At last my cousin Mourad said, Get down. I want to ride alone.

Will you let me ride alone? I said.

That is up to the horse, my cousin said. Get down.

The *horse* will let me ride, I said.

We shall see, he said. Don't forget that I have a way with a horse.

Well, I said, any way you have with a horse, I have also.

For the sake of your safety, he said, let us hope so. Get down.

All right, I said, but remember you've got to let me try to ride alone.

I got down and my cousin Mourad kicked his heels into the horse and shouted, *Vazire*, run. The horse stood on its hind legs, snorted, and burst into a fury of speed that was the loveliest thing I had ever seen. My cousin Mourad raced the horse across a field of dry grass to an irrigation ditch, crossed the ditch on the horse, and five minutes later returned, dripping wet.

The sun was coming up.

Now it's my turn to ride, I said.

My cousin Mourad got off the horse.

Ride, he said.

I leaped to the back of the horse and for a moment knew the awfulest fear imaginable. The horse did not move.

Kick into his muscles, my cousin Mourad said. What are you waiting for? We've got to take him back before everybody in the world is up and about.

I kicked into the muscles of the horse. Once again it reared and snorted. Then it began to run. I didn't know what to do. Instead of running across the field to the irrigation ditch the horse ran down the road to the vineyard of Dikran Halabian where it began to leap over vines. The horse leaped over seven vines before I fell. Then it continued running.

My cousin Mourad came running down the road.

I'm not worried about you, he shouted. We've got to get that horse. You go this way and I'll go this way. If you come upon him, be kindly. I'll be near.

I continued down the road and my cousin Mourad went across the field toward the irrigation ditch.

It took him half an hour to find the horse and bring him back.

All right, he said, jump on. The whole world is awake now.

What will we do? I said.

Well, he said, we'll either take him back or hide him until tomorrow morning.

He didn't sound worried and I knew he'd hide him and not take him back. Not for a while, at any rate.

Where will you hide him? I said.

I know a place, he said.

How long ago did you steal this horse? I said.

It suddenly dawned on me that he had been taking these early morning rides for some time and had come for me this morning only because he knew how much I longed to ride.

Who said anything about stealing a horse? he said.

Anyhow, I said, how long ago did you begin riding every morning?

Not until this morning, he said.

Are you telling the truth? I said.

Of course not, he said, but if we are found out, that's what you're to say. I don't want both of us to be liars. All you know is that we started riding this morning.

All right, I said.

He walked the horse quietly to the barn of a deserted vineyard which at one time had been the pride of a farmer named Fetvajian. There were some oats and dry alfalfa in the barn.

We began walking home.

It wasn't easy, he said, to get the horse to behave so nicely. At first it wanted to run wild, but as I've told you, I have a way with a horse. I can get it to want to do anything *I* want it to do. Horses understand me.

How do you do it? I said.

I have an understanding with a horse, he said.

Yes, but what sort of an understanding? I said.

A simple and honest one, he said.

Well, I said, I wish I knew how to reach an understanding like that with a horse.

You're still a small boy, he said. When you get to be thirteen you'll know how to do it.

I went home and ate a hearty breakfast.

That afternoon my uncle Khosrove came to our house for coffee and cigarettes. He sat in the parlor, sipping and smoking and remembering the old country. Then another visitor arrived, a farmer named John Byro, an Assyrian who, out of loneliness, had learned to speak Armenian. My mother brought the lonely visitor coffee and tobacco and he rolled a cigarette and sipped and smoked, and then at last, sighing sadly, he said, My white horse which was stolen last month is still gone. I cannot understand it.

My uncle Khosrove became very irritated and shouted, It's no harm. What is the loss of a horse? Haven't we all lost the homeland? What is this crying over a horse?

That may be all right for you, a city dweller, to say, John Byro said, but what of my surrey? What good is a surrey without a horse?

Pay no attention to it, my uncle Khosrove roared.

I walked ten miles to get here, John Byro said.

You have legs, my uncle Khosrove shouted.

My left leg pains me, the farmer said.

Pay no attention to it, my uncle Khosrove roared.

That horse cost me sixty dollars, the farmer said.

I spit on money, my uncle Khosrove said.

He got up and stalked out of the house, slamming the screen door.

My mother explained.

He has a gentle heart, she said. It is simply that he is homesick and such a large man.

The farmer went away and I ran over to my cousin Mourad's house.

He was sitting under a peach tree, trying to repair the hurt wing of a young robin which could not fly. He was talking to the bird.

What is it? he said.

The farmer, John Byro, I said. He visited our house. He wants his horse. You've had it a month. I want you to promise not to take it back until I learn to ride.

It will take you a *year* to learn to ride, my cousin Mourad said.

We could keep the horse a year, I said.

My cousin Mourad leaped to his feet.

What? he roared. Are you inviting a member of the Garoghlanian family to steal? The horse must go back to its true owner.

When? I said.

In six months at the latest, he said.

He threw the bird into the air. The bird tried hard, almost fell twice, but at last flew away, high and straight.

Early every morning for two weeks my cousin Mourad and I took the horse out of the barn of the deserted vineyard where we were hiding it and rode it, and every morning the horse, when it was my turn to ride alone, leaped over grapevines and small trees and threw me and ran away. Nevertheless, I hoped in time to learn to ride the way my cousin Mourad rode.

One morning on the way to Fetvajian's deserted vineyard we ran into the farmer John Byro who was on his way to town.

Let me do the talking, my cousin Mourad said. I have a way with farmers.

Good morning, John Byro, my cousin Mourad said to the farmer.

The farmer studied the horse eagerly.

Good morning, sons of my friends, he said. What is the name of your horse?

My Heart, my cousin Mourad said in Armenian.

A lovely name, John Byro said, for a lovely horse. I could swear it is the horse that was stolen from me many weeks ago. May I look into its mouth?

Of course, Mourad said.

The farmer looked into the mouth of the horse.

Tooth for tooth, he said. I would swear it *is* my horse I didn't know your parents. The fame of your family for honesty is well known to me. Yet the horse is the twin of my horse. A suspicious man would believe his eyes instead of his heart. Good day, my young friends.

Good day, John Byro, my cousin Mourad said.

Early the following morning we took the horse to John Byro's vineyard and put it in the barn. The dogs followed us around without making a sound.

The dogs, I whispered to my cousin Mourad. I thought they would bark.

They would at somebody else, he said. I have a way with dogs.

My cousin Mourad put his arms around the horse, pressed his nose into the horse's nose, patted it, and then we went away.

That afternoon John Byro came to our house in his surrey and showed my mother the horse that had been stolen and returned.

I do not know what to think, he said. The horse is stronger than ever. Better-tempered, too. I thank God.

My uncle Khosrove, who was in the parlor, became irritated and shouted, Quiet, man, quiet. Your horse has been returned. Pay no attention to it.

Beautiful and Free

Carolyn St. Clair King

GIL Bronson was in the mow, forking down the last of the treasured hay to the cows that could no longer forage on the drought-browned range. When he heard the rumble of wagon wheels, he knew his father was back from town. So very soon now, Gil would know the best, or the worst, that could happen to him.

If there was someone with Dad, it would be the cattle buyer. Cattle buyers, in this hard year, were as scarce as grass, and the news that there was one in town had sent Dad off as fast as he could hitch the team. But if his father was alone, it would mean that he had had no luck. And that meant the end of Gil's long-cherished dream of going off to school in town.

He was fifteen, now, and a year had passed since his graduation from the one-room school which served their district. But going to school in the city meant boarding out, buying books and getting clothes that were different from overalls and his father's castoff, high-heeled boots. What with the drought and loss of cattle, and then no market for the steers they had saved, Dad simply had not had the cash. But if Dad sold the steers today, he had promised Gil that he could go to school.

There were no voices in the yard—just Dad saying, "So, there, Bess. Up a little, Ben." Then the rattle of loosened traces.

Gil knew the worst. But he forced his stiff legs down the ladder and even managed a frozen smile. "Hi, Dad. No luck in town, I guess."

Ben Bronson shook his grizzled head. "Young Fealy was there, in that car of his, and he took the cattle buyer off with him. Fealy's been able to feed this summer, after the range dried up, and he has a lot of beef for sale—all the buyer's going to want, I reckon. I might have saved myself the trip." He cleared a husky throat. "I did manage to buy some hay to tide us over with those cows we're feeding, Gil."

"That's good," Gil said. "I had to scrape the mow this morning." His cheeks felt stiff, and his voice was wooden. Dad buying hay—that meant he had had to use the money they had all been hoarding, a dime or a dollar at a time, in the old tin can on the kitchen shelf. There had not been enough there yet to get Gil started off to school, but it had been a nest egg, anyhow.

Ben Bronson sighed and rubbed a hand across the stubble on his chin. "I'm sorry, Gil," he said.

Gil knew that was true, and he felt ashamed to be adding trouble to the load his father had to carry.

"Sure, Dad," he said. "I've sort of given up the notion of going off to school. I'm getting kind of old for that, and besides I reckon you need me here."

His father's look of pleased relief was pretty chilly comfort, though. At dinnertime the potatoes stuck in Gil's tight throat, and he wasn't hungry.

Ben Bronson, trying for a cheerful note, broke the painful silence. "Everyone in town is agog over the wild-horse hunt tomorrow. Protheroe has offered a thousand bucks to whoever captures that outlaw stallion they call Black Prince. Five hundred dollars for his mate."

They had known about the hunt, of course. It had been organized by the wealthy rancher who had a covetous eye on the two wild creatures—the last of the bands of horses that had roamed these hills since the early days when the Spaniards had come in search of the fabled golden cities.

Gil's mother looked at him with a sudden bright and hopeful smile.

"Gil," she said, "you ought to go. You've always been crazy about that stallion. When you were younger, I couldn't keep you home from the Hesperus flats, where you could watch those two wild horses. Knowing their habits as you do, you might be the one to win that money and put yourself through a year of school."

Gil's laugh was hollow. "Gosh, Ma," he said, "the finest riders in the country will all be there. What chance do you figure old Rex would have against—well, say Jim Fealy's Scamp? That thoroughbred will leave the other bangtails standing still.

"Jim Fealy should be barred," Ma said. "All the money those Fealys have."

"No, he shouldn't," Gil protested. "Jim's entitled to his fun, just as much as anybody. Although I can't imagine its being fun. It makes me sick to think of someone's rope around Black Prince's neck. He's a beauty, sure enough, but it's something that's sort of all tied up with his running wild and being free. And the mare—you never saw her like, nor the way the two of 'em stick together. If one or the other is out of sight, they act as crazy as our old Bess with an unweaned colt."

"Protheroe aims to keep Black Prince," Ben said, "and send the mare back east to his married daughter. Just the same, Gil boy, I'd have a try at that prize. Someone's going to win it. Might as well be you."

Ben cleared his throat and left the table. Ma sat there, anxiously watching Gil, who was staring blankly into space.

It really hurt the folks, Gil knew, not being able to send him off to the school he had planned on for so many years. There really wasn't any chance of his winning the Protheroe prize—let alone the fact he could never bear to put a rope on Black Prince's neck—but if it would make the folks feel better. . . .

"All right, I'll go," he told his mother.

Gil didn't sleep well that night. He dreamed of going off to school, leading Black Prince by a fine new halter. But it wasn't a pleasant dream and when Gil woke up he wished he hadn't said he would ride in the Protheroe hunt.

As soon as breakfast was over, however, he saddled his old cow pony, Rex, and put the thick meat sandwich Ma had fixed for him inside his buttoned denim jacket. He wore scarred and scuffed old leather chaps to protect his legs if the chase should lead through heavy brush, and his father's old broad-brimmed hat.

The sun was lifting a cautious eye above the eastward peaks when Gil, completing the five-mile climb, reined his pony through the dew-drenched grass of the high flat meadow where the Protheroe hunt was now assembled.

Gil knew everybody there, except a short and bulbous man who was riding with the elder Fealy. Young Jim Fealy was there, of course, on his thoroughbred, and several other cowboys rode mounts that were notable for speed. It was just as Gil had thought it would be, and it sort of let him out, he reasoned, feeling glad deep inside. Raising his hand in silent answer to the shouted greetings, he took his place with the other riders.

Then Lou Protheroe came riding up, important on his tall, black horse, and raised a large authoritative palm.

"Now, folks," Lou said, "just a few instructions. I've had some boys out there all night keeping tabs on the two wild horses. They're grazing in a little draw, up near the head of Canyon Creek. We're going up there, and when I signal, the boys will start the outlaws down our way. When they break from cover, we'll chase 'em up across the flats toward the fence I've built across that narrow neck of land between Devil's Gulch and Big Arroyo. With you *hombres* coming up behind, we'll have 'em neatly trapped. Then it's just a question of who will be the lucky jigger to slip his noose around a thousand dollars—or half of that, if you snag the sorrel."

Protheroe's smile flashed, and the assembled cowboys yelled and waved their broad-brimmed hats.

Gil thought: I hope the Black Prince fools 'em.

And it wasn't sour grapes, either, for the closer the moment came when those two wild creatures would be imprisoned, the less Gil could bear it.

He tailed the laughing bunch up to the flat below the gulch where the outlaws grazed, pulling Rex to the farthest end as they ranged their horses in one long line.

When Protheroe raised his gun and fired, the following minutes seemed to Gil to stretch as tight as banjo wire. Every eye, along with his, strained toward the opening of the draw where the Prince and his mate would appear. And it wasn't long until Gil saw them, bursting startled from the brush.

On a grassy knoll, limned against the cobalt blue of the morning sky, they paused at sight of that line of riders.

The stallion's coat gleamed black as water under winter ice, the heavy mane floating like a dusky cloud from the high arched neck, the long black tail barely clearing the rocky ground. And by his side, just as beautiful in her way, stood the clean-limbed, round-bodied little mare, glowing embered where the sun's first rays touched her sorrel coat; her sweeping mane and fanning tail the color of a cup of well-creamed coffee.

A gasp of awe and admiration ran down the line of waiting riders. Then, like dynamited earth, suddenly and with a roar, the line burst forth in hot pursuit.

As the outlaws stood for another second, it seemed to Gil that the mare looked doubtfully toward her partner. But every line of the Prince was defiant, his head flung high and nostrils flaring, while clear above the cowboy yells and the thunder of their horses' hooves, Gil could hear his challenging trumpet call.

Black Prince dipped his nose to touch the mare's. Then the two were off like triggered bullets, leaving the scattered field of riders streaming far behind.

Gil, on his ancient horse, transfixed, incapable of motion, knew that the speed which had so often saved them would only bring them faster, now, to the fate in store for them.

And now Gil, too, spurred his pony across the flat. As he topped a little rise, he could see the race strung out ahead.

Black Prince was just a thin black streak, the mare a flash of tossing mane; and Jim Fealy on his thoroughbred was still a good half mile behind. There was no one close to Jim, and Gil knew that the Prince was already his. For when the outlaws reached the fence and, finding themselves hemmed between the two deep gulches, were forced to turn, Jim would be there with his lariat.

That was something, Gil decided, that he simply could not bear to see. On sudden impulse, he reined his mount across the rim of Big Arroyo, which was shallow here at its lower end. Having gained the sandy bottom, Gil spurred Rex up the smooth, flat floor with no other purpose in his mind than to feel the clean, cold rush of morning wind against his face and forget a little, if he could, what was happening up there on the flat.

As Gil rode up it, the arroyo deepened, till finally its eroded banks rose sheer and clifflike to the rim, and all his upward glance could find was a slice of sky with a small white cloud adrift on its untroubled blue.

Then he saw the fence where it joined the gulch to make a trap for the two wild horses. He listened for some sound from above. But all was quiet, and Gil surmised that when the cornered outlaws struck the fence they had turned away toward Devil's Gulch, on the other side—or they might even be racing back, in sheer defiance, toward that line of riders.

Gil left his saddle and found a seat on a nearby rock. Perhaps, if the outlaws did break back and Fealy missed them, it would give the tail-end men a chance. If that happened, Dad would blame him for not being there. Someone would rope the horses sure enough, and maybe he had been a chump, sneaking off like this. A chickenhearted guy like him probably never would get to school.

Then, so suddenly it made him jump, he heard a close-up repetition of the great black stallion's unforgettable, trumpeting challenge.

Leaping hastily to his feet, Gil gazed upward, and there above him on the rim saw the wide, red nostrils and gleaming eyes of the cornered Prince. Beside that proud black head appeared the froth-flecked nose of the little sorrel, quivering nostrils widespread in terror, and panic-stricken, liquid gaze fixed intently on her mate.

For one brief, disdainful instant, Black Prince glanced back across his shoulder, then touched the sorrel's nose with his, in command and encouragement so clear that it seemed to Gil the Prince had spoken. In the next split second, the stallion leaped—a jump that no man in his wildest fancy would dream a horse could make.

Not a dozen feet from where the boy stood, the outlaw stallion struck the arroyo bottom, a blur of black, slashed by four whitely gleaming hoofs. Gil shut his eyes, believing that when he looked he would see the Black Prince lying dead.

Then he heard the stallion call again and, opening his eyes, saw the Prince unhurt, and realized that the streak of red flashing downward between himself and the strip of sky was the mare, who had followed her lord and master.

But now, as the red streak came to earth, both the slender forelegs buckled, and with a little moaning cry, the mare went over on her side.

Black Prince, already turned for flight, was caught back instantly by the sound, and Gil stood frozen as he saw the stallion dip his nose and hold it long against his mate's. There was no hope for the mare, Gil thought, and believed Black Prince knew it, too.

Gil could have run to fetch his rope from where his prick-eared pony stood, not a dozen feet away. He could have flung his loop easily about Black Prince's drooping neck, and the stricken stallion would not have stirred. The thought flashed into Gil's mind, but he didn't ponder it long. All his attention was centered on the dreadful plight of the sorrel mare.

A sound, intruding from above, broke the spell—for Gil, at least. Looking up, he saw Jim Fealy on his thoroughbred, and other men behind him—Protheroe, and the elder Fealy, and the short fat man Gil didn't know.

A sudden rage welled up in Gil as he saw Jim Fealy grab his rope. The Prince had heard—he must have heard, with those ears attuned to the slightest sound—but he stood his ground by the fallen mare, an easy and certain target for the loop that Jim was hastily building.

In a blur, Gil saw Jim swing and throw, saw the rope uncoil and angle downward. In another instant, that hissing and distended loop would close about Black Prince's neck—that drooping black neck, no longer proud and arched with triumph.

In that instant, Gil came to life. Leaping wildly from the clump of brush which had sheltered his observation point, he swung his father's old black hat, jumping wildly up and down and screaming as if his lungs would burst, "Run! Run, Black Prince! You've got to run!"

Startled, the stallion turned his head, and Jim Fealy's hissing loop slid harmlessly down a sleek black shoulder.

Gil could hear Jim's shouted curse. Protheroe was swearing, too. But Gil didn't care. For mingled with their shouts was another sound—the sudden flurry of scrambling hoofs, as the red mare, panicked by all the noise, rose to her unsteady legs—legs not broken, after all—legs she could move on slowly now—then more swiftly, as the Black Prince, circling, nipped her gently on the flank. And then, in a wonderful rising thunder of drumming hoofs, the two of them were making off down the sandy floor of Big Arroyo.

It was some time before the men above could circle down to the spot where Gil was numbly waiting. He wasn't sure what they would do. They might even put him in jail for this. Yet he had never felt so glad, and sort of right and good inside. And when they all came pounding up, Gil stood his ground.

"The Prince was really mine," he said, in answer to Jim Fealy's accusation. "I could have put my loop around his neck long before you showed up. But I wanted him to get away, and I'm glad he did."

Both Protheroe and the Fealys were black with anger and making threats. At last, however, they drifted off. Then the short, fat man came up to Gil with outstretched hand.

"I'm fond of horses, too," he said. "I'd like to know you better, son. I've made excuses to Fealy, and I'd like to ride along to your place for dinner if you'll invite me."

Gil said, "All right. I know the folks will be glad to have you." But the folks, Gil thought, would be disappointed in their son, and sorry about the prize—not understanding how a boy could want a thing as much as he had wanted to go off to school, then have his chance, and let it go.

The fat man's name was Myers. But it wasn't till late in the afternoon that Gil learned he was the cattle buyer whom Dad had failed to land.

At the dinner table, all the talk had been about the hunt and the two wild horses. Finally Gil had left to do his chores. Myers was gone when he came back, and his father was waiting impatiently to tell him that though Myers had signed for the Fealy cattle, he had bought theirs, too, this afternoon—every last one that was fit for market.

When Dad handed the check to Gil, his voice was husky. "It's yours—for school," he said. And Ma's eyes were brimming with joyful tears.

That made it pretty hard for Gil. After all, when a fellow is almost a grown man, and going away to school, he can't be blubbering in front of his folks.

A Horse in Her Future

Margaret Burrage

DARLENE Manners leaned one shoulder against the wide doors of Barn One and watched wistfully as Hank Cenno, riding master of the 7-Hills Riding Academy, led his pupils on another ride.

"If only I had a horse," Darlene thought longingly, "I could be going with them."

Ever since she could remember Darlene had loved horses. It had begun at the age of two with her first hobbyhorse and progressed to riding her nextdoor neighbor's Shetland pony until her legs grew too long. Now, at fifteen, her love of horses was so deeply ingrained that for some time she had been doing barn chores at the riding academy just for the privilege of handling and exercising the horses. At first Hank had protested from time to time over her working so hard, but now, in his absent-minded way, he had come to depend upon her.

Darlene shifted her shoulders against the rough boards of the barn. Not having a horse was, at the moment, only one of her problems. Overlying her deep wish for a mount all her own was the knowledge that, unless a miracle occurred, next Monday would find her working in a stuffy office. Her heart constricted at the thought. It wasn't that she didn't want to help Dad by earning her own allowance and her school clothes for fall, it was just that she couldn't bear to leave the horses!

It had all started the night before, at dinner. "Money's going to be tight for a while, Chicken Little," her father had told her reluctantly. "I'm branching out into real estate for myself, so

215

instead of a regular salary, I'll be on my own. It won't leave much except for necessities. I'm afraid your allowance . . ."

"That's all right, Dad," Darlene had reassured him quickly. "Perhaps I can find a job."

Both her father and mother had looked relieved. "I was talking with Chuck Wilcox the other day," her father said. "He needs someone to do simple filing at his insurance office. I'll call him if you like. At least that'll save you from job hunting." His voice was husky.

At the look of hurt pride on his face, Darlene tried to act pleased. "That'll be neat, Dad," she said, her voice as gay as she could make it.

Her mother reached across the table and patted her hand. "Personally, I'll be relieved to have you stop playing around that riding club," she said. "Why, you talk, eat, and breathe horses! You have no friends any more. You actually seem to like horses better than you do girls your own age."

Darlene plopped jelly on her bread. "I *do* like them better," she said flatly. "They're not silly; they do what you want them to; and they don't fight with you like that hateful Michele Adams!"

Mrs. Manners looked at her husband and raised her hands in a gesture of despair. "Your mother's right," Bob Manners said. "You do need friends your own age. Perhaps this is for the best."

Darlene's heart constricted now just thinking of it. How could it be "best"—to be cooped in a stuffy insurance office all summer? I can't do it, she thought in despair. I just can't.

As the gay cavalcade rode past, Hank broke into her thoughts. He turned, straight and tall, in his saddle, raising his riding crop in a little salute. "Watch out for Michele, will you, Darlene? She's practicing out on the track."

Darlene made a wry face. "Okay," she called back in flat resignation.

Ever since they first had met, she and Michele Adams had kept up a running feud. Michele owned the most magnificent of all the quarter horses boarded at the stables, and her tack, studded with glittering silver *conchas*, was expensive, but she was an indifferent rider. Worst of all, she infuriated Darlene by the slipshod manner in which she groomed both her horse and tack.

Darlene could see her now in the distance at the far end of the practice track. She was riding slumped in the saddle instead of with heel, hip, and shoulder in a straight line as Hank taught.

"Doing everything wrong, as usual," Darlene said to herself. "She shouldn't hold Lobo back like that! It's okay on the turns but on the straightaway she should know enough to give him his head."

Hank had worked as hard with Michele as he had with the others. First they had been given classroom work. This consisted of a talk on horses and their reactions and an illustrated lecture on care of equipment—Michele had sure failed that one, Darlene thought wryly—then they were given thorough instruction in saddling up, followed by the do's and don'ts of riding. After that came the actual practice work of saddling and unsaddling, done over and over until it became automatic, and only then came the mounting of their horses.

For the more backward of his pupils, Hank put a saddle on a wooden sawhorse and required them to mount over and over until they could do it with ease. Of course, Michele had been one of these.

That really must have hurt her pride, Darlene thought with sympathy. But it needn't have stopped her from listening to Hank's advice and following it when riding!

At least Michele was in no trouble at the moment. Darlene went back to her barn chores and her depressing thoughts. When a shadow darkened the door, she looked up to see Michele carrying in her saddle. She draped it carelessly across an empty stall door, the saddle blanket dragging on the floor.

"Hi, Darlene," she called in greeting. "Hank tells me you're leaving and going to work in an *office*." Her voice held a sort of shocked disapproval.

Darlene continued to spread shavings carefully in an even thickness on the floor of the stall. "Maybe I will and maybe I won't," she answered. "I talked with Mr. Miner this morning and he half-promised me a job working evenings at his drugstore. I'll know for sure tonight. If my father will let me take that, I can keep on here days."

"I can't imagine why you want to," Michele said spitefully. "You work like a stableboy and you don't even own a horse!"

"You forget that Hank lets me exercise Gay!" Darlene shot back. The moment she said it, she was sorry. Her own love of horses made her realize that it wasn't fair to remind Michele that Darlene was the only one Hank ever permitted to ride the beautiful but treacherous black mare Michele admired so much.

"I have to check on the horses in the paddock," Darlene said quickly, and dashed out of the barn. At the paddock fence, she stopped to catch her breath, her cheeks hot with embarrassment. How could she have said such a mean thing!

Dusty, her favorite of all the stable mounts, mane and tail flowing in the breeze, trotted over to nuzzle her shoulder. She patted his gleaming chestnut coat, admiring him extravagantly.

"Aren't you the beauty, though," she crooned. "You're stacks handsomer than that old Gay!"

As if in answer to her name, Gay separated herself from the other horses and darted toward the paddock fence. Her movements were swift, effortless, and flowing. As she reached the gate she wheeled, and lashing out with both hind feet, kicked viciously at Dusty's sleek flank. With a quick, instinctive maneuver the other horse evaded the flashing hooves.

"Shame on you," Darlene scolded, admiring in spite of herself the spirited small mare with her slender legs, muscular neck, and deep chest. "How can you look so beautiful and be so mean?"

Gay put her ears back, snaked her slender neck forward, and nickered loudly. Darlene gave both horses an extra pat and went back into the barn. Michele was gone.

From the last stall, Lobo whinnied softly. Darlene hurried to him down the cool, dark aisle. Lather coated his flanks and his neck was wet. Anger exploded in Darlene's chest. That Michele!

She had done it again! She had put Lobo in his stall without bothering to cool him off.

If that isn't just like her, Darlene fumed to herself. She knows I'll walk Lobo for her rather than let him get all stiffened up. As soon as she had finished with Lobo, Darlene hurried to complete her regular chores. When Hank returned with his group of riders, she was nearly through for the night.

The young people tended their mounts, then raced for the clubhouse to buy snacks. Darlene watched them wistfully. What fun it must be to go on a real trail ride instead of just exercising horses alone. She gave herself a small shake. What was she complaining about? She was lucky to have this chance to work with horses at all. At least, she was with them for today, anyway. All the gloomy thoughts she had been keeping in the back of her mind returned in a dismal cloud. What if she couldn't persuade her father to let her take that job at Miner's Drug Store? What if she had to work in an office all day and never have a chance to ride or be with horses at all?

"I can't bear to leave," she thought desperately. "I just can't"

She dropped her now empty water pail and threw both arms around Belafonte, the golden palomino she had just watered. "Oh, Bella," she cried, her voice choked with tears, "how could I ever leave and never see you again? You and Dusty and the others?"

Behind her Hank entered the dim barn. "Almost through for the night?" he asked cheerfully.

Darlene kept her back turned while she hastily dabbed at her eyes. "Hi, Hank," she said steadily. "Have a good trail ride?"

"So-so," Hank answered. "Most of the class is catching on pretty well. Not one is a natural like you, though!" His face lighted. "What a way you have with horses! Why, with you even Gay almost behaves."

"I wouldn't say that exactly," Darlene said dryly. "I have to master her every minute."

"I said almost, didn't I?" Hank laughed. Then his face sobered and he laid his hand lightly on Darlene's shoulder. "I know how you feel about leaving the stables, Funnyface," he said. "But it's a strange thing about something you really want to do. If you want it bad enough, you can always find a way."

"I hope that's true," Darlene said fervently. "I hope somehow I can find a way." Later, as she walked slowly along toward Miner's Drug Store she kept on hoping it with all of her heart.

Mr. Miner stepped from behind the counter as soon as he saw Darlene. "Came about the job, didn't you? I'm awful sorry, Miss Manners," he said regretfully, "but my wife's nephew took it. I couldn't help myself. My wife—well—you know how it is."

He was so obviously distressed that Darlene hastened to reassure him. "It's all right, Mr. Miner," she said. "I'm sure I can find something else."

"Hope you do." Mr. Miner's round face puckered with concern. "Sure hope you do. You know that."

"Thank you." Darlene left quickly, swallowing desperately at the lump that was beginning to form in her throat. She mustn't cry here on the street. Safe at home in her own room, however, she buried her face deep in her pillow and let the sobs come.

Next morning Hank met her at the barn door. There was a worried pucker on his forehead. "Listen, Funnyface," he said hurriedly, "I'll have to ask you to exercise three of the horses this afternoon. Think you can squeeze in all that riding after the barn chores?"

Ordinarily, Darlene would have been overjoyed at such an opportunity, but today she was too discouraged to show any enthusiasm. "Yes, of course I'll do it, Hank," she answered soberly.

Hank tapped beneath her jaw lightly with one forefinger. "Hey, chin up there!" he smiled. "Remember what I told you. There's always a way." He set off quickly for the clubhouse.

Darlene's jaw tightened. "Sure there's always a way," she told herself, "and I just won't let one setback discourage me. I'll find some way, wait and see!"

Today when the riding club members left on their trail ride, Darlene, thinking of the three horses she had to exercise, felt only a momentary pang of envy. From the corner of her eye she saw Michele listlessly riding Lobo on the now empty practice track.

"Why, it must be hard for her, too, to see the trail riders go out," Darlene realized suddenly. "If only she'd try harder she'd be able to ride well enough to go along."

By mid-afternoon the barn chores were done. "Now to exercise those horses," she thought with satisfaction. Unlocking the tackroom, she filled her pockets with carrots. As she crossed the wide area to the paddock, Dusty came sweeping up to the gate, nose extended. She fed him a carrot. The other horses crowded about the fence, too, and she fed them all, petting each in turn.

"Funny Gay isn't right in the front row," she thought in surprise. "I think I'll exercise her first, while my hands and wrists aren't tired."

Carefully she searched, looking over the horses one by one, but she saw no star-faced black mare. There was no doubt about it, Gay was gone. "That rascal," she thought in exasperation. "Now how could she ever have jumped the fence?" Then from out on the track she heard the thundering sound of hooves.

Whirling about she saw Gay, ears tight against her head, her body stretched low—and on her back, obviously already in danger of losing her seat, was Michele!

For one moment Darlene stood frozen, her hands pressed against her mouth. Then she sprang into action. Dusty! There was no time for a saddle. Springing up on his bare back, she clutched his halter. With a flying start the chestnut was off up the track. Guiding him by knee pressure alone, Darlene bent low over his neck. Ahead of her Gay stretched out as if flying. Despite the danger of the moment, Darlene felt a thrill of admiration for the black tornado.

"Stretch yourself, Dusty," she urged, "or you'll never catch her!"

Dusty put on another spurt of speed. He had found his stride now, and the pines at the far side of the track passed in a blur. Michele had lost her stirrups and was clinging desperately to the saddle as she bounced about.

If only she can hang on, Darlene thought. She urged Dusty onward. Michele will fall—she'll be killed—faster, Dusty, faster! With a surge Dusty reached the mare's flank. For what seemed years to Darlene they stayed there, not gaining, not losing. Then they began to creep up.

If only Michele doesn't panic—if only I'm strong enough! As they drew up beside the black mare, Darlene reached out and grasped Michele about the waist. Michele grabbed her shoulder, almost unseating her. Then Michele was free of the saddle.

Dusty slowed to a smooth, even stop. Darlene let Michele drop lightly to the ground. Ahead of them, Gay stopped too and began nibbling unconcernedly at the grass in the center of the track.

"You all right, Michele?" Darlene asked shakily.

Michele's face was subdued and white. "I—I guess so."

"Then you lead Dusty while I catch Gay."

When Darlene returned with the black mare, Michele was plodding along the track leading Dusty. Something about the droop of her shoulders touched Darlene.

"Go ahead and say it," Michele said. "I had no business taking Gay and I'll never make a rider."

Darlene tried for a light touch. "You'll never *live* to make a rider if you try Gay again! Until you've ridden a lot more, that is. I've got a good knee grip and strong hands, but that horse gives me plenty of trouble."

Michele's shoulders drooped even lower. "Let's face it," she said. "I can't even ride Lobo, let alone any other horse. I'd better sell him and just give up trying to ride."

Darlene laughed. "You give up?" she said. "A girl with nerve enough to tackle a horse like Gay? You know you won't do that. Listen, I'm supposed to exercise Paint, Rebel, and Gay today. I guess Gay's already had her share of exercise, so how about your riding Lobo while I exercise the others?"

For the remainder of the afternoon the two girls rode together, Darlene patiently coaching and directing. When Hank returned with the Trail Riders, Darlene showed off her pupil's progress. Hank was delighted. "You're doing just fine, Michele," he beamed. "You're really getting the feel of your mount now. Say, we'll have you on trail ride in no time!"

"You know something, Darlene?" Michele said when Hank had left for the clubhouse, "that's the first time he ever praised me. Listen, when I can ride well enough, will you take one of the track horses and ride the trail with me?"

At the look on Darlene's face her voice faltered and stopped. "Oh, Darlene, didn't you—you mean you didn't get the drug-store job?"

"Mr. Miner gave the job to his wife's nephew," Darlene said flatly.

"Oh, Darlene, what will you do now? Why, you can't give up coming to the academy. Not now when we can have so much fun riding together!"

Darlene squared her shoulders. "I'll find some way," she said, trying to sound confident. But the confidence was all in her voice. What was there that she could do now? Monday was only one more day away.

Later, alone in the barn, she fed and watered the horses. The day, and perhaps her work at the stables, too, was at an end. She was tired. "Not that I mind being tired," she told herself quickly. "Not when I get tired doing what I like to do—even if I *don't* get paid for it," she added ruefully.

A sudden thought struck her and she made some rapid mental calculations. I do believe it would work, she thought slowly. Yes, it would—I'll bet it would. *Yippee*! She threw the oat measure she was holding high up into the air and caught it. Then she sought out Hank.

"Hank, may I talk with you?" she asked. "It's business and it's important."

An hour later, Darlene raced home and burst into the living room where her father was reading the paper.

"Dad," she breathlessly, "what would Mr. Wilcox pay me at the office?"

Her father laid down his paper and picked up his pipe. "Oh, about ten dollars a week, I guess."

Darlene took a deep breath. "Dad, I can earn twice that at the 7-Hills Riding Academy. Now, wait, Dad—hear me through before you say anything." Swiftly she outlined all the barn chores that she had been doing at the track. "And," she went on, "all of a sudden I decided that no matter how much I enjoy doing those chores, they're worth good hard cash. For just a minute," she chuckled, "I was afraid Hank didn't feel that way, but he was so embarrassed because he hadn't thought of paying me himself that he's going to pay me a lump sum for the work I've done these past weeks. Isn't that super?"

Her father puffed thoughtfully on his pipe. "And what do you plan to do with all that wealth?"

"I've got it all figured out," Darlene said promptly. "The back pay goes into my college and so does five dollars a week. Five dollars will go towards school clothes for fall. The rest I'd . . . I'd sort of like to save up for a horse. Then I could go on trail rides, too. Michele wants me to ride with her. She's doing just swell!"

Her mother interrupted from the doorway. "Michele?" she said. "Isn't she that girl you can't stand?"

Darlene felt her face grow hot. "It's different now that I've got to know her." She added shamefacedly, "I guess I never tried to understand her very much."

"Seems to me," her father said, "that there's been some misunderstanding all around. It strikes me now that you'd better take this stable job, since you like it so much."

Darlene rushed at him and hugged him tight. "Oh, Dad, you're out of this world."

Her father held her close. "Well, I think you're pretty great yourself," he said.

On the Hoof

Ann Spence Warner

KAY Benning always groomed Red Wing last, just as she saved until last her favorite piece of candy. Then she could give extra brushes to the sorrel mare's glinting tawny mane and tail. Kay had little time to ride Red Wing these days, but just to work around her was a joy.

A final brisk rub along the haunches—ah, now the gleaming coat was perfect. But those thin ribs! Faster than she could build up the mare, Mr. Todman wore her down. If he rode her a few more times as he had last week, Red Wing was going to be in really bad shape.

Clarke Grant's bicycle bell sounded from down the driveway. Kay's thin face lighted. Clarke, a schoolmate of hers in wintertime, lived on the outskirts of the city, near the road to the Benning place, and came to the stables often. Here was someone with whom she could talk over her troubles. Her mother understood horses so little that it was no comfort taking business problems to her. Clarke got the point.

"How's the big boss?" he greeted her.

"Oh, Clarke! We hear Dad won't be back for weeks yet. And I simply don't know what to do until he gets back."

"Same as you've been doing." He was always quick with encouragement. "Everything looks ship-shape to me."

"It's Red Wing."

"So Mr. Todman's back again."

"I'll say. And a man like him—how can I refuse him the horse he wants? Especially when we still owe him on the last feed bill.

Clarke!" She grabbed his arm desperately. "That's his coupe coming up the road now. Look—Red Wing in plain sight. No chance of getting her out of his way."

"Tell him she's promised."

"He'll see no one comes for her. Anyhow, you know lying never gets you anywhere. And I can't have trouble with him while Dad's away—sick, and worried to death with me in charge when he feels I'm just a kid."

There had been no one else her father could call upon. Her mother—well, as Mr. Benning always said with a laugh, you could take some people out of the city but you never took the city out of them. Mrs. Benning was afraid of horses and understood nothing about the livery business.

"Oh, I wish I knew what Dad would do if he were here," Kay whispered. Mr. Todman was stepping out of his coupe in riding togs. "He always hated to let Mr. Todman have Red Wing but he felt he had to do it. Still, Red never used to get so completely upset as she has lately. I just can't understand it."

Mr. Todman would bring the sensitive mare in wet, nervous, completely unstrung. He always rode too hard, handled a horse too roughly; yet that should not account for the quivering nerves that lately could not be quieted for hours, for days. After he left, Kay would walk Red Wing up and down, cool her and rub her. But still there were the shuddering twitches.

"Ha! I see you have my horse for me," he declared in his heavy jovial voice. "Give me the same saddle I had the last time I rode."

There was nothing Kay could do except get the mare ready.

"Come over here," Clarke called to her. "I've got something to show you."

"Be with you in a minute," Kay answered as she watched Mr. Todman start off.

Clarke had a wounded pheasant, holding it covered up in the basket on the handlebars.

"I saw him in the field as I rode by—hopping and flopping."

Kay's gentle exploring fingers quickly located a place where a shot had gone into its body. "Oh, if only that dumb hunter could aim straight! It's bad enough having him break the law protecting pheasants. But he doesn't even kill them. His aim . . ." The grinding of her teeth was more expressive than words. "I found two last week. Feel how thin this bird is. I'll bet it was shot at the same time and it's been suffering ever since."

Days of suffering had so weakened and bewildered the wild creature that it welcomed the shelter of her arms. Kay's tender fingers gently caressed the red feathers about its bright eyes, the dark head set off with the showy white collar, and the body plumage glinting with brilliant greens, reds, saffrons, and blends of other rich hues.

"I'd love to get a picture of that bird," Clarke declared, "but I left my camera at home. It wouldn't take me long to get it, though."

They both saw the flat tire at the same moment. "Aw, heck!"

"This bird's drooping so the picture wouldn't be much anyhow," Kay offered cheerfully.

"You never think any picture is much," Clarke grumbled.

It was true that Kay found it hard to share his absorbed enthusiasm for photography. She saw no sense in poking around in a stuffy, spookily-lit room when she could be riding in the sunshine!

"Who do you suppose can be doing the shooting?" Clarke wondered. "The law's so strict."

Suddenly Kay's eyes narrowed. Red Wing's quivering nerves. And how the mare hated a gun! Kay had found the wounded bird in the pasture the day after Mr. Todman last took Red Wing out.

"Mr. Todman!" she exclaimed. "I noticed today how awkwardly he got into his saddle. Do you suppose he could have had a gun concealed under his coat and breeches?"

Clarke's face reflected the excitement in hers. "He'd be the sort. Say, if we could just catch him!"

"Lot of good that would do!" Kay replied bitterly. "Who'd believe our word against his? The highly respectable Mr. Todman!"

"They would if . . ." He broke off, scowling in the direction of his flat tire. "That pesky tire! If it didn't take so doggone long to patch it!"

"Gabbing and fussing won't hurry it up." Kay had missed the connection in his mind. She finished with a comradely grin. "Better get busy."

"I'm going for a ride first," Clarke announced abruptly. "Mind if I take Dundy?"

"He isn't spoken for this afternoon," Kay said slowly. Dundy was a wise, reliable horse and the temptation was to send him out too often. Whatever else, Kay did not want Dundy out of condition. Still, Clarke handled a horse right. And it was late for more calls. "All right. Take him."

Kay was so intent on her painstaking care of the wounded pheasant that she did not even notice in which direction Clarke rode away. She bedded the bird down in a comfortable straw nest in an empty grain room, hopeful that it might be saved.

Would Mr. Todman never get back? Heartsick with concern, Kay had to keep her hands occupied. Jack, a neighborhood boy who helped her with the heavy work, had appeared to begin his evening chores. She got him to lend a hand in yanking off Clarke's flat tire so she could patch the damaged tube. Mr. Todman had been out more than his customary two hours. Poor, poor Red Wing! Too bad this tire had had to be flat when Clarke wanted his camera.

Ah, there at last was Red Wing. Kay held her breath as the mare came nearer. Sweat streaks all over her. Drying foam on her bit, her nostrils, her neck, her flanks. That twitch of her drooping head.

Kay's eyes avoided Mr. Todman's face. She answered his remarks briefly, struggling to control the anger surging through her. Now, now while it meant so much to avoid trouble with her father away, she must not let her temper get uppermost. She must not say things to anger him.

She watched the man closely. If he had carried a gun earlier, it was not in evidence now. She had to let him inspect the wounded pheasant and not tear into him for the brute, the pheasant killer she suspected him to be. She had to stand debating with him who the hunter might be. He even suggested Clarke.

Oh, no, Kay disagreed; not possibly. Would the man ever go? At last he started for his car, but her relief was short. For as he left, he informed her that he was taking his vacation at home. He would be out the following afternoon, every afternoon that week.

By the time his car had circled the driveway, Kay's hands were trembling so that she was frightening Red Wing more than she was soothing her. If she could only take a ride on the mare, together they could outrun the horror of that man. They could lose themselves in the joy of the swift trot, the rhythm, the music of its thudding beat. But Red Wing was too tired. She must be quieted, blanketed, and put in her box stall to rest; Kay's brush stroke widened in a soothing measure.

Still the mare quivered under her touch. Another ride tomorrow with Mr. Todman! Red Wing could never stand it. Something must be done to prevent it. But what?

Clarke was coming up the lane. She stared incredulously at the horse and the rider. Dundy was limping. His body was streaked with sweat. He was in the worst shape any horse had been returned in years. And Clarke—Clarke!—was the offender. And he wasn't even saying he was sorry. He swung off the horse and dropped the reins.

"Mind putting Dundy up for me? I've got to get home in a hurry."

Kay could not speak. For Clarke to do this to Dundy! Mr. Todman had suspected him of doing the shooting. Could he have done that, too? But Clarke was a good shot. He—oh, Clarke wouldn't . . . Yet old Dundy here . . .

"Say, you fixed the tire!" Clarke's voice was excited, happy. "Atta girl!"

Kay touched Dundy. Yes, his coat was caked, growing chilly now. He lifted one hoof; as if his leg ached. Kay saw that the shoe was worn off half an inch in front. On top of everything, Clarke had been riding him on a hard road. Clarke!

"You were swell to fix it," Clarke's pleased voice was telling her. "Now I can get away without losing a sec."

A hard road! If he had cut across Fletcher's pasture and then taken two miles of the highway, he would have been home.

"Clarke," she called after him, "did you ride after your camera?"

"How did you know? I didn't want to get your hopes up till I found out if I did get a picture to show up Mr. Todman."

Kay ran toward him. "Did you snap him?"

"Have to let you know later," Clarke called as he left.

Kay hurried back to Dundy. She must rub him down, put on poultices. Her mind raced her hands. Suppose Clarke had a picture of Mr. Todman firing a gun. What would that prove? It would be too wild to hope that the same picture could show the pheasant, too. Clarke in his excitement had never stopped to think.

But suppose she got evidence to support the picture. Suppose she found traces of the slain bird. Only where would she look? It would soon be dark. By the time Clarke reached home so she could ask him over the telephone it would be too late to start.

Her eyes fastened on the leg she was beginning to sponge. Dundy's hoofs had given her one clue. Carefully she studied the fetlock. That blackish-red clay could be found only in Smith's creek pasture. And the bridle path passed it.

If she found evidence of freshly killed pheasants and if the picture turned out, they would have a chain of convicting evidence. They would not need to take it to the sheriff. Her father might not want her to do that. It was for him to decide. But if she let Mr. Todman suspect what they had, he would not press a request for Red Wing.

Hastily finishing her work with Dundy and blanketing him crookedly, she saddled a big rawboned roan horse.

As soon as he was warmed up, Kay encouraged him to do his best. Within a short time they were inside Smith's pasture. She found recent traces of hoofs. She followed them, looked eagerly on every side.

Ha! Here the horse had stopped, milling about. Kay dismounted. On the other side of the fence were more tracks. The brush on her side was trampled down. Kay followed the broken line. A plain footprint of a man's shoe. Yes, and here under this brush—what luck! He'd hidden the dead bird. And, yes, his gun! Maybe he had been afraid she would see it. It was not far from here to the highway. He probably had intended to stop for it. But if he had caught a glimpse of Clarke riding Dundy, he might have thought it better to wait until tomorrow. He was an early riser, she knew.

Kay left the gun untouched and carefully replaced the slain bird, minus its tail feathers. Then she started home with a light heart.

It was dark by the time she reached the stables. She called to her mother that she'd come to dinner in a minute. She had to telephone first.

Clarke's mother answered, and she was not at all cordial. No, he was not at home. Mrs. Grant disapproved of girls calling up her son. Kay tried to explain to her that her business with Clarke was important.

His mother answered tartly, "Is there any of your business that you young people do not think is all-important?" And she hung up.

Kay lacked the courage to call her back. She would have to suppress her impatience until morning.

It was less than an hour after sunrise when Clarke's bicycle came rattling up the driveway.

"Hey," he called to Kay, "look what I got!"

"Oh, did the picture turn out?" She ran toward him.

"Take a look." He thrust a cardboard at her.

As plain as could be was Mr. Todman taking aim. And in the picture was the very bush under which he had hidden the bird.

"Only I didn't get the follow-up," mourned Clarke. "I thought I was surely early enough this morning. I cut across the field to that bush you see there in the picture. But the dead bird I'd watched him hide was gone. So I couldn't get a picture of that.

He must have caught a glimpse of me—got on his guard anyhow."

Kay pulled a handful of tail feathers out of her pocket. "He didn't find these on his bird, early as he came," she exulted. Quickly she told Clarke her story. "And now it's not too early to call that gentleman and inform him that Red Wing is not available today—or any day. Not till Dad gets back."

While she put through the call, Clarke took a carrot in to Dundy, then brought him out to brush and rub him, making the best amends he could for his rough treatment of the day before. His whistling slowed as Kay talked on the telephone, then shrilled out with pleased satisfaction as she replaced the receiver.

"He'd missed the tail feathers, all right," said Kay triumphantly. "He wasn't at all anxious for me to talk about a picture I had to show him. In fact it seemed to be quite agreeable to him to stay away from the place entirely. He agreed yes, yes, Red Wing did need a rest. And that is that."

With her heart at rest, Kay brought the mare out of her stall, took off the blanket, and began to groom the lovely coat. Soon she was going to have every horse in the stable in perfect condition. Only happy days were ahead for Red Wing.